PAINTING GRACE

PAINTING GRACE

MARY HESTER

ISBNs: 979-8-9933935-6-8 (paperback); 979-8-9933935-7-5 (ebook)

Library of Congress Control Number: 2026931799

First Printing: 2026

Printed in the United States of America

Published by Silent Clamor Press, Los Angeles CA

PRAISE FOR MARY HESTER

In Mary Hester's moving debut novel, *Painting Grace*, the past and present fuse as an esteemed art history professor moves toward the end of her life. Uprooted by memories and regrets, she is long past allowing herself love and forgiveness, only to slowly find redemption through art, and in a young caretaker who will become her last student. Hester reminds us that one life can make a difference to so many. A poignant and compassionate story that will resonate long after it's over.

— GAIL TSUKIYAMA, AUTHOR OF *THE SAMURAI'S GARDEN* AND *THE BRIGHTEST STAR*

Painting Grace is a compellingly rendered portrait of striving and success and the cost to a young woman's life. Purely told, tremendously affecting, a read that reminds us how human we are, how fallible, and ultimately how fortunate if grace descends.

— MICHELLE LATIOLAIS, AUTHOR OF *WIDOW* AND *SHE*

Hester explores the rich dynamics of human bonds: families of blood, families of choice, and the families of the heart. I can't promise you'll feel peaceful after reading this book, but you'll certainly feel wiser.

— JOHN MATTHEW FOX, AUTHOR OF *I WILL SHOUT YOUR NAME*

PART I
THEN AND NOW

CHAPTER 1

TIES THAT BIND

"I don't see why we have to celebrate our first wedding anniversary with your parents, for God's sake, Miriam," Tom Johnson muttered that hot night in July 1979. "Your father will be harping on my lack of publications again." He was dressing in the single cramped bedroom of their apartment near Louisiana State University, where both were assistant professors. Miriam was in the bathroom finishing her makeup, but the rooms were close enough that she could hear him, even above the hum and rattle of the ancient window unit in the bedroom. She wished he were in any department but the one chaired by her father.

"Oh, Tom, they just want to wish us well," she answered. "What's so wrong about that? We have the rest of the weekend to ourselves. They want to give us a gift—Mom hinted it's something we'll love." She joined him in the bedroom, giving her shoulder-length blond hair a final brush.

"Did she tell you what it is?" Tom asked, watching her in the mirror as he put on a seldom-worn tie for the upscale steakhouse Miriam's father had chosen.

"No, but she was all a-dither with excitement."

Tom rolled his eyes and grinned. She knew he'd always liked her mother. He was handsome in the brown plaid sports jacket, his dark hair longer than her father liked, but pulled back in a neat professorial ponytail. Miriam adjusted his tie, feeling Tom's eyes lingering over her body in the red silk sheath that, yes, fit her perfectly. She reached around his neck to smooth his shirt collar, and he pulled her to him, kissed her, then released her, giving her his slow, sexy smile. He was right. Having this night alone together, even staying home, would've been nice.

"I saw in *Cablecast* that the original King Kong movie is on tonight," Tom said. "We could get takeout Chinese and watch it in bed. We already know how it ends so we wouldn't have to pay attention."

"Very tempting, but they'll be on their way by now," Miriam said, walking toward the door. But as she navigated the long outdoor wooden staircase in her heels, she thought of them, cuddled together in bed, ignoring the big gorilla on the small black-and-white television, sure and gentle hands beneath the sheets making everything else fade away.

At the restaurant, Tom held her hand as the hostess guided them through the sea of starched white tablecloths to where Miriam's parents, Rosemary and William Landry, waited. Miriam glanced at Tom when his hand gripped hers tighter—he was frowning, jaw set— yes, he was nervous. Her mother waved to them from the table, elegant in her black dress and pearls, still beautiful at fifty-eight. Her father smiled when he saw Miriam, but the smile disappeared when he nodded at Tom before turning, with his customary air of authority, to summon the waitress.

They began with stilted conversation about the weather and how their semesters were progressing, but the old-fashioned in front of her father meant he'd loosen up soon. The waitress poured them each a glass of the wine he'd ordered, and Miriam took a welcome sip and Tom a larger swallow. They ordered appetizers.

Rosemary talked a little about having their large mid-city home

kitchen. She knew he was anticipating the unflattering comparison and hoping the steaks would arrive to interrupt the conversation. Predictably, her father launched into a description—that interested no one—of Franklin's latest work on some arcane medieval poet. Rosemary cut her eyes to William and covered a yawn, not subtle about it.

"When Franklin was working on his doctorate," William said, "he was in my office every Saturday morning to update me on his research or give me a new chapter from his dissertation. He had two publications out before he'd finished graduate school."

"Oh, here are the steaks," Rosemary said, shooting William a pointed look.

He registered it, Miriam saw, but ignored it. "I once thought Franklin and Miriam might become romantically involved," he said, oblivious to Tom's raised eyebrows and Miriam's exasperated sigh. "But I suppose it was not to be. His intellectual sophistication and her younger age probably prohibited conversing on a level that would have engaged him."

"If you save room, we can split a dessert, Mom," Miriam said, a shade louder than necessary. Franklin had been an insufferable ass-kisser, socially inept, and no one's idea of good-looking. She still winced, remembering her nineteen-year-old horror at her father's deluded assumption that she would be attracted to Franklin. She glanced at Tom to share a secret smile, but he was engrossed in loading butter and sour cream on his baked potato. She took a deep breath, trying to exhale the fear that these people she loved most in the world would never live in harmony.

Rosemary whispered that she'd love to share a dessert. They ate in silence for the next few minutes, then Rosemary turned to William and said, "It's a good thing our Miriam didn't marry Franklin or she'd now live far away in Massachusetts."

Her father looked as if he hadn't quite put that together. "Well, yes, I suppose you're right, Rosemary. And that would have been quite a loss to LSU as well as to us personally." He turned to Miriam and said, "Are you still planning to submit that chapter of your dissertation to *Impressionist Art?*"

Miriam hesitated, unwilling to be another example of professional success outstripping Tom's. "Yes," she finally answered, "but I'm struggling with converting the piece from a dissertation chapter to a freestanding article."

Her father assured her she'd do fine, reminding her that it would be her second major publication since graduate school. Not subtle, Dad, Miriam thought, poised to change the subject, when Tom spoke.

"The journal editor will love it. Miriam is an amazing writer as well as a teacher. A rising star in her department." Her father was effectively paused by Tom's voicing the words he would have said. Miriam smiled at Tom, grateful.

To Miriam's relief, her mother guided the conversation during the rest of the meal through innocuous topics, discussing possible Thanksgiving venues (Miriam patted Tom's thigh under the table) and the new minister (they all agreed he'd never match his beloved predecessor). After the coffee and crème brulèe, when Tom was covertly checking his watch, Rosemary lifted her purse to her lap. Tom, hoping that this meant dinner was over, scooted his chair back.

Her father glanced at her mother, who nodded at him.

"Miriam," he began, focusing on her as if Tom weren't in the room. "Your mother and I have purchased a cottage on Azalea Street—and we'll be moving into it later this month."

Miriam forced a smile through the stab of disappointment. She'd never contemplated her parents giving up their beloved home on Magnolia Lane, had always assumed that it would one day be hers. Reading the knowing empathy in her mother's eyes, Miriam said Azalea was a lovely street, the best response she could manage.

"William is right that it's time for a smaller place," Rosemary said, eyes misty, "but it still feels strange to be leaving a house with so many memories." Turning to Tom, she said, "Miriam was only a little girl when we bought it, but she worked on all the house projects with us. It wasn't in very good shape then."

"Which is why we could afford it," William said.

Miriam could tell her father was about to launch into the story of how he'd learned the house was being sold from an estate, the heirs eager to convert it to cash as quickly as possible. He liked to recount how he'd stepped in and made an offer before it went on the market.

Rosemary headed him off, saying, "I fell in love with the house the first time I saw it. Remember, Miriam, when you and I went over with the realtor after our offer was accepted?"

Miriam smiled. "You let me run upstairs and pick out my new bedroom."

Rosemary turned to William, smiling, and said, "You took so much time off that year."

He grunted, but smiled back at her. "Yes, well, you and Miriam were quite the worker bees and needed my supervision." William chuckled, then looked around the table, smiling expansively, his gaze settling on Miriam. "Your mother and I have a gift for your first wedding anniversary. Rosemary, did you bring the package?"

Rosemary fumbled in her purse and drew out a small wrapped box topped with an elaborate silver bow, and handed it to Miriam. She opened it carefully and drew out keys she instantly recognized as those to her parents' home on Magnolia Lane. She looked up to find them beaming at her. She turned to Tom, whose brows were raised, mouth slightly agape, as if he'd just witnessed a car wreck. Did he realize what it meant?

"We want you to have the house, Miriam," her father said, in the tones of a despot adding an unexpected five acres to a peasant's farm.

Miriam glanced again at Tom, who'd closed his mouth into a tight line, his face now scarlet. She reached for his hand under the table, but it was clenched tightly. For his sake, she offered, "It's a wonderful gift, but it's too much." Tom nodded emphatically.

"No, no," her father said, waving away her objection. "We gave this quite a bit of thought and want you to have the house." He picked up the check and glanced around to be sure everyone noticed.

Miriam's mother wished them a happy anniversary and told them to go and enjoy the rest of their evening. She remained seated while William examined the check, and Tom stood and pulled out Miriam's chair. He stepped back to the table when he noticed his forgotten wine glass, still half full, and stood lifting it to his lips just as Miriam bent to pick up her purse. They collided and the glass slipped from his hand. It fell at the edge of the table in front of William, spilling wine onto his lap.

"What the hell?" William cried, jumping back from the table, nearly overturning his chair, but not before wine had spilled onto his trousers.

Tom said, "Sorry, sir, the glass slipped out of my hand."

Rosemary grabbed a napkin and tried to blot the wine from William's trousers. He pushed her hand away, saying, "Just leave it, Rosemary," and muttering, "bumbling idiot."

Miriam said, "Oh, Dad, I'm so sorry, it was my fault—I bumped into Tom." Her father didn't acknowledge her apology, just leaned over the table to sign the check, angrily stabbing the paper with the pen, ignoring them. Rosemary assured William she could get the stain out with white vinegar.

Miriam said, "Thanks for everything, Dad," and attempted a quick hug. Her father remained stiffly upright and didn't hug her back. Tom stood by awkwardly. Miriam blew Rosemary a kiss and took Tom's arm, heading for the exit. Tom held her arm close and shot her a sly wink.

As they left, Miriam heard her father tell her mother, "He probably did it on purpose. Truly ungrateful."

In the car, Miriam found herself giggling. "What is it?" Tom asked.

"Did you see my father's face? And the way he jumped back? He almost fell on his ass!" Miriam was laughing now, and Tom joined her.

"His face was redder than the wine!" he said. They laughed louder.

With a wicked smile, Miriam said, "Tell the truth. Did you do it on purpose?"

Tom flashed his pirate's grin and said, "Nah, but I should have."

Miriam felt some of the tension dissolve with the laughter, and, encouraged, she asked, "Aren't you excited about the house?" She watched his face, hoping for a glimmer of excitement.

Tom's smile disappeared, and he stared straight ahead, as if the familiar road required his full concentration, white knuckling the wheel as if it might wriggle free.

"Um, well, I wasn't expecting it."

Miriam stayed quiet, waiting, still hoping.

Tom glanced at her and said, "Do you really want to live there? The utility bills alone will eat us alive, and we don't have time to care for a house that size—you're not a full-time housewife like your mother, and even she has a maid. It's just not what we need at this stage of our lives." He paused, then added, "And we might not want to live here forever."

Miriam froze. It was the first time he'd said it, though she realized it had always hung in the air between them.

Tom said, "We might want to consider positions at other universities before we settle down permanently. Most academics move several times."

Miriam nodded, looking out the passenger window. This was generally true, but not for her. Baton Rouge was home; LSU was her university, always had been.

FOR SEVERAL DAYS, THEY DIDN'T SPEAK OF THE HOUSE. MIRIAM WAS afraid to broach the subject, and she thought Tom was probably hoping it would miraculously go away. She left the box with the keys on their dresser. On Wednesday evening, the phone rang as they were cleaning up after dinner, and Miriam rushed to the kitchen extension. She saw Tom look up from drying dishes as she said hello to her mother. Miriam smiled at him over the receiver, told her mother she'd call back to confirm the time. She hung up and turned to Tom, who'd remained motionless, waiting, dish towel in hand.

"It was Mom. They want to know if we can meet them downtown tomorrow afternoon to sign the papers for the house." She went back to the sink and gave the pan a final scrub, afraid to meet his eyes.

Tom waited, silent and stiff, as she rinsed the pan, then handed her the dish towel to dry her hands. She looked up at him, questioning. He frowned, took the dish towel back from her, dried the pan while she waited, as if considering his answer, no trace of anticipation or happiness. Finally, he put the pan in the cabinet, then looked at her and said, "You really want this?"

She held his gaze, knowing he wanted her to say no, that she'd realized he was right, the house wasn't what they needed. But she couldn't. She nodded, mute, but let her eyes plead. He sighed, surrendering, put his arms around her, and said quietly, "Okay, baby, we'll take the house. But promise me it won't mean we'll never consider moving—that you'll still keep an open mind?"

She'd promised, though she didn't mean it, and he probably knew that. Tom regarded her, dubious. He opened his mouth to say something, then closed it, keeping his arms loosely around her, but drawing back to watch her face, his eyes a silent appeal. She had nothing further to say though, and pulled away, telling him she needed to put in a couple of hours on her paper.

THEY MOVED INTO THE HOUSE BETWEEN THE SUMMER AND FALL semesters, Miriam giddy with excitement, Tom trying to share her happiness. They painted rooms and bought furniture for their bedroom, the only room her parents had left empty. Miriam insisted that Tom take her father's study downstairs, and she took as her office the sunny corner room upstairs that her mother had used as headquarters for her civic activities. Tom was quickly proved right about the time the house required. Miriam struggled to keep it as her mother had, and Tom struggled with new duties, including maintaining the large yard. Going to a movie on Saturday afternoon became a thing of the past.

"Miriam, you're exhausting yourself," Tom said as she rubbed lemon oil into the dining room furniture late on a Friday night. "You're trying to be both your mother and your father, and even they were never more than one or the other."

"I'm not. I just want the house to be a home for both of us, to be nice." Why couldn't he see that? And why didn't he want the same thing? If he was worried about her doing too much, why didn't he help more? They could have worked together on the household chores on Friday night, before the weekend began, made a domestic ritual of it.

He didn't treat the house as truly theirs, kept his distance, wouldn't embrace it.

Miriam had dreamed of hosting dinner parties in the home, but when they did, there were raised eyebrows and jokes about the "mansion" where they lived. Reciprocal visits to friends' apartments or small rented houses brought more comments and jokes about the contrast. Tom was embarrassed, far less relaxed than when the same friends had visited their little apartment.

And, yes, Tom was right that the house was a bald assertion that they would stay.

CHAPTER 2

A WORLD DIMINISHED AND A STRANGER IN THE HOUSE

In 2015, when Miriam would turn sixty-five, she'd hoped for an unhurried transition into retirement, but the diagnosis abruptly changed those plans. Instead of traveling and visiting the great museums of Europe, she'd be dismantling her life. She looked out her kitchen window at the late-summer slant of sunlight filtering through the leaves of the old oak. She'd spent many hours beneath its spreading branches, planting and tending bright flowers—pansies in the fall, petunias in early spring, impatiens in the summer—savoring the dappled sun on her face and the birds' melodies. She envisioned herself there, on her beloved patch of earth, gradually fading out, disappearing.

Now would be the time to rely on faith—if she believed. In the years since she'd lost Tom and Rosie, her faith had worn gossamer thin, as insubstantial as cobwebs. She rarely thought about faith, God, or prayer. That day she felt the lack, the emptiness remaining when she was forced to surrender all that had filled her life. Well, she'd made her choices. She couldn't fill that void now, even if she wanted to.

And, yes, she was afraid. She'd be facing it alone—the cancer, the loss of her independence, her body's betrayal and deterioration. Her parents were both gone, along with her dear neighbor, Mac. Her few friends were fellow academics scattered around the country, more colleagues than friends, their interactions limited to conferences and email or exchanging Christmas cards.

She'd expected the usual brief report on her annual physical exam and test results when her doctor's office called on a sunny July afternoon, the kind that made life seem easy and all problems solvable. When the nurse said Dr. Landreneau wanted her to come in to discuss the test results, she had asked to discuss them by phone, begrudging the time an appointment would take when she was busy preparing for the new academic year. But the nurse had insisted. That, she'd thought, would teach her to think twice before mentioning something as trivial as a little indigestion and the occasional twinge of abdominal pain. She wouldn't have said anything, but Dr. Landreneau, her long-time physician, had been persistent during her physical, a change from his usual relaxed, jovial manner. When she'd questioned the need for what seemed to her an unnecessary battery of tests and imaging, the nurse merely said that Dr. Landreneau had ordered them after her examination and would discuss the results with her when they were received. Typical. Dr. Landreneau had always been thorough to a fault. She'd assumed his insistence on a follow-up meeting had more to do with the medical profession's self-importance than with anything actually wrong.

When Miriam had arrived for the appointment, she'd been surprised and somewhat gratified to be taken back immediately, but then felt a quiver of anxiety when she was brought directly to the doctor's private office. Dr. Landreneau nodded to her from behind his polished mahogany desk and gestured to a chair in the pleasant room with soft lamplight and watercolor landscapes interspersed between bookcases and medical certificates.

"Thank you for coming in, Miriam. How have you been?"

"Fine." She waited, hands clasped in her lap, and studied the Oriental rug. Exquisite, and the polished finish on the hardwood floor was immaculately maintained. She glanced up at Dr. Landreneau. His somber expression belied her hope that he'd pronounce her healthy.

He finished flipping through the file on his desk, looked up, and said, "Miriam, you have a growth on your pancreas that is probably cancerous."

Wait, what? She leaned forward as if she hadn't heard correctly.

"I'd like you to see Dr. Viator, an oncologist who specializes in pancreatic cancer." He handed her a card. "I've sent him your labwork and scans. He'll decide what other testing is needed."

Miriam struggled to catch up, to keep her expression calm, clamp down the rising panic. Dr. Landreneau knew she was unusually healthy and fit, never missed classes due to illness. This couldn't be right.

He paused, as if waiting for questions, but she couldn't speak. She looked away from his concerned kindness.

"You have an appointment with Dr. Viator at eight tomorrow morning."

"I'm sorry, but I'm meeting with a new graduate student then." Couldn't she just continue with the plans she'd had an hour ago?

"Miriam, this is your life we're talking about. Postpone your meeting. At my request, Dr. Viator is coming in early to see you. He's fully booked the rest of the week, probably the rest of the month."

"If he's so busy, will he have time for me?" She heard the childish petulance in her voice. She didn't want an oncologist.

"He's the best, Miriam, and I want you to have him. He commits to his patients, and he won't be too busy once he takes you on. You'll like him."

Dr. Landreneau stood and walked with Miriam to the hallway, assuring her that she would be in the best hands. Not the assurance she wanted. She walked to the lobby in a daze, clutching Dr. Viator's card. She realized she'd left her purse in Dr. Landreneau's office. The nurse fetched it, and Miriam checked out. She drove home, numb, frozen—like that water pipe last winter, silent and splitting on the inside. As soon as she closed her front door, tears seized her.

. . .

She'd arrived at Dr. Viator's office the next morning, frowning at the words "Oncology Associates" on the sign. She filled out the new patient form, hesitating at the reason for the visit, writing "pancreatic cancer," then inserting "suspected."

Despite her expectations, she liked Dr. Viator immediately, finding him direct and compassionate, an admirable combination. He said he'd confirm with further tests and procedures, but that she almost certainly had advanced pancreatic cancer.

"Can you, um, estimate how much time before, uh, before. Um, how many years . . . I have left?" She sounded like an idiot and to make it worse, felt tears rising.

Dr. Viator tapped a pen against his desk. "I'm sorry, but in your case, it's probably months rather than years. Maybe six, maybe twelve. It could be longer. With this kind of cancer, it's always a guess." But the sympathy in his eyes told her he believed the estimate accurate.

He'd said more, but she hadn't absorbed it all, snagged on the part about months.

Two weeks later, Dr. Viator's initial opinion was confirmed. Given the swift decline predicted, he'd directed her to begin "integrating a caregiver into the household." That would be hard. She'd lived here on Magnolia Lane most of her life, alone for the last thirty-three years. Baton Rouge had grown up around the neighborhood, shaded by century-old live oaks arched over the narrow streets, branches from opposite sides meeting in the middle, the leaves a green mosaic between shadowed limbs. Only the old neighborhoods had this air of solid tranquility, though the university was only ten minutes away in one direction and downtown ten minutes in the other. Many of the original houses remained, some, like hers, stately two-story stucco and brick, others airy wood-sided homes resembling farmhouses in Andrew Wyeth paintings (but better maintained). Most had generous porches and wide, manicured lawns. Sprinkled among the larger houses were neat wooden cottages painted in pastel shades with porch swings.

Now with the diagnosis confirmed, eliminating her last hope that it had all been a terrible mistake, she had to begin the process of reordering her rapidly shrinking world. She entered her sunny sitting room (probably a "den" in the current vernacular, as if a pack of animals inhabited the place; maybe a "family room" if one had a family). She settled in the leather recliner with her phone and watched Petey, with his feline nonchalance, saunter in through the curved archway framed in gleaming white millwork. As always, he navigated confidently despite his blindness; the vet said cats used their whiskers, but she thought it was more than that. She wondered with a panicky sadness what would become of him when she was gone. She'd have to think of something, couldn't leave her old friend bereft and homeless. Petey strolled past the built-in maple bookshelves flanking the fireplace, filled with the works she and Tom had loved—Jane Austen, Henry James, Edith Wharton, the Brontë sisters, Charles Dickens, Shakespeare, and Emily Dickinson. Maybe she could find some comfort in rereading them now; she'd have time on her hands with her fall semester suddenly empty. The thought of those unfilled hours frightened her. She'd always been so busy, eager to fill every moment with productive work.

Petey jumped into her lap and she stroked his soft coat, white except for his gray-striped tabby tail, as if God had whimsically taken it from another cat kit. "Faithful friend," she murmured, "I'll take care of you." She gave him a scratch under the chin, then picked up her phone to begin making calls.

She started with the chair of the LSU Art History Department, Alice Barrett. Thirty-eight years Miriam had taught there, she thought as the phone rang. It hardly seemed possible.

Alice's perpetually chipper secretary offered Miriam a cheery greeting and passed her through.

"Miriam, how are you?" Alice asked. "Getting ready for another fall?"

Miriam faltered, realizing how unprepared she was for this. "Oh, well, I've had some bad health news, Alice." Miriam paused, as if Alice could divine her meaning, making further explanation unnecessary. But Alice was silent, waiting. "Pancreatic cancer," Miriam said. "It doesn't look like I'll be able to return this fall." However irrational, she felt ashamed, apologetic, as if she'd somehow allowed the cancer to invade, to exploit a weakness stemming from an inner flaw.

"I'm so sorry, Miriam. We can certainly cover your fall classes. Will you be able to return for the spring semester?"

Miriam realized she'd been too cryptic. "No, I'm not going to get better and probably won't last through the spring."

"Oh, I see. I'm so sorry, Miriam, please let me know—"

"About my graduate students," Miriam interrupted, wanting the call to be over, not wanting to break down, "two completed their doctorates last spring. One is continuing, and two new ones are starting this fall. We should meet about reassigning them." Miriam wavered for a moment, almost offering to continue part-time for the fall. But no. It wouldn't be fair to get involved, knowing she might not be able to complete even the semester.

They set a meeting date and ended the call. Miriam blinked back tears. However unreasonable and unfair, she felt abandoned and bereft. The waters would close around her sinking ship without a ripple.

She shook off those thoughts and called the department secretary about her campus office. Before the gravity of the diagnosis had fully sunk in, she'd planned to keep the office that fall, continue her research, perhaps counsel the graduate students she'd handed off to other professors. She realized now that she'd been envisioning her original plan for easing into retirement—dropping by her office at will, perhaps serving on the committees of the more promising graduate students, and undertaking research guided only by genuine interest without concern for ease of publishing or competing work of other scholars.

But now, with only months remaining and those tainted by encroaching illness, she realized she wouldn't be using the office and advised accordingly. The office was one of the best in the department, second only to the chair's, comfortable and bright with windows looking out on the mossy old campus oaks. Its release would set off a round of tussling among the tenured professors, who'd doubtless coveted it as they prowled by, eyeing the closed door. She pictured the removal of the brass nameplate reading "Dr. Miriam L. Johnson." She could get her remaining personal papers when she dropped off the key. Her books and journals could be made available to other faculty members.

She leaned back in her chair and gazed out the windows at the sunlight illuminating the iris plants by the back fence, the white blossoms with their delicate blue markings like hand-painted Delft china. Sadness washed through her. She contemplated the brevity of that time of serenely enjoying professional achievement, past the years of doubt and striving, of leveraging the small victories and accomplishments into reputation and respect. A few years, maybe fifteen, of frequent citations of her work, enviable speaking engagements, graduate students vying to study under her. Then it all ended abruptly, not even a gently fading light for her, only a sputtering flicker before oblivion.

Back to the caregiver. Miriam shifted in her recliner and sighed. She'd been planning to call her attorney, Duncan Theriot, about updating her will, a chore she'd put off before the diagnosis gave it new urgency. Maybe he could help. His wasn't the most brilliant legal mind, but he was a good judge of character. She took a deep breath and called him. When she relayed the news, the sadness in his voice touched her; she hoped it wasn't only that he'd be losing a good client. Duncan promised to ask around and call her back.

Before she had a stranger in her house, looking through her things, she'd have to clean out those bottom two dresser drawers in her bedroom. She dreaded the task. She returned to the kitchen, made a cup of green tea, though the antioxidants hadn't quite lived up to their reputation in her case, and brought it upstairs to her bedroom. She opened the first drawer, surprised at how much it still hurt to see the things—the December birthday drawings, each lying on top of that year's dress.

She pulled out the neatly stacked contents of the first drawer and flipped them, beginning with those that had been on the bottom—the drawings of the baby and toddler, each paired with a small pastel or gingham dress. Next were the drawings of a young child, hair longer, loose and curling, or in pigtails or a ponytail, under each drawing a crisply pressed dress in bright solids or prints, some with sashes or ribbons. From the second drawer, she pulled drawings and dresses for the school years, ending with the more sophisticated fashions a teenager might condescend to wear. A lovely pale blue silk dress lay beneath the last drawing. Miriam separated the drawings from the dresses, finding that she remembered every line of each drawing, even the ones she hadn't looked at in years. When she'd added a new drawing and dress each year, she'd never contemplated removing them. These tangible artifacts of her guilt and sorrow, the sole relics of her lost daughter.

She couldn't throw the dresses away, all good quality and practically new, so she packed them into shopping bags to take to the Goodwill Store, where she could leave them anonymously at the back-intake area. She carried the drawings down the hall to the shredder in her office and fed the first one through, barely glancing at it. The drawing for the next year had been with a little pink ruffled dress. She shouldn't have, but she paused for a final look at the detailed image of the baby wearing the dress, big eyes like Tom's, the lips and smile resembling hers, plump hands reaching out as if asking to be picked up. "Rosie," she murmured, and the heavy paper shook in her hand. She started to thrust it into the shredder but stopped short. She could put that one aside for now; there was no rush. She put it on the desk and swallowed hard, feeling the heat on her face. She closed her eyes, seeing the images she'd created for each birthday, her annual—what? Ritual? Penance? She took a few deep breaths to still the tremors.

She continued shredding, faltering again on the fifth drawing, the one of the little girl in pigtails wearing a polka-dotted dress, and put it aside too. Finally, she came to the last drawing, the one paired with the blue silk dress. A young woman, smiling with the promise of the future, stood on Miriam's front porch, perhaps on the way to her high school graduation, perhaps dressed for a special date. Miriam sobbed as she shredded it, shoulders shaking, in pointless mourning.

Petey rushed into the room, meowing loudly. He raised himself on his hind legs, rested his front paws on her knee, and lifted his face to her. She paused to scratch his head, and he jumped into her lap and nuzzled her, as if determined to rub out the sadness.

Miriam stroked Petey to reassure him, then lifted him off her lap and returned to her bedroom, Petey trotting beside her. She took out the last thing left in the bottom drawer, the painting. Her hands shook again and her breath caught. She couldn't just feed it through the shredder. She'd keep it, at least for now. Besides, Mac's garden was the primary focus, she told herself disingenuously, remembering with a faint smile her dear neighbor laboring over his precious roses. The mostly hidden blond child peeking out from behind the red rosebush was only a small part of the composition. Miriam carried the painting back to her office and put it on the top shelf of the closet where her other paintings were stored, and put the two drawings in her bottom desk drawer beneath some folders. She would need to pack all of the paintings in boxes, address them to someone, but who? Well, she didn't have to decide today. She picked up the bags of clothes in the bedroom, trudged downstairs, into the garage, and loaded them into her trunk.

CAMILLE CAILLOUET, MIRIAM'S NEW CAREGIVER, RECRUITED BY Duncan from his office's nighttime cleaning crew, arrived promptly at the appointed time of one o'clock. Although Duncan had said that Camille was a student in the community college's nursing program, Miriam had expected a woman more typical of the caregivers she'd hired for her parents—at best competent and kind, at worst sullen and inattentive, often slow-moving, and none too bright. That was what minimum wage paid to a worker in a dead-end job bought you. But Camille was only nineteen, attractive, slender, and fit, with Cajun French dark eyes, shiny black hair, and creamy skin.

Camille's eyes widened as she entered the living room, hesitating before stepping onto the thick hand-carved wool of the Aubusson rug.

"Should I take off my shoes, Dr. Johnson?"

"No need," Miriam answered, though she herself generally wore slippers in deference to the hardwood floors. "And please call me Miriam."

"Your house is beautiful," Camille said, gazing around the living room at the antique furniture and draped valences of the ivory silk curtains. "It's like the inside of a genie's bottle," she said, then flushed. "My grandmother used to love old reruns of *I Dream of Jeannie.*" Camille edged closer to the large oil painting of a Louisiana wetlands scene, water lilies blooming on a lake edged with cypress trees, snowy egrets resting in the branches, backed by a brilliant sunset. Miriam and Tom's only addition to the room.

"It's lovely, isn't it?" Miriam said and pointed to the fox crouching at the edge of the lake. "Sometimes I half expect him to twitch his ears and run into the woods."

Camille laughed. "Yes, it's awesome." Miriam winced. She hated the overused word.

"I've always valued realism in painting," Miriam continued, "though it's been out of vogue for many years. Come see an example in the dining room of the same sort of scene, but in a loose-brush style." As they crossed the foyer, Miriam realized she was slipping into professor mode, but felt more comfortable.

Camille followed, pausing at the threshold to gaze appreciatively at the Oriental rug, timeworn yet still beautiful, its durable silk threads fading gracefully to a more subtle harmony than the original radiant hues. Miriam switched on the crystal chandelier, and Camille took in the gothic china cabinet with leaded glass doors and the elaborately carved Victorian sideboard, two of the better pieces Miriam's parents had purchased decades ago. It was hard to think of these things being carted away, destroying the synergism that had complemented and enhanced the beauty of each, creating the work of art that was this room, this home.

"It's like a museum," Camille said reverently. Miriam ignored the misguided "compliment" and turned on the art light above the large oil painting, gesturing to Camille to stand with her on the other side of the gleaming Chippendale table for the best view. The girl apparently had a genuine appreciation of art, however unschooled. Camille's breath caught at the sight of the painting, escaping in a soft, "Oh, it's beautiful."

"Yes, this is a good example of a more Impressionistic rendering," Miriam said. Moss-hung trees encircled glittering waters, clouds hung lazily from a blue sky, wild fuchsia azaleas were a blur on the shoreline. Miriam remembered the day she and Tom bought it, spending two hours in the gallery, leaving to breathlessly discuss over lunch how they could afford it, then drawn back irresistibly for a final look that had ended with their working out a payment plan with the gallery owner. They'd never bought a painting without thinking it beyond their means, and they'd never regretted buying a single one, had only regretted not buying a few she still remembered, including a lovely bayou scene they'd returned for, determined to make the necessary sacrifices to own it, only to find a blank space on the gallery wall where it had hung.

But enough of this, the girl wasn't here for an art lesson. "Duncan told me you're studying nursing at the community college, and I thought you might like to have the study for your schoolwork since your main function—at least initially—will be simply to be present if needed." Camille nodded and followed Miriam back down the hallway.

Camille glanced around the study's dark wood paneling and bookcases, the heavy velvet drapes over the long windows, probably noticing the annoying, self-satisfied ticking of the grandfather clock Miriam still wound daily. Artwork her father had chosen hung on the walls: somber portraits of unsmiling men in long coats and women in tightly corseted gowns, along with a few daguerreotypes of Civil War soldiers. She should have removed Tom's battered old Smith Corona typewriter sitting awkwardly on the polished burled wood of the immense desk. Camille looked less than thrilled with the study. But she'd find it quiet and comfortable, and she'd be out of the way if Miriam wanted to watch *Downton Abbey* without Camille rustling around at the kitchen table on the other side of the wall.

On the way back to the living room, Camille glanced down the hall to the back windows. "What a beautiful backyard. Is it fenced?"

An odd question. Miriam said yes and raised an eyebrow.

"Oh, I just got a dog, Hanks," Camille said. "I was just thinking how much he'd love a big yard like that. He stays inside or in my little backyard all day while I'm gone."

And? Surely Camille wasn't angling to bring the dog here. Miriam didn't respond to the remark, but gestured Camille to a chair in the living room.

"Let's talk about scheduling, then I think we'll be finished for today."

Camille looked startled, perhaps concerned that she wouldn't be paid for the full day. Then she said, "Just one question, if I could?" Miriam nodded assent. "I wasn't sure from the interview why you needed a caregiver. Is there an illness?"

"Oh, well, I've had some health issues arise that may lead to further, uh, needs. I'll know more as time passes, but the doctor thought it would be advisable to have a caregiver on hand as a precaution, particularly since I live alone." Camille was silent, waiting for her to say more. Miriam realized the explanation was inadequate, but preferred not to divulge her diagnosis, at least not yet.

"As discussed in Duncan's office, you will receive full-time compensation regardless of the number of hours you work," Miriam said, "and while you are in my employ, you will not work for anyone else."

"Yes, ma'am."

"I don't expect to need you eight hours a day initially. Perhaps you could come by in the morning before your first class, then return in the afternoon after your last one."

Camille nodded and said, "I could come at lunch too. It would be better for you not to be alone for too many hours in a row."

Miriam paused. Probably true, though she disliked admitting it. Camille was watching her, attentive, dark eyes compassionate and knowing, despite the lack of information. The girl seemed more familiar with illness than one might expect for someone her age. She'd mentioned a grandmother.

"Do you have anyone at home to consider in your schedule?"

"No, I live alone now. My grandparents raised me, but my grandfather died of cancer two years ago, and my grandmother died of pulmonary disease in June." Camille blinked rapidly, clearly still grieving. "Caring for my grandparents is part of what made me want to be a nurse."

Miriam nodded, unexpectedly comforted that Camille knew the

ugliness of illness and hadn't shied away from it. "I'm sorry for your loss," she murmured.

Petey approached Camille's chair and sniffed her shoes. Camille leaned down, offered him her hand to smell, then stroked him. Petey purred and tilted his head up, as if inspecting her, though his eyes were permanently closed.

"Your cat is so sweet."

"Yes, Petey is an exceptional boy. Everyone falls in love with him."

"How did he lose his sight?"

"Glaucoma. I paid the LSU Vet School Clinic thousands of dollars for treatment and surgery for him, trying to save his eyes. I had to give him eye drops that hurt and medicines that tasted bad. But he came every time I called him, even though he'd wail when he saw the eye dropper. He didn't run and hide or fight me." She wouldn't have been able to bear it if he had.

Camille reached down again to scratch Petey under the chin. He seemed quite taken with her.

"After I dosed him, he'd pace around, flicking his tongue, as if trying to escape the evil taste, or paw at his poor eyes. Eventually, his eyes had to be removed to spare him intense pain, but after that, Petey got right on with his life. He didn't waste time sitting in a corner feeling sorry for himself."

After they went over the scheduling details, Miriam stood to signal that they were finished. Camille seemed reluctant to leave, and Miriam had to keep edging her toward the door. She reached behind Camille to open it, nodded goodbye, and closed it before Camille left the porch. The visit had tired Miriam, and she wanted to return to her chair. The disease was already making her quite lazy. But of course, it wasn't only the disease. No, she was tired on many levels.

She was pleased with Camille. As Miriam had divined from years of teaching, Camille was intelligent with a good work ethic. When they'd met in Duncan's office, Camille's navy blue interview dress had seen better days, but was carefully pressed, her black pumps well-worn but freshly shined. Miriam had hired her on the spot and offered a good salary too. No point in scrimping now.

Miriam paused in the hall at the study. She knew people found it strange that she'd continued to live in this house, alone. Her parents had tried to dissuade her from returning only days after Tom died, the back porch still stained by his blood. Sometimes at night, she heard echoes trapped in the walls—Tom's pacing, the creak of the large leather desk chair, the clatter of the typewriter, then soft cursing as he yanked the page out, crumpled it, and tossed it aside. Maybe she'd stayed to be with the ghosts. Maybe guilt chained her here.

CHAPTER 3

UNEXPECTED FRIENDSHIPS

Another two weeks passed, and Miriam and Camille settled into a routine. Tonight, Miriam was tired, and after dinner, Camille, who always knew when the weariness set in, told Miriam to go upstairs while she cleaned up. She did, appreciating Camille's cheerful energy, glad not to be alone. She went first to the front bedroom and peered between the curtains at the dark street below, leaning against the windowsill. Saddened by the arrival of fall without her students, she felt the creeping frailty invading her tall, thin frame, once so upright and strong, aging her beyond her years.

The full moon rode low and lovely over the quiet old mid-city neighborhood, the air still humid and heavy, though autumn was creeping in on the cooler breezes and falling leaves. The live oaks' thick branches screened the streetlights and cast long shadows over the narrow streets, deepening the darkness. Lights had gone out in the front rooms of the houses and come on in the back or upstairs windows as beds were turned down, stories read, and the day put to rest. Brick walkways led through yards brightened by fall-blooming azaleas to front porches illuminated by flickering gas lanterns. Rocking chairs and porch swings under hanging fans sat motionless in the moonlight.

When she heard Camille ascending the stairs, Miriam crossed the hall to her bedroom. She slipped out of her clothes and into her nightgown while Camille fussed over the bed, turning down the sheets, plumping up the pillows, and propping them against the headboard, knowing that Miriam liked to read before turning out the light.

"I told you that you needn't do that, as if you were a hotel maid," Miriam said. "I half expect you to leave a mint on the pillow."

Camille laughed and said, "I guess I should be getting home to walk my dog."

Miriam wasn't comfortable with the idea of Camille walking at night, even with a no-doubt protective dog. Although Camille's neighborhood was only blocks away, it was a different world from Miriam's.

"Do you really think it's safe for you to walk alone at night?" Miriam asked, not for the first time.

"I'm not alone; Hanks is with me. And he needs his walk after being by himself all day."

"Can't you walk him in the morning?"

Camille smiled. "I walk him in the morning too, and soon it'll be dark then as well."

Miriam hadn't thought about that. Camille's thinly veiled hints about letting Hanks stay in Miriam's spacious backyard had continued, despite Miriam's lack of response. To forestall a return to that subject, Miriam asked, "What kind of dog is Hanks?"

"He's a pit bull," Camille said, "but he's very gentle and sweet."

"How did you, uh, acquire him? From a shelter?" Surely Camille hadn't deliberately chosen that type of dog. Miriam slipped into bed, clearly signaling that any response should be kept brief.

"No, I rescued Hanks myself."

"Oh?" Miriam wasn't really all that interested, but Camille sat down in the bedroom reading chair and launched right into the story. Miriam leaned comfortably against the pillows.

"I first saw Hanks when I was cleaning in an office building on the Acadian Thruway. I was on the seventh floor when I looked out the window and saw this brown-and-white dog at the edge of the road."

Camille chuckled. "Well, I found out later he was brown and white. He was so dirty then that the white looked tan."

Miriam nodded permission to continue.

"You know how big and busy that road is, and cars go so fast. He looked like a stray—no collar, with his ribs showing. I was wondering why he was out there so late at night, and then I saw these three guys at the all-night gas station on the other side of the road calling him. Hanks ran across all four lanes of traffic to get to them, dodging cars."

Camille frowned, remembering. "At first, I thought they were going to help him, and when he got to them without being run over, I turned around and plugged in the vacuum. But then I heard hooting and hollering. I went back to the window and saw those men charging at the dog as he walked toward them, yelling and waving their arms."

"Oh, no," Miriam murmured, picturing the starved, terrified dog.

"They chased him back into the road. They were laughing while this poor, scared dog ran back across in all that traffic, cars beeping at him. Then, as soon as he got across, they started calling him again, holding out their hands like they had food."

Miriam shook her head in disbelief.

"Poor Hanks was scared, but so hungry. He started back across the road, but as soon as he got close, they charged him again, yelling and waving their arms. Hanks ran back into the road, and this time he almost got hit. The men were laughing so hard they were hanging onto each other and stumbling around the front of the station."

Camille glanced at her watch—probably thinking about Hanks waiting for her now. "I didn't want a dog, but I wasn't going to just watch their sick game. So, I ran down—so scared I'd be too late—to where Hanks was all huddled up on the side of the road. I held out my hand for him to sniff and he let me pet him. Then I took off my belt and put it around his neck like a leash."

"What did those men do when they saw you?" Miriam pictured her there, alone at the dark intersection.

"They started shouting, 'Hey, baby, come over here with the doggy, we got something for both of you.' I was going to yell at them to go to hell—sorry." Miriam waved the apology away. "But I was afraid that might scare Hanks. So, I took him into the building and let him stay with me while I finished cleaning. Then I brought him to my car—he was afraid to get in, but he wanted to stay with me, so he did—and I got dog food on the way home."

The story was more compelling than expected; Miriam was moved. "Did you let Hanks stay in your house?"

"No, I put food and water and a blanket for him on the back porch —it seemed better to wait until I was awake to watch him. And he needed a bath too."

A good, practical solution.

"My house has long windows looking out on the porch, and after I went back in, I watched Hanks settle down on the blanket beside the window," Camille said. "Hanks saw me and sat up. I knelt and pressed my palm against the window in front of him, and Hanks licked the pane on the other side, looking at me with his big brown eyes. I'd planned to find him a home, but right then, I knew he was my dog now."

Impressively bold and kind. As Camille stood to leave, Miriam reconsidered letting the dog come. After all, having Camille here early in the morning and later in the evening was convenient.

"I suppose if you brought your dog here, you could walk him after you arrived," Miriam said, thinking that perhaps Camille should arrive earlier to accommodate that. "You could give him his evening walk after dinner. In between, he would stay in the yard, of course. I wouldn't want him upsetting Petey." Miriam gazed fondly at him, curled up in his accustomed spot beside her.

Camille leaped at the offer, assuring Miriam that she would arrive half an hour earlier for the walk.

"Let's try it tomorrow," Miriam said, her tone more resigned than gracious. She hoped the dog wasn't given to barking.

THE NEXT MORNING, MIRIAM WATCHED FROM THE LIVING ROOM window as Camille opened the car door for Hanks, so clearly thrilled to be with her, tail wagging madly, jaws stretched into a wide grin. Dogs certainly had more expressive faces than cats. Why had she been so reluctant to allow him to come? She went out and sat in the rocker on the front porch. She waved at Camille, who called out that she'd be back in half an hour and set out with Hanks. Miriam watched Hanks sniffing the new street, almost prancing in his delight, looking up at Camille and grinning at her. Then Miriam returned to her chair in the sitting room.

When Camille and Hanks returned, they were both grinning. Miriam listened from her chair, Petey curled in her lap, as Camille led Hanks down the hall to the French door that opened onto the back porch. Petey lifted his head at the heavy clomping on the wood floor. His nose twitched, and then he sprang up, hissing and yowling as he tore toward Hanks. Sounds Miriam had never heard from him before. Miriam lurched out of her chair and followed. Hanks jerked back toward the front door to escape, bumping into the foyer table. The antique oriental vase on it wobbled, then fell, and the crash of broken china momentarily stunned Hanks and Petey. Miriam, afraid the big dog would snap at Petey, hurried toward them as Camille regained control of Hanks.

"I'm so sorry, Miriam!"

Miriam scooped up a squirming Petey, muttering to herself that she knew this was a bad idea, and retreated back to her recliner, blood dripping from a shallow scratch to her forearm. She turned to see Camille leading Hanks back to the French door instead of out to her car. Hanks, now subdued, walked close to Camille, head lowered, looking ashamed. On the porch, Camille removed his leash (why?) and returned to fill a water bowl she'd brought.

"Aren't you going to take him back home?" Miriam said loudly from the sitting room. Obviously, having him here wasn't going to work.

"Please let him stay, just for today. It's already late, and I need to get you set up before I leave for class. He'll be outside now."

Miriam couldn't think of an adequate protest to that. Camille knew Petey didn't go outside; this morning's drama was over. And she heard the edge of tears in Camille's voice and didn't want to make the girl cry. After all, Miriam had given her the long-awaited permission to bring the dog. Camille was in the foyer now, sniffling as she picked up the pieces of the vase.

"I'm so sorry about your beautiful vase, Miriam. Please withhold payment for it from my check, and I can help you find a replacement."

Right. Camille clearly had no idea what a replacement would cost, in the unlikely event that they could find one. But then, Miriam thought, so what? She'd enjoyed the vase for many years; she didn't need a replacement now.

"Camille, please don't worry about it—just a bauble I picked up at a garage sale years ago," Miriam lied. She was more worried about Petey's reaction.

Camille finished picking up the shards, took them to the kitchen, and brought Miriam a mug of tea. "Maybe we could try again tomorrow if I bring Hanks into the backyard through the side gate instead of through the house?" Camille said, pulling out a tissue to blot at her face. The tears touched Miriam—clearly, Camille loved Hanks as much as she loved Petey.

"Well, let's see how he does today and we can think about tomorrow," Miriam finally said and was rewarded by Camille's brilliant smile, which didn't seem to allow for the possibility of failure. Well, they'd let this play out for the day, as promised.

Hanks now sat obediently on the porch, as if awaiting further instructions. Camille, with great care, squeezed out the door and patted Hanks' big head, murmuring words Miriam couldn't hear, but that Hanks apparently took to mean that he was free to enjoy the yard. Camille returned inside, and they watched through the long sitting room windows as Hanks explored, leaping forward to chase a squirrel up the large oak, then trotting around the perimeter. They laughed at Hanks' antics in his new domain—his energy and joy, big doggy grin.

After Camille left for her morning classes, Miriam continued watching Hanks, Petey again ensconced on her lap, satisfied to have Hanks banned from his immediate domain. She dislodged Petey gently and went to the kitchen to fix another cup of tea. She saw the shards of the vase on the counter—Camille maybe thinking she could glue them back together, but a glance told Miriam that was hopeless. Miriam's mother had given her the vase as a housewarming gift, and it had meant something to both of them. But her mother, lost to heart failure over ten years ago, would never see the broken pieces or mourn the loss of the vase. And before another year passed, neither would she. Miriam gingerly put the shards into a bag, then into the garbage, not wanting to upset Camille further with the sight of them. Not important, only a remnant from the past. She moved a painted porcelain bowl to the foyer table where the vase had been. Then she put her keys in the bowl, as if they had always belonged there.

She returned to the sitting room. Hanks was still bounding around the yard as if he'd found his own paradise. Then he leaped onto the porch, flying over the stairs, and stopped short in front of the window, looking in at her, still grinning, tail wagging. Miriam put down her mug, gave Petey a reassuring stroke, then slipped out the French door onto the porch Hanks had just vacated to chase another squirrel. His big head swung around when he heard her, and she sat down quickly on the porch swing when he charged toward her, afraid he might jump on her. But Camille had evidently trained him well. Hanks halted before her, as if reporting for duty, and she cautiously scratched behind his ears. He regarded her soulfully, tail wagging so hard his hind quarters wiggled back and forth.

AFTER THE FIRST WEEK, MIRIAM BEGAN LETTING HANKS INSIDE after Camille left for classes—always putting him back out before she returned, not ready to admit that he was allowed in the house. To Miriam's surprise, Petey fascinated Hanks. Petey remained uneasy with Hanks' attentions but was unwilling to surrender his place on Miriam's lap. He'd wail and hiss at the large panting beast in his face, and Hanks persevered through a few swipes across the snout. But the dog showed admirable restraint, even gentleness. Now, when Petey heard Hanks come in, he sometimes approached him. Hanks would wait, deferential, lowering his snout to Petey's upturned face to sniff noses. Then Hanks would go too far, slurping his tongue across Petey's head, earning a hiss as Petey retreated. Still, they seemed to be developing an improbable friendship.

It was windy and rainy this morning, and Miriam let Hanks in as soon as Camille left. He flopped on the rug with a contented sigh. Miriam returned to her recliner, leaned back, and closed her eyes, thinking she might doze in the cozy room. But her mind drifted into those corners she'd habitually blocked with a wall of busyness. She looked out to the porch where Tom had died. Funny how time honed some feelings to a razor's edge rather than dulling them. For years afterward, she couldn't sit on the porch, though it had been a favorite spot since childhood. She'd gradually reclaimed it, but some days the house was like a minefield. She had to tiptoe around the trip-wire images so easily detonated—crimson spreading from Tom's body on the gray porch floorboards. The gun's explosion and her screams. Those days, infrequent now, but never entirely gone, could still trigger heart tears like blood, so hard to staunch the flow once started.

Hanks, who'd been watching her, got up and rested his big head on the couch beside her, looking at her, as if in sympathy. Petey stirred, then resettled, no longer bothered by Hanks' proximity. Miriam alternated between stroking Petey and scratching Hanks behind the ears. Hanks curled up at her feet, and Petey nuzzled her, circled once in her lap and resettled. The sad memories and hard regrets faded in the sound of Petey's purring and Hanks' snoring, and Miriam dozed too.

PART II
THEN

CHAPTER 4

DIVERGING PATHS

Miriam and Tom each had their fourth-year reviews. Tom's was more warning than encouragement, but he'd been reappointed (barely, her father told her), which meant he'd have two more years before mandatory tenure review. Miriam's review committee had encouraged her to apply for early tenure the next fall. Although Tom had, in his dependably generous way, rejoiced with her, his continuing struggle dampened her pleasure in the achievement.

He wasn't only struggling with publication. His teaching wasn't going well either. She'd seen his dismal student evaluations and they'd observed each other's classes. Hers had gone well that day, and she'd basked in Tom's obvious pride and compliments.

Tom's class had been a different story. Unlike her students, who often greeted her as she arrived or stayed after class to talk or ask a final question, his students had filed in and out of the room, barely acknowledging him, silent or talking among themselves. An exception was a plump but pretty young woman who gazed at him adoringly when she lingered after class, her tight sweater and miniskirt straining as she leaned over his desk to ask a hastily formulated question. Tom's efforts to stimulate classroom discussion were met with disinterested silence (except for a couple of fumbling attempts by his admirer), one student snored in the back row, and another belligerently questioned the current relevance of the novel—Dickens' *Bleak House*—asking if they could read a Vonnegut or Updike novel instead, missing even the basic fact that this was a British literature course and unimpressed by Tom's strenuous attempt to convey the book's historical and literary significance.

After his class, Miriam and Tom had gone to the cafeteria for coffee, and she'd tried to offer something useful. Compliments were easy; helping without hurting was harder, she thought, seeing the frustration behind his eyes. She suggested that he pause to ask questions during the lecture, attempting to soften the implicit criticism by pointing out that she'd had the advantage of being raised by a professor.

"It's easier for me because my father talked about his classes and students almost every night at dinner. I sat in on his summer courses too. His classes taught me as much about teaching as about the subject matter."

"Yeah, the graduate students say your father's a great teacher," he said, voice flat, face expressionless. Stupid to make her father the good example. She wasn't helping.

Back at her office, she sat tracing her fingers over her desk's scarred surface, wondering whether good teaching could be learned or was an innate talent you had or didn't. For her, the greatest reward was that excitement on a student's face when an idea took hold, and the parts suddenly became a whole.

Tom wasn't feeling that. What if he never did? What if he became like one of those old tenured professors shuffling around the department, back bent prematurely from habitual slumping, lines carved by perpetual disappointment, cynicism hardened to bitterness, classroom jabs at students deteriorating from challenging to petty and cruel, watching the clock during lectures more than the students, and living for the breaks between semesters. She sighed and rubbed her temples, trying to push back a growing headache. Maybe she wasn't giving Tom enough credit. Beginning professors and graduate students received little or no instruction in teaching; the university adhered to the unrealistic theory that they would learn by doing. She pulled a pad from her desk and composed questions generic enough for Tom to tailor to the topic at hand. Maybe they'd help, but he'd need to work on the timing and how to ask them.

ON FRIDAY MORNING, MIRIAM WAS THRILLED TO RECEIVE A REVISE-and-resubmit from the journal *Impressionist Art* for her paper on the evolution of Berthe Morisot's paintings during the years Morisot exhibited in the prestigious Salon de Paris before she began exhibiting with the Impressionists. But as Miriam labored over the revisions on Saturday, her initial euphoria turned to frustration verging on panic. Yes, the paper was too long, but the editor was demanding that she cut nearly half, with no suggestions about what to omit. Tom found her an hour after lunch in her home office, slumped at her desk, head in her hands, amid scattered pages.

"I don't know how to cut half the article and still have a coherent paper within my organizational structure," she said. "And if I change the whole structure, will it still be the paper they accepted? What if they reject the revised version?"

Tom rubbed her shoulders and said, "Why don't I take a look? A second pair of eyes might help."

She gathered the pages and handed them to him, both dubious and grateful. He took them with the editor's letter downstairs to his study, where he stayed the rest of the afternoon. She switched to working on notes for the week's lectures, but her mind kept returning to her paper. Nothing productive, just random anxiety. At sunset, she went down to Tom's study.

He looked up from the pages spread across his desk, covered with annotations written in the margins and between the double-spaced lines and bracketed chunks maybe marked for cutting. He blinked at her as if emerging from a trance.

"Tom, you did so much," she said, trying to sound appreciative. Was he editing or chopping? Would she recognize what was left?

"I'm almost done. Pizza tonight? Give me another half hour." He offered a vague smile and returned to the paper, pencil hovering, immersed.

"Um, okay. Let me know when you want to order." She trudged back upstairs, yearning to quit for the night. She tried to return to her lecture notes, gave up, and picked up her new John McDonald mystery novel.

Another hour and a half passed before Tom came upstairs and handed her the manuscript. When he left to pick up the pizza, she started reading the notes that seemed to fill every blank space, then put the paper aside, overwhelmed. She went down to the kitchen, opened a bottle of wine, and put out plates and napkins. They spent a pleasant evening watching sporadically humorous television requiring only minimal concentration.

As they sat in church the next morning, Miriam's mind wandered during the hymns and sermon, maybe even during the prayers, to Tom's comments. Toward the end of the hour, as if her inattention were forgiven, even rewarded, she suddenly understood how Tom's cuts, moves, and shifts fit together to form a tighter, more concise whole. After the service, she was eager to work on the new draft.

"Could we skip the restaurant brunch today and just have sandwiches at home?" she asked.

"You want to get back to your paper, don't you?"

"Yes—I see what you're doing with the editing. Brilliant, Tom. If I can just put it all together."

"You can. Go on upstairs when we get home. I'll make the sandwiches."

Miriam sat at her desk and began working, the sounds of Tom in the kitchen and everything else fading away as she reread carefully through his comments, deletions, and where he'd moved text around. She began the new draft. Yes, his direction better informed her argument and what he'd trimmed honed rather than diminished her thesis. When she paused at the end of a section to read the new version without looking at the old, she didn't miss what he'd cut. He'd left one section bracketed and untouched, suggesting that she omit it, but preserve it to use in another paper. He was right; the section was less integral to this paper, and she'd been trying to cover too much.

She was vaguely aware of Tom entering her office and quietly putting a sandwich plate and a Coke on her desk, then leaving without an interrupting word. Grateful not to have to stop, she continued on, munching the sandwich when she stopped to read over a revised section. A couple of hours later, Tom came back with a mug of coffee and cookies. She smiled at him as he collected her empty plate; he stooped to kiss her and left the room. She sipped the coffee, reconsidering a sentence, then lined through what she'd written, reworded it, and continued.

By evening, she had a new draft within the editor's length limits. She was mildly astounded to find that nothing had been lost—half the length, but the omissions sharpened rather than obfuscated her significant points. She glanced at the forgotten clock—nearly seven. She grabbed the pages and rushed down to Tom's study.

"Thank you, Tom," she said, showing him the revised paper. "You're a brilliant editor. I never would have been able to do it without you."

"Nice to get something right," he said, and winked at her.

TOM WAS ALREADY UP WHEN MIRIAM WOKE ON MONDAY MORNING. He turned and smiled at her when she joined him in the kitchen and handed her a cup of coffee. Maybe his success with editing had rejuvenated him. She hoped the energy she sensed from him would carry over to his own work.

They sat at the kitchen table together with toast and coffee. Tom handed her some typed pages with handwritten notes in the margins and said, "Look, I added some questions to my lecture notes using your suggestions."

She took the pages and read through them, feeling his gaze on her. She looked up, cringing inwardly, but keeping her expression neutral.

"What do you think?" he asked.

She looked down again at the pages and forced a smile. She told him he'd made a good start with the questions, and he took them back with a sigh, frowning. She wanted to say more, to bring back his initial hopeful expression, the revived energy he'd had. But she knew the questions he'd laboriously concocted (and she could visualize him rising early to struggle over them) were likely to draw only blank looks (perhaps a bumbling effort from that plump girl).

She should help him edit them, but she was exhausted after the weekend's work on her paper and not up to engaging in his struggle.

They finished their coffee in silence. Before leaving for their classes, they kissed and Miriam said she loved him, knowing he wanted her to say more, something he could tell himself to deny that he was failing in the classroom. She hugged him again and left. When she turned before getting into her car, he was still standing in the doorway watching her, shoulders sagging, looking defeated. She raised a hand to wave, but he'd already turned back into the house.

ON SATURDAY MORNING, MIRIAM CAME DOWNSTAIRS TO FIND TOM behind his desk, holding the grip of her Smith & Wesson .38 caliber revolver gingerly with his thumb and index finger, barrel dangled downward, as if it were a small dead animal. He looked up, eyebrows raised, questioning, and said, "Hey, I found the key to the mysterious locked desk drawer and look what was in it. Did you know it was here?"

Miriam glanced at the open drawer and the black gun case on the desk and said, "I'd forgotten, and actually it's mine. My father gave it to me."

"Oh," he said, and replaced the gun in the case with distaste. "Kind of old school, isn't it?"

"Yes, my father likes revolvers better than pistols. He also collects Civil War firearms, but this is his gun of choice for functioning weapons. He used to take me target shooting out on his country property—there's still a cache of tin cans in the garage even though I haven't gone shooting in years."

The sun emerged from behind a cloud, light flooded through the crack between the drapes into the dim room. Tom blinked, sunlit and beautiful, and she yearned to be with him in the bright, cool day.

"Let's go shooting—it'll be fun. Dad's between tenants for the property, so the pasture is empty and we won't accidentally kill anything. I have a key to the gate."

Surprised, he said, "Well, I've never shot a gun before, so you'll have to teach me."

A shard of guilt pierced her, knowing he should be working on the paper he was planning to submit to *The Henry James Review*. But surely they'd both benefit from a break after working so hard last weekend. She tried to ignore that the hard work had all been on her paper, not his.

"I'm actually a pretty good shot," she said. "Southern woman and all that."

Tom nodded and said to give him twenty minutes to finish up, looking sly and calculating. He liked to surprise her with little enhancements to their outings, so she dawdled and took her time upstairs. She changed into black hiking pants with deep pockets for the bullets, a red-and-black plaid flannel shirt over a black tank top, and black leather half boots. She heard him moving between the garage and kitchen, so she took a few minutes more to brush out her hair and freshen her makeup. She was applying bright red lipstick when she caught Tom watching her from the bathroom doorway.

"You look like a cross between a Vogue cover girl and an Orvis catalogue model," he said, pantomiming taking her picture. He ducked back into the bedroom to change into black jeans and the forest-green hiking shirt that brought out that color in his hazel eyes.

"And you look like a cross between the lead guitar player for a hot band and a fishing guide," she said, putting her arms around him. He gave her a quick kiss, and they were on their way. She directed him to the interstate, her hand on his thigh, his hand over hers, exhilarated by escaping for an unplanned afternoon of pleasure.

On their way to the property, they stopped for a fried chicken lunch at a country diner, then drove ten more miles and turned off the highway onto the gravel road to the property. Miriam unlocked the chain on the gate, and they parked at the edge of the pasture. Tom pulled the bag of tin cans from the trunk, and Miriam took the revolver from its case and put the bullet pouch in her pocket.

They walked through the mowed grass of the wide pasture ringed by mature oaks to a defunct cattle trough. She set tin cans on the edge of it, then backed up about ten yards. She faced the cans, and feeling Tom's eyes on her, took her time assuming her stance. She aligned her feet shoulder-width apart and extended her arms straight out, elbows locked, right hand gripping the pistol with her left hand wrapped around it. Flexing her knees slightly and leaning forward from the waist, she sighted in on the first can and began shooting, hitting five of the six cans.

"Pretty good, Annie Oakley," Tom said, raising his eyebrows and nodding.

"Now let's give you a turn," she said.

"You know, I'm okay with just watching. I've never liked guns."

What? Why hadn't he told her? They could've done something else, maybe a movie? They still could. She looked at him, ready to offer, but he was smiling, as if he'd only been teasing.

"Ready and awaiting your expert instruction," he said.

She ejected the spent casings into one of the larger tin cans. "We'll do some dry firing first so you can focus on how to hold the gun, sight it, and—the most important thing—pull the trigger." She expected him to laugh at that, but he remained somber, intent as she positioned his arms and hands in the proper grip for shooting. Maybe guns did make him nervous; shooting might not be the enjoyable, cathartic experience for him that it was for her.

"Always point the gun at the target before you put your finger on the trigger." She leaned in closer, putting her hands over his to help him correct his aim, explaining how to adjust the sight so it was level and centered with the revolver's notch. Her breasts brushed his arm, and she savored the feel of his hands under hers. "Now hold the trigger at your first distal joint—that's right. Envision the trigger finger as actually touching your nose while you look through the sight.

Compress the trigger smoothly, then release it slowly after the hammer comes down, letting your finger slide up and down the trigger."

She stepped back to observe; he looked good standing in position, concentrating on getting it right. She let him dry fire a couple of times, then showed him how to release the barrel, and load the gun, then unloaded it and had him reload it.

"You'll have recoil with the bullets that you didn't have with the dry firing," she warned, "the gun will kick upward a bit." Sure enough, the first shot went high. She leaned in again, putting her hands over his, showing him how to adjust the aim. He paused to nuzzle her, making her laugh, but prompting a warning not to fool around with a loaded gun. He shot and missed, which she assured him was usual for a beginner and suggested moving closer to their targets. After a few more tries, he hit one of the cans.

"Tom, that's great for your first session! You're a natural."

"Even if it wasn't the one I was aiming for?"

"I don't think I hit any of the cans until the third time my father brought me out."

"Must've been blind luck then." He missed the last shot.

He handed the gun back to her with a crooked smile, and she knew he'd had enough for the day. He hadn't felt the exhilaration she did in target shooting. She ejected the casings into the can, and they gathered the remaining cans and remnants into the bag. She took his hand and squeezed it as they walked back to the car; he squeezed back and leaned over to kiss her cheek, and she bumped her hip against his. At the car, she gave him a final lesson.

"Never leave bullets in the gun, ever," she said, putting the gun and bullets away. She was headed for the passenger side when she saw Tom taking a blanket and a cooler out of the trunk.

"I thought we might need some refreshment after our exertions," he said, with that slow smile. She laughed, delighted, and followed him back into the pasture, where he spread the blanket out near a small pond reflecting blue sky interspersed with fluffy white clouds, the tranquil silence broken only by the birds singing from the trees on the perimeter and the breeze rustling the leaves. She sat down, watching him take from the cooler a bottle of wine, crackers, and cheese slices arranged neatly on a plate. This, she thought, was Tom, always ready with a secret indulgence to share at the right moment.

"This merlot shouldn't be chilled, but it'll warm up if we give it a minute," he said, pouring the wine and handing her a glass. The sun went behind the clouds, and she sat leaning against him in the cool air, sipping the wine and nibbling on cheese and crackers. He pointed to a cloud and said it looked like one of the old, tall wooden sailing ships in the Boston harbor. She said it looked more like a pirogue in the bayou backed by towering cypress trees.

"My little coonass," he said, putting his arm around her and pulling her closer.

"Glad you're finally learning some Louisiana terms, but no one born and bred in Baton Rouge is a coonass. You have to be way farther south in Cajun country for that."

"Ah, I'll keep working on my Louisiana lingo."

She gathered the empty wine glasses and the remnants of their snack and put everything back in the cooler. He watched her, then patted the blanket beside him, and she lay on her side, propped on an elbow, looking at him. He reclined too, facing her.

"You could have told me you didn't want to go shooting," she said.

"The thought of being alone with you in an empty cow pasture was just too tempting."

"Seriously, we could have done something else."

"I liked watching you shoot. And I liked the lunch before and this part after even more."

She reached for him and sank into the feel of his arms around her, pulling her close.

After a long kiss, she leaned back and said, "You know, next time we want to get out of town, we could go hiking again in Port Hudson State Park."

He laughed, kissed her again, and said, "A very fond memory." He slipped his hand under her tank top and rubbed her back, pulling her closer again. Then he leaned back, looked at her with mock serious-ness, and said, "But we narrowly avoided disaster. Lucky for us that Boy Scout troop didn't deviate from the trail."

"You rascal," she laughed, remembering the blanket from his backpack spread on the soft grass in a copse of trees off the trail, how she'd clung to him, eager for more kisses.

Safe in the pasture's solitude, they took their time, lingering in kisses and each other's tender places. Afterward, they lay close together, sweat drying in the fading sun and cool breeze of the late afternoon.

Tom rolled to lie on his side facing her and stroked her hair. "You know, Miriam, you could succeed anywhere," he said, his voice low and husky.

She looked at him, dreading what was coming.

He cleared his throat and continued, his eyes on hers, "I mean, sometimes I wonder if you're afraid to try somewhere new, away from all that you've known."

"But I love it here, Tom."

"I know, I'm just saying, you could love other places too."

She didn't think she could love anywhere else the way she did her home. Here.

"Don't you think you might love it here too if we stayed?"

"Well, I love being where you are," he said and left it at that.

CHAPTER 5

On a Wednesday afternoon in March, Miriam returned home smiling and humming to herself. Her lectures had gone well, and a favorite student, Marcie Bienvenu, had come by her office to discuss majoring in Art History. Miriam found Tom in his study, bent over typed pages, pencil in hand. The pages had been erased and written over again so many times that they were worn through in places. A pile of crumpled paper lay on the floor. She stood behind him, rubbing his shoulders, feeling the tension. Tom reached back and covered her hands with his.

"Bad day?"

Tom mumbled that it had been a tough one, but stopped there.

"What happened?" She sat down on the couch across from him and said, "Talk to me, Tom."

He leaned back in his chair, sighed, then said, "Your father called me into his office. He said I'm not producing the way they expected when the department hired me. Said I'd better get some publications out before my next annual review. 'Some,' not 'one.'" Miriam eyed the stack of student evaluations on his desk, and he added, "Yeah, those were bad too."

"Do you want to talk?"

"Not now, maybe at dinner."

She kissed his cheek and quietly retreated to her office. They were past the early days when their departments were still giving them the benefit of the doubt, still confident that they would validate the foresight of those on the search committee who'd championed them. She and Tom had imagined a future of philosophical discussions, eager students, wise and welcoming older professors mentoring them, and academic journals keen to publish their articles on esoteric topics known only to scholars. Life, they'd thought, would be similar to graduate school, but with a steady paycheck and better offices. Their dreams had aligned when they'd met at LSU, both fresh from promising graduate school triumphs, proud of obtaining tenure-track positions in crowded fields.

She heard the clank of the mail slot downstairs and the soft fall of letters on the rug, rapid steps, an envelope ripping open, and quick strides up the stairs. Tom came in, face shining with excitement, waving a letter, pointing to the name of the college on the envelope.

"Miriam, remember, I told you that when they called last week, they said they'd like me to come up for an in-person interview? Well, they've confirmed, and they want to fly both of us up! They want to meet you too and show us the town! It means I've made the short list!" He stopped to catch his breath and study her with mixed hope and anxiety. She couldn't hide her dismay. She vaguely remembered his mentioning the call, but she'd thought of it as only a tentative contact, nothing definite. She hadn't acknowledged to herself that he was still scanning the postings of academic positions, still seeking to relocate, preferring to believe that he'd reconciled himself to staying.

Tom forged ahead. "It's a good small liberal arts college in upstate New York. It could be a great place for us." His eyes searched hers, imploring. "We could breathe there."

"I don't want to move. This is our home." She turned back to her paper on Berthe Morisot's first forays into what was then an exclusively male Impressionist group, hoping to escape into her work, end this.

"But I'm not making it here," he pleaded, leaning over her desk to catch her eye, voice hoarse. "I don't fit in at the department, and it's affecting my work."

She looked past him for a silent, suspended moment before giving the only answer she had, the one he must know by now.

"Tom, I love it here, and New York is so far away. It would kill my parents if we moved. My mother depends on me—I'm an only child." She shoved her paper in a desk drawer, slammed it, and walked past him downstairs to the laundry room. She yanked clothes from the washer and threw them into the dryer as if they'd offended her. Tom trailed behind. He wasn't going to leave it.

"If I get an offer, you said we could at least consider it."

Had she? Maybe. She didn't remember. If he'd asked when she was deep in revisions or composing lecture notes, she might've responded without listening, wanting him to leave before she lost the thread she was following. If she'd heard, she'd probably assumed he wouldn't get an offer in the competitive academic market and forgotten about it. Her selfishness appalled her for a moment. But she was needed here; purpose justified her desire. Didn't it? She turned back to him.

"So you want to leave our home and go live in New York, where we don't know anyone?" she said, hearing the shrillness in her voice. "And what would I do, Tom? I've been told that my chances for early tenure here are excellent."

"Well, I've been pretty clearly told my chances for tenure are dismal. If I wait to apply until after I've been turned down, it could hurt my chances anywhere else."

"This little New York college probably doesn't even have an art history curriculum. It's too small."

"With your talent, you could teach anything in the art department —they obviously have one of those."

"Would you be happy at a teaching college, Tom? Their graduate program is probably limited if they even have one. You'd have double the teaching load and no time for research and writing." Neither would she.

"I wouldn't be under constant pressure to publish either. Will you at least agree that if they make me an offer, we'll consider it?"

She nodded, wordless, and hoped he wouldn't get an offer. Then she asked, "Who did you list as references? Won't you have to tell my father about this?"

Tom looked troubled. He said he'd given the names of two of his graduate school professors and Herb Rothschild, his only real supporter in the department. If he got an offer, they could tell Miriam's parents then.

SHE DIDN'T FLY UP WITH HIM FOR THE INTERVIEW, SAYING SHE couldn't miss even a single class so close to midterms. When she returned to the empty house after taking him to the airport, she was unprepared for her sadness, disproportionate to his brief absence. That night, he called from New York, describing the picturesque small town and lakeshore in glowing detail. But that excitement was gone when he called Friday night, replaced by a despondent monotone and short sentences describing the formal interview. She told him Saturday's more casual lunch with department faculty and dinner with search committee members would probably be easier (though she didn't believe it).

She missed with surprising sharpness their weekend rituals—Friday night pizza with a movie on cable, early Saturday morning gardening, leisurely café dinner. She buried herself in research. Uninterrupted by their familiar pleasures, though, the hours dragged. She yearned to discuss her paper's emerging outline with Tom, craved his insightful comments and reliable encouragement.

When he called Saturday night, he described his responses to questions about teaching and research, saying he didn't know how well it had gone, clearly hoping she'd say it all sounded fine, promising even. She didn't. She knew he'd lie awake after they hung up, replaying every meeting and interaction, agonizing over each word said. She almost called him back, pitying his long night alone, but didn't. She allowed herself a moment of elation that this episode was probably ending.

MIRIAM MET HER FATHER FOR THEIR WEEKLY LUNCH ON THE following Tuesday in the elegant dining room of the LSU Faculty Club. The room's tall windows and French doors, the lazy turn of the ceiling fans, and the music student's skilled playing on the shiny black grand piano in the corner should have relaxed her, but she was tense, an unfocused foreboding gnawing at her.

Her father strode to the table, scowling. He began speaking as he pulled out his chair.

"Tom's fourth-year review was a disaster. I've warned him repeatedly that he needs to shape up or he's going to be shipped out. He needs to get *at least one* publication out pronto. He's got a lot of work to do if he wants a chance at tenure."

"Yes, he knows that. He's working on a manuscript."

"The Tenure and Promotion Committee's report made it damn clear that they'd just as soon push him out of the nest and be done with it," he said, his face reddening.

The server appeared and took their orders. Miriam sipped her water, focusing on the sunlight sparkling on the small crystal vase on the table holding a red rose and white carnations, wishing she were back in her office, eating a sandwich at her desk, with her manuscript.

Her father took a deep breath and lowered his voice, which had gotten loud for the genteel Faculty Club. "I have some good news for Tom," he said. "Herb Rothschild, who took over as editor of the *Southern Literary Journal* when I had too many competing commitments, has been looking for a copy editor. I suggested Tom—Rothschild is one of the few who like him. Or at least tolerates him." He said it as if this made him think less of Herb.

"How would that work with Tom's teaching?" Miriam asked, wary. "Would he be released from part of his class load?"

"Well, I don't know about that, Miriam. We're all expected to do more than the bare minimum. This would be a feather in Tom's cap—if he does a good job."

"Well, he's really busy with the manuscripts he's submitting from his dissertation and writing his lectures. You know we're both teaching new courses this semester."

"For god's sake, Miriam, I thought you'd be thrilled. Your mother keeps asking me why I don't do more to help Tom. Here I get him a plum position on a well-established scholarly journal that most assistant professors would kill for, and you're worried that he might not be able to fit it into his busy, albeit completely unproductive, schedule."

"Dad, I'm sure he'll be thrilled. I just don't want him to be too distracted from getting his tenure package together."

Her father sighed loudly. "I'll ask Rothschild if his last copy editor had a reduced teaching load, and if so, we'll see if we can do the same for Tom. But I'm not asking Herb to do anything more."

"Of course not."

Miriam feigned surprise when Tom told her about the position that evening, not wanting to mention talking with her father, which might lead to questions about the rest of the conversation. Tom was more excited than she'd seen him in months, maybe years. By the next week, he was in his study, editing through a large stack of manuscripts, referring frequently to a collection of style manuals on his desk. His own manuscript lay in exactly the same position as it had the week before.

"Tom, don't you think you should work on your own paper too?"

"I'm under a tight deadline to finish editing the articles for this quarter's issue. We're taking it to the printer next week."

She was glad to see Tom's engagement in the editing, his clear sense of accomplishment and purpose. She was grateful too, for Herb's mentoring and friendship. But Tom's paper remained untouched, even after that first pile of manuscripts went to the printer and a new one took their place. She knew academic journals were chronically under-staffed and that this one was highly respected, the result of dedicated work from a series of professors, including her father, over the last twenty-five years. She also knew that no matter how well Tom performed his editing duties, it wouldn't save him if he didn't have any publications to list in his tenure package.

She was still thinking about that when she arrived at Tom's office to meet him for lunch and found his office door closed, unusual when he knew she was on her way. She hesitated, wondering if he was having a private conference with a student, and listened. She heard his voice, low and soothing, intimate even. Like when he spoke to her.

"No, no, of course you're no trouble," he said. "I always love talking to you, Agatha. It's my pleasure. Yes, we can go over that part again."

Who was he talking to? He shouldn't be talking to a student that way—what if it was the plump girl, his admirer? No, surely not. Finally, she opened the door a crack. He was on the phone.

Tom waved her into his office without a trace of guilt. He scribbled a note that he was talking to a journal author and could meet at her office in 15 minutes. She gave him a thumbs up and turned to leave, still wondering at Tom's intimate, solicitous tone. Was this a local scholar he knew personally? She hoped not. She hoped it was someone who lived in a distant city.

She was so distracted that she nearly ran into Herb as he was rounding the corner to his office next to Tom's.

"Whoa, Miriam, I'm sorry," he said, stopping short to avoid colliding with her. He glanced at Tom's closed door, cocked his head, listening, then said, "Tom told me he was having lunch with you, but it looks like he's stuck on the phone with Agatha."

"Oh?" Miriam asked.

"Agatha's one of our best literary critics, nationally acclaimed. In her eighties, with little formal education, but a brilliant mind. Her papers always require heavy editing, and she can get pretty feisty about the changes."

Miriam nodded, beginning to understand.

"From the first phone call, Tom had her purring like a kitten. Now she won't talk to anyone else. If Tom isn't here, she'll ask me when she can call him back."

Miriam walked back to her office, picturing the elderly critic's frowning dismay at the myriad of editorial revisions softening to acceptance, maybe even gratitude, as she listened to Tom's gentle explanations, informed by respect and empathy, making the changes palatable.

ON SATURDAY AFTERNOON THE NEXT WEEK, MIRIAM WAS IN HER office upstairs when Tom came in and handed her a letter from the college he'd visited. It politely thanked him for his interest in the position and said another candidate had been selected. Miriam said she was sorry, trying to sound sincere (and she was, for the sadness in his eyes).

"Remember, we have the potluck party at Herb and Emily's tonight," she said. An English Department event wasn't generally greeted with anticipation, but being with Herb and Emily Rothschild was, whatever the occasion. Tom nodded, morose, returned to his office downstairs, and closed the door.

Tom was still brooding that evening when they walked to the door of Herb and Emily's modest brick home carrying a bottle of wine, a casserole dish filled with a five-layer Mexican dip, and chips. Miriam was tired of the heavy silence and hoped the party would lighten his mood. She scanned the parked cars for her father's, relieved not to find it. He rarely attended these events, although her mother would've enjoyed them. Music and laughter drifted from the house, and voices greeted them as they walked through the living room to the kitchen amid chatter about classes, department gossip, and the baseball team's performance. They greeted Emily and added their dish to the others she was arranging, poured wine into plastic cups, and found a place together at the end of a worn green-and-brown plaid couch. After some initial conversation with the department's newest hire and his wife, Tom said he was going to help Herb at the grill. Miriam noticed he took his already-empty plastic cup with him and ducked into the kitchen for a refill before heading outside. When Herb returned with a platter of burgers and Emily called everyone into the dining room to serve themselves, she saw Tom refill his cup again before joining her.

They served themselves on paper plates and sat down. The group quieted while everyone dug into the food, complimenting Herb on the burgers. Tom caught her glance at his cup and said, disingenuously, "Oh, did you want me to get you a refill?" He drained his and added, "I could get it for you now."

What was this? She'd never seen Tom have more than a couple of glasses of wine sipped over a couple of hours. She tried to ignore his drinking and participate in the conversations around them. Tom sat back with his wine, mostly silent. She finished her meal and rose to gather empty plates and napkins, then chatted with Emily in the kitchen. When Herb clinked a spoon against a mayonnaise jar for attention, Miriam returned to her seat.

Herb raised his cup to a man with snowy hair and bright blue eyes wearing a tweed jacket with suede patches at the elbows, and said, "I'd like to make a toast to Professor Emile Berthelot, our esteemed colleague and one of the best professors in the department. We'll miss you after you retire at the end of the semester and hope you'll come around frequently, but not too often so that we know you're enjoying yourself." Cups were raised around the room. Tom began clapping loudly, though no one else did. Miriam grabbed his wrist to stop him, embarrassed by the looks he was getting. Tom pulled away from her, irritated, but ceased clapping.

Emile thanked everyone, put his arm around his wife, and said they were looking forward to having time to travel.

"Do you think you'll move to your Florida house full time?" asked a woman in her late forties with dyed black hair and heavy eyeliner, wearing a tight (unflattering) burgundy dress and shiny black vinyl boots.

Tom leaned over and, in a loud whisper, said, "She reminds me of a cheap bottle of wine poured into that dress." Miriam frowned and shushed him.

Emile glanced at Tom, cleared his throat, and said, "We'll probably go to Florida more often and spend more time there. But we've lived in

Louisiana all our lives, and our son and his family are in Baton Rouge. They just had their fourth child, so we're pretty well rooted here."

"He married a Louisiana girl," Emile's wife said with a smile. "She told him, 'You don't leave Louisiana!'"

Everyone laughed. Except Tom, who said, too loudly, "It's true. Did you know South Louisiana has the highest share of natives in the nation? About 75%, even 90% in some places. God only knows why." Tom glanced around at the now-silent group, then continued. "The great Louisiana writer Ernest Gaines said that in all his stories and novels, no one ever escapes Louisiana. But Gaines himself moved to California and stayed there, writing about Louisiana from a safe distance."

Emile shot his wife a look with a slight shake of his head, as if to say, I told you what he was like.

Tom continued, without encouragement. "Maybe there's a literary advantage to living in the South? Flannery O'Connor said whenever she was asked why Southern writers particularly like to write about freaks, she'd say it's because they are still able to recognize one."

Hoping to end Tom's monologue, Miriam said, "Where in Florida is your vacation home, Emile?" He opened his mouth to answer, but Tom broke in.

Looking at Miriam intensely and taking her hands, as if they were alone, Tom said, "Flannery O'Connor also said that where you come from is gone, and where you are is no good unless you can get away from it." Miriam felt her face redden and pulled her hands back. People looked away from them, awkward, embarrassed.

"Hey, Tom, can you give me a hand cleaning up out here?" Herb called, gesturing to the back door, adding, "Don't go away, folks, dessert is coming." Tom followed him out. People returned to chatting. Miriam spotted Emily in the kitchen and escaped there, offering to help.

"Thanks, I could use you in here," Emily said in her perfectly organized kitchen. "Herb told me it's been hard for Tom in the department. But Herb also said how much he hopes Tom will stay." Miriam nodded her thanks, forcing a small smile, and Emily handed her a platter and box of miniature desserts to arrange on it.

Miriam and Tom stayed long enough to choke down dessert, Miriam trying to act as if all was well. No one attempted to engage Tom in conversation. When they walked out to the car, Tom started toward the driver's side, and Miriam pushed him aside and said she was driving. As soon as they pulled out and started down the street, Tom said, "I'm sorry, I shouldn't have said all that. Not the time or place. I get it."

"Well, chugging the wine didn't help," Miriam said, staring straight ahead as she drove, furious, seething, the burger twisting her guts.

"I said I was sorry. I wasn't thinking. But, really, Miriam, if you weren't from here, you'd see how much better our lives could be somewhere else."

Ignoring that, she said, "You might want to remember before you act like a jackass that most of the people who'll vote on your tenure are at these parties."

"Yeah, except for Daddy Dearest, who didn't make an appearance."

"Thank God for small favors," she muttered.

By the end of the fifteen-minute drive home, Tom had fallen asleep and was snoring loudly. He jumped awake when Miriam slammed the car door and followed her inside.

"You can sleep in the guestroom."

"Fine, I'd rather sleep there." He got his pajamas and retreated.

Miriam showered and went to bed, read for thirty minutes, comprehending little of what was on the pages she turned, then clicked off the lamp and closed her eyes, feeling a deep weariness, but sleep wouldn't come. She rolled over and resettled herself. She tried to empty her mind and drift off, but kept returning to Tom's stubborn conviction that everything would be better if they moved. If she shared that belief, it might be different, but she didn't. The college in New York would have been a disaster. Any benefit of decreased publishing pressure would be eclipsed by his lackluster pedagogy, which would weigh heavily against him at a teaching college.

He could succeed as a professor here regardless of his shortcomings as a teacher because research and writing trumped teaching evaluations. Several examples came readily to mind of well-respected professors with national reputations built on their publications who were snore-worthy teachers. Tom's work on her paper had been outstanding, his editing so skillful; how could he not succeed as a writer? In graduate school, inspired by a linguistics course, he'd published a paper in *The Literary Linguist,* a small journal in its first year of publication. Having the publication had helped him when he'd interviewed at LSU, especially with Herb Rothschild, who considered the piece creative and original, a precursor of innovative research to come. (Her father had dismissed the paper as not "true" literary scholarship.) She'd hoped Tom might be encouraged to explore the emerging area further, but he'd lost interest in the analytical linguistic approach, returning to the overcrowded field of traditional literary criticism.

She got out of bed, hearing Tom snoring as she passed the open door to the guestroom and went downstairs to his study. She looked at his unfinished paper, comparing the characterizations in the novels of James and Wharton. Maybe she could help him the way he'd helped her.

It took less than twenty minutes for her to realize that she couldn't. English literature wasn't her field, but even she could see that the ideas didn't merit publication. The paper read like what it was, a chapter from a dissertation good enough for a graduate student's committee, but without the substance and original thought required to publish.

She thought again of Tom's editorial work on her paper, and it dawned on her for the first time how distinct the talents and skills of an editor might be from those of a writer. Baton Rouge's opportunities for professional editors were quite limited, particularly for literary editors. LSU had a good university press, but, like most, it was thinly funded. Editorial positions were likely few. Cities like New York, Boston, Chicago, or San Francisco probably had many more such positions. That didn't mean Tom would be hired; she had no idea how difficult it was to secure one of those positions or the background required. She didn't think Tom did either.

She realized, of course, that all of those cities had prestigious universities with art history departments. But successful candidates for professorships probably held Ivy League degrees, perhaps augmented by connections in the academic world far outshining her University of Virginia degree, her father's position as chair of the LSU English department, and her few years of experience here, publications or not. Positions outside of academia might exist, such as being a curator for a museum. But that would mean no teaching, and she couldn't accept that. It might also mean only limited time for research and writing compared to that offered by a university professorship. She'd worked single-mindedly for years to earn the right to follow those pursuits.

Why should she be made to feel selfish for clinging to what she'd built? She'd never hidden from Tom that she loved it here. Wasn't he the one being selfish to ask her to throw it all away? She'd never wanted more than to live and work here—in this house, at LSU, in Baton Rouge, Louisiana, The South. It was part of her; leaving it would be like losing a limb.

She didn't want to live without Tom either, or to see failure dull and rust his potential, or for him to be trapped in a life where he woke dreading each day. But wasn't it magical thinking to believe that by leaving, he could break an evil spell and find happiness? She put the manuscript back on the desk, trying to position it just as she had found it, and returned to bed. Her mind twisted down paths of different choices as she lay awake, always returning to her yearning to stay.

CHAPTER 6

Retired general Arthur Mackenzie and his wife, Coralee, had moved next door when Miriam was fifteen. Despite the gap in their ages, she and Coralee became good friends. Miriam visited Coralee when Mac was working in his garden, occupied with woodworking projects in his garage, or away for reserve duty. She sensed Coralee's loneliness and admired her steadfast cheerfulness and unfailingly positive outlook. Coralee greeted her with obvious pleasure and served fresh-baked cookies and Darjeeling tea from a blue-and-white porcelain teapot purchased in Germany. She told Miriam tales of the active, encapsulated social world of the military bases where she and Mac had lived, illustrated by framed photos on the living room walls. Miriam thought how isolated and quiet their neighborhood must seem in comparison.

Coralee had found a satisfying hobby in painting, and Miriam eagerly accepted the offer to join her. Mac built a second easel for Miriam, like the one he'd made for Coralee, and Miriam would arrive to find the easels facing a crystal vase of roses from Mac's garden centered on the polished cherrywood dining room table. Coralee painted with more enthusiasm than talent, but her joy in the work was contagious. She taught Miriam how to mix the colors on the palette and use them to evoke the sunlight filtering through the windows on the leaves, the shadows, and the promise of the buds, generously praising Miriam's efforts.

When Miriam brought her first canvas home, her mother was delighted and set it on the foyer table to bring it to the framer. When her father came home, though, his only comment was, "Well, now we know Miriam's calling isn't as an artist." Rosemary had the painting framed anyway, but hung it in the corner bedroom that served as her office. Miriam didn't share any more of her paintings with them. To save money on materials, she painted over canvases, as Coralee taught her, and stored any paintings she kept in her bedroom closet. Years later, when her parents moved out of Magnolia Lane and into their cottage, Rosemary hung Miriam's painting in the small guest bathroom.

When Miriam and Tom moved into the Magnolia Lane house, Tom joined the friendship with Mac and Coralee. He shared Mac's interest in history and respected the older man's knowledge, including his first-hand experience in the Second World War. Mac enjoyed having a new listener for his stories and offered Tom wise counsel without judgment or criticism when consulted about departmental politics or recalcitrant students. Coralee loved to cook, and her dinners were not to be missed.

Two years after Miriam and Tom moved next door, Coralee was diagnosed with breast cancer, far advanced by the time it was discovered. Mac was beside himself. "But she's only sixty-three! We had so much left to do. We were going to visit our son at his base in Japan this fall." He was stunned, almost in a stupor of grief.

At first, Coralee seemed like her usual self, and Miriam divined Mac's desperate hope that the diagnosis—or at least the prognosis—

was wrong. But within weeks, Coralee's health declined sharply; soon she was mostly bedridden, and the doctor ordered hospice care.

Miriam managed to visit every day or two, though it was hard to witness her friend's suffering. Coralee loved old-style romance novels, populated with characters like the mysterious British aristocrat—a secret philanthropist with a vast country estate who abandons his rakish ways to throw himself at the feet of a beautiful, independent American art student studying in London. Coralee also liked the Western-themed novels, featuring characters like the wealthy rancher, a broken-hearted widower and confirmed loner until a lovely and virtuous young woman answers his ad for a housekeeper. Miriam read the bodice-rippers to Coralee as she lay in bed, sometimes dozing lightly in a medicated haze, but always reaching out to Miriam when she said goodbye, tremulous smile and eyes telegraphing her gratitude for the diversion of the novels she now found difficult to read herself.

At eight o'clock on a Thursday night near the end, Miriam was in her home office, working on a paper accepted for publication contingent upon revisions, when she heard a knock downstairs. She paused, unwilling to be interrupted—the two weeks the journal had given her had passed swiftly; the paper had to be sent back tomorrow, and she was far from finished. She heard Tom open the door and greet Mac. She walked down the hall and from the landing heard Mac say, in a voice raspy with heartbreak, that Coralee was having a bad night.

"Do you think maybe Miriam might read to her for an hour? Maybe Coralee could get through it easier if she were distracted from the pain. I can't give her more medicine for two hours—I called hospice to make sure."

Miriam went downstairs, hugged Mac, and told him, of course, she would come, ashamed of her panicked frustration at being torn from her article when her friend lay dying. She told Mac she'd be there in five minutes.

As soon as the door closed, Tom asked, "Don't you have to finish revising your paper?"

"Yes, but I have to go. I'll finish when I get home. I'll only be gone an hour or so."

"Would the journal give you an extension?"

"I hate to ask for one. They said if they had it by the deadline, they could put it in the fall issue. Otherwise, it won't be out until next spring. It's alright, Tom, I'll get it done." She kissed him and left.

Mac hadn't exaggerated. Coralee's face was drawn with pain, perspiring skin clammy and pale. Miriam ran cool water over a cloth in the bathroom and put it on her brow. Mac, tears in his eyes, handed Miriam a paperback he'd bought that afternoon at the drugstore, *Taming of a Frontier Man.* On the cover, a muscular, bare-chested, ruggedly handsome man pulled a woman with flowing locks and a low-cut dress toward him—you could almost see the bosom heaving. She imagined Mac standing awkwardly in line at the drugstore, his big hands hiding as much of the cover as possible, the cashier smiling at him as she rang up the purchase.

"Oh, this looks like a good one—you did well, Mac," she said, and was rewarded by a feeble smile from Coralee. Miriam glanced at the medication schedule on the bedside table. Yes, Mac was right, two hours to go. Well, she would make it pass as quickly as possible.

She'd been reading for only ten minutes when she heard Mac open the door downstairs and greet Tom. She heard the murmur of their voices followed by steps in the hallway. She paused in the reading when Tom entered the room, Mac close behind him.

Tom approached Coralee's bedside and asked how she was doing. She nodded, attempted a smile, and said, "Your lovely wife here is keeping me entertained."

"Well, about that," Tom said with his most charming smile, "I don't see why she should have all the fun. I'm the English professor, and I think it's high time I got a turn reading these racy novels." He waggled his eyebrows and, unbelievably, Coralee giggled softly.

Tom held out his hand for the novel. Miriam gave a mock sigh of resignation, rolled her eyes, and said, "He's been telling me this for days. I hope you don't mind if he reads for a while. I think he's been feeling left out."

Coralee was no fool. "Thank you both," she said. "I'm grateful. But I don't want to take too much of your time. Mac may be an old military dog, but he does know how to read." Mac nodded vigorously, but didn't speak, eyes shiny.

"Miriam, why don't you talk to Mac about those big gardening plans you have for Saturday and let Coralee and me enjoy this fine novel? Who knows, maybe I'll learn something," Tom said with a rakish grin of his own.

Downstairs, Mac said, "Tom told me you have a big deadline tomorrow. I'm so sorry—I didn't even think about your schedule."

"Of course you didn't, Mac, your thoughts were right where they should be—on what would help Coralee. Never hesitate to come to us."

They both paused, listening to Tom's dramatic reading.

"'I told you not to come here again!'" Tom read in his best falsetto, then, lowering to a commanding baritone, "'Since when do I do what you tell me? Come here, woman, and I mean *now.*'" Switching to narrator voice, Tom continued, "'He grabbed her arm firmly, yet gently, and pulled her to his chest. Suddenly his lips were pressed to hers, his hands running down her body, spreading fire, and—,'" Tom's voice lowered dramatically, "*'all resistance left her.*'" Tom added, "I bet Mac was like that when he was a young buck, especially with a beautiful lady like you, the belle of the base."

They heard the soft giggle again. Mac whispered, "Bless him. I'm sure he's got work he should be doing tonight, too."

"Nothing more important than this," Miriam said softly. They talked briefly about the plans for Saturday, and Mac sent her home.

Tom didn't return until nearly eleven. He said Coralee had finally begun to drift off after Mac gave her the medication. When Miriam tried to thank him, he stopped her with a kiss, then went into his study to finish the next day's lecture.

AFTER CORALEE DIED AND MAC'S SONS HAD CONCLUDED THEIR visits for the funeral and returned to their respective bases, Mac spent whole days without emerging from the house, except to get the paper. When he did, he was still in pajamas and a robe, even though the paper now remained in his driveway past eight, no longer snatched up immediately after its six o'clock delivery. Miriam had never seen Mac when he wasn't wearing a polo or sport shirt tucked into pressed and belted khakis, the only concession for gardening a switch to jeans or, on particularly hot days, shorts. She or Tom called daily and invited him to dinner, but he always declined, mumbling that he was cleaning out Coralee's things or sorting through the medical bills to figure out what needed to be paid. Miriam offered to help, but he declined that as well. Rosemary came by with casseroles and cookies, attempting to gain entry to sit with Mac and offering to help with the house, but he never let her past the front door. She said he seemed glad to have the food, but not ready for company.

After a month of this, Tom hatched a plan. He showed Miriam two LSU baseball tickets and said, "I'm going to invite Mac to the game."

"But you hate baseball!" Tom disliked all team sports, considering them a waste of time.

"Yes, but Mac loves Tiger sports. He watches every game that's televised, but I don't know if he's ever been to one in the stadium. I'm going to take him out for a steak dinner too."

Miriam thought it might work and offered to come.

"Nah, it'll be a guys' night. You can come to dinner with us if you want."

She laughed and said she wouldn't intrude on the manly outing.

Mac agreed to go. He arrived at their house fifteen minutes early, wearing a purple button-down-collar shirt with "Louisiana State University" embroidered in bright yellow above the pocket and the first real smile she'd seen in weeks, if not months.

Tom came down in his own LSU shirt. "All right, my man! Let's go root for the Tigers!"

The outing broke the spell of despair. The next morning, Miriam looked out her bedroom window and was overjoyed to see the once-familiar sight of Mac kneeling between his rose bushes, a five-gallon bucket already half full of weeds.

After that, she began spending time gardening with Mac, worried that he might sink back into depression, and slowly, he began to heal. Tom continued to take him to games, and Mac never declined those invitations. Rosemary was finally able to lure Mac to dinner and sent him home with containers of leftover pot roast and vegetables in gravy. Miriam and Tom had him over as well, barbecuing on the back porch, Mac outside with Tom, probably advising. At dinner, Tom drew stories from Mac about his years in the Army. Mac didn't like to talk about combat but spoke of life on the bases around the world with Coralee, their sons, and the friends they'd made. Sometimes he choked up when he spoke of Coralee, but the memories were becoming comfortable old friends again.

Miriam began painting in Mac's garden while he worked, bored with the still-life painting she and Coralee had done indoors. Mac was gardening with renewed passion, taking master classes at the LSU Agricultural Center and studying rose horticulture. With military precision, he reconfigured his large backyard into a formal garden. He planted azalea bushes interspersed with bridal wreath shrubs and camellias along the wooden fence around his property. He left a five-foot strip of manicured grass between the fence plantings and neat rows of rosebushes in the center of the yard. Between the rows, he laid stone pathways he could use to tend the bushes and stroll to enjoy the fragrances and extravagant beauty of the blossoms. He installed a tiered fountain in the center of the rows, the glinting, cascading waters cooling the air and splashing down into the sunlit pool in the bottom tier. On paving stones laid in a square around the fountain, he placed two small benches, leaving room for Miriam's easel. The fountain attracted birds, and the familiar songs and chirping of Cardinals, Blue Jays, sparrows, Mourning Doves, and the occasional Chickadee filled the air in the morning and evening.

Being in the garden inspired Miriam, and she slowly developed her style of focusing on a single rosebush, painting the background with Impressionistic suggestion, accentuating the natural light, and making the sky a vital part of each composition. Mac was the perfect companion—unobtrusive, offering only admiration when he stopped to see her progress. Both Mac and Tom respected her desire to keep her work private, although neither agreed with it.

"Honey, you should put this in a show or a gallery," Mac would say when she completed a painting.

"I tell her that all the time, but she won't do it," Tom would say.

"She won't even let me hang them in our own house." They'd both shake their heads.

"Well, I guess it's her work and she can do as she pleases," Mac said.

"I guess," Tom agreed with a frown and a shrug.

As Mac's sixty-seventh birthday approached, his first without Coralee, Miriam and Tom talked about how to celebrate.

"What do you think about giving him that painting he likes?" she asked Tom as they sat at the kitchen table together, making the shopping list for the birthday dinner the next night. Miriam's parents were joining them, and her mother was baking Mac's favorite, a red velvet cake.

"Which one? He loves them all," Tom said, maybe envious.

"I'll show you." Miriam ran upstairs, retrieved the painting from her office closet, and carried it back to the kitchen. "I think this is his favorite," she said, holding it up for Tom.

The painting was an evening scene. In it, the sinking sun reflected flame-gold on the undersides of popcorn clouds clustered above the horizon. The light faded upward, first to a pale tangerine glow and then to soft purple-tinged cloud tops. Tropicana roses clustered in the foreground echoed the colors back to the sky. Behind the rosebush, she'd loosely painted in soft focus the azalea and camellia bushes, the tiny white flowers of the bridal wreath shrubs bright in the gathering twilight, the shiny green camellia leaves reflecting the last rays of the dying light, fat pink blossoms blurred in the shadows. The painting was a favorite of hers too, but what of it? She wanted Mac to have it.

Tom nodded. "I hate to give that one away, but no one will appreciate it more than Mac. It'll mean the world to him."

Miriam packed it carefully in a box with tissue and wrapped it in red-and-purple birthday paper sprinkled with tiny silver stars and affixed a large red bow. She and Tom agreed to wait until after her parents left to give it to Mac, knowing that he often lingered, having a last cup of coffee with Tom or drying dishes in the kitchen. Her mother would have liked to do the same, but her father was always ready to go after dessert, saying sharply that he had an early morning.

That night was the same, and her father ushered her mother out the door, precluding any lingering in the foyer.

After Miriam and Mac finished the dishes while Tom boxed up leftovers, Miriam held the bottle of wine up to the light. "Just enough for half a glass each before you leave, Mac." He smiled and agreed, sitting down at the kitchen table. Tom winked at her and set out glasses as Miriam slipped out of the kitchen.

When she returned with the package, Mac's eyes widened in happy surprise. He said they shouldn't have, glancing at the gift they'd given him earlier, a handsome pair of leather gardening gloves and a pair of clippers.

"This is something else, Mac," Miriam said quietly, "and we hope you like it."

He opened it solemnly, knowing it was special. Miriam smiled to see how his face lit up when he saw the painting, his sharp inhale. He turned, blinking, wet eyes to Miriam and took a deep breath before thanking her. She glowed with his happiness.

When she came home the following Monday afternoon, Mac must have been waiting for her because as soon as she pulled into the driveway, he burst out of his front door, gesturing for her to come over. She parked the car in the garage and joined Mac on his front porch. He ushered her into his living room and pointed to the wall, where he'd hung her painting and installed an art light above it. He showed her how the light had a dimmer switch and moved it up and down.

"Look, it's almost like we're seeing the scene over several hours as the light fades in the sky," he said. And it was. He'd hung the painting opposite his big recliner, next to the large television Tom had persuaded him to buy, then encouraged him to enjoy, regularly watching games with him after Coralee's death.

"I can sit in my chair and just look at your beautiful painting, Miriam," Mac said with gratitude that surprised her. "Honey, you teach about all those other artists, but you don't appreciate your own work." His expression turned serious, and he put his arm around her shoulders. "I pray that someday you'll truly see the beauty in it."

She'd lowered her eyes and laughed, embarrassed. "Oh, Mac, now you're just being silly. But thank you—I'm so glad you like it." She couldn't explain why she held the paintings so close. They were precious to her; it was almost as if they might fade away if she exposed them to the light of others, Mac and Tom being the only exceptions.

Mac looked out the window and said, "Well, the light's fading fast. I'd better get out there if I want to finish weeding that last row." He walked her to the door, saying, "If you ever want me to, I'd be glad to install some lights like this in your house. We could put them in your home office, and you could hang some of your work in there at least."

She smiled and thanked him, and neither ever mentioned it again.

CHAPTER 7

FIGHTING QUICKSAND

As the summer passed, Miriam couldn't deny the changes in Tom. A heavy sadness extinguished his old spontaneous delight in small escapes like hiking in nearby Port Hudson Park, planting the summer impatiens and caladiums around their oak trees, or seeing a new exhibit at the planetarium. Even a dinner out at Vinny's, their beloved neighborhood Italian restaurant, or Sunday brunch with Emily and Herb, barely sparked his interest or appetite. He spent his time at home in his office, and she had to coax him out even for their usual Friday night pizza and a movie on television. When she entered his office, he was often sitting at his desk, staring blankly into the middle distance, absorbed in thoughts that he didn't share. Now that the fall semester had begun, the more relaxed days of summer were over, and Miriam could feel the weight of disappointment and anticipated failure pulling Tom further down.

Sunday afternoon, after a futile attempt to find their former pleasure in sharing a lazy diner brunch, Miriam was in her home office trying to focus on her lecture notes for the next morning. Tom had only picked at his omelet and, as soon as she finished chewing her last bite, said he needed to get back to work.

If she were awarded early tenure, she would be promoted and begin next fall as an associate professor. She hadn't said much about it to Tom. His mandatory tenure application date was also next fall, and he'd been warned of the consequences if he didn't have publications to list before then. Denial of tenure would mean the end of his tenure-track position at LSU. He might be offered a position as an instructor—humiliating and unlikely, given his dismal student evaluations—or his contract would be terminated. She didn't like to think of the choices they'd have to make if that happened.

Tom had gone to the library to do some research, and the house was quiet. No distractions except that she kept remembering how disheartened he'd looked when he left, his wistful glance at the back-yard sunlight. She forced her attention back to her notebook and headed the page with the chapter number for tomorrow's class. She tapped her pen on the desk and looked out the window. She looked back at her pad. She wasn't going to obsess over the changes in Tom. Everyone had bad days, and everyone felt down in the dumps now and again. She knew firsthand the pain of rejection by the fickle, even cliquish, academic journals.

Miriam glanced at her watch. The time she'd allotted for preparation was slipping away. She gripped her pen and scanned the pages of the text for the most salient points to cover. She jotted notes. Tom would work his way out of this; he was intelligent and insightful. Not uncommon for some young professors to take longer than others to hit their stride. No doubt that Tom was a diligent scholar, constantly reading and rereading his beloved authors and criticisms of their work. Surely that would spark his own creativity and lead to an original thesis he could develop into an article that would succeed. A single good publication would lift the intense pressure, give him confidence, and open the door to others as it had for her. Herb Rothschild had been awarded early tenure and built a national reputation as a Melville scholar. Like Tom, Herb loved the novels of Henry James, and they could discuss *The Golden Bowl* for hours. Tom told her that Herb had offered to work with him on his manuscripts and had been generous with his time. Herb's popularity with both students and other faculty gave him influence in the department that Miriam knew he would use to help Tom. If Herb had confidence in Tom's ability to succeed in academia, surely she should as well.

Miriam worked until Tom returned from the library at six, looking defeated and exhausted rather than exhilarated. She kissed him and suggested that they put away their books, heat up the gumbo her mother had dropped off on Saturday, and watch *Sixty Minutes* and then something lighter, like *Archie Bunker's Place*. He gave her a tired smile and agreed.

ON MONDAY MORNING, MIRIAM CAME HOME AFTER HER EARLY CLASS to get a book she'd forgotten and saw Tom's car in the driveway. She opened the front door and called to him. He didn't answer. The kitchen was just as she'd left it. Tom's study was dark; the textbook for his course and his lecture notes were still on the desk. Why? He should have been up and on his way to class if not already there. She dropped her things on the kitchen table and rushed upstairs to their bedroom. The curtains she'd opened that morning were drawn, and Tom was in bed, eyes closed.

"Tom, your class starts in twenty minutes—what are you doing?"

"I can't go," he answered faintly, not opening his eyes.

"Why, Tom? Are you sick?"

"Miriam, please, just leave me alone."

"Did you call in?" He didn't answer, didn't open his eyes. She sighed, went downstairs, and called Lily, the long-time English Department secretary.

"Let me guess," Lily said, "I have to go and cancel Tom's class again."

Again? "Yes, I'm sorry—he's still sick. We think it's the flu," she said in a choked voice. Lily snorted and hung up. Miriam trudged back up the stairs.

"I called and said you were sick, but Lily wasn't happy. How many classes have you missed?"

Tom didn't answer or open his eyes.

"Tom, tell me—how many?" Her voice rose; she wanted to shake him. He turned his head slowly and looked at her, but didn't get up.

"You don't understand how bad I feel."

"How many, Tom?" she almost shouted.

"I missed last Wednesday and Friday," he mumbled.

So this was his third day of missed classes. She'd never missed a lecture and couldn't imagine canceling that many. She was angry, frustrated, and, yes, afraid. And helpless. So she ran.

"I'm going back to campus to work on my paper before my afternoon class."

He knew she could've worked at home, but he only rolled over, saying nothing. Did he even consider, or care, about what his failure would do to her future as well as his? She felt better back in her office at the university, where the air wasn't thickened by Tom's misery, and she could bury herself in the paper, polishing the syntax, rechecking a point she'd already spent hours researching. Focusing on the pages until everything else disappeared, including the memory of Tom's face in the darkened bedroom.

MIRIAM WOKE AT SEVEN ON SATURDAY TO A BEAUTIFUL LOUISIANA fall day, cool, clear, and sunny. She looked out the bedroom window and saw birds frolicking around Mac's fountain, surrounded by blooming rose bushes. She leaned over Tom, gently shook his shoulder, and said, "It's lovely outside. Do you want to go to the rose garden at the Capitol? Then have breakfast downtown?"

Once he would have eagerly agreed to wander the paths through the blossoms in the early light, but now he only mumbled that he was tired and rolled away from her. She leaned over and kissed his cheek, whispering, "Please?" Tom only burrowed his head deeper into his pillow.

She could tell herself that he didn't love her less, that he was caught in a morass that had nothing to do with her. But it hurt to feel how little response she could evoke in him now. She blinked back tears, dressed, and gathered her easel and paints. She couldn't face the thoughts she'd have in her home office, a room away from Tom in the dim bedroom. She'd catch the early light in Mac's garden.

She was in front of her easel when Mac came out with his gardening tools, glad to find her there. Mac paused to examine her half-finished painting of a rosebush illuminated by early morning rays, covered with soft blossoms, pink like the dawn sky.

"It's going to be a real beauty," he said, then straightened and walked to a corner of the garden, calling out to her, "Miriam, did you see this one?"

She joined him, facing another pink rosebush a few rows over from where she'd been painting. Mac pointed to a blossom opening on a shoot edging out above the foliage, lit up by the early morning sun.

"It's perfect," she said, and hurried back to get her easel.

Mac chuckled and carried her stool and the small paint table. Then he returned to his gardening, and they worked in companionable silence for the next couple of hours. Miriam tried to let herself escape into her painting, but her gaze kept returning to the bedroom window above them. It remained dark, the curtains closed. Mac caught her looking when he brought her a cold bottle of water.

"Tom's still asleep?" he asked, following her gaze with a worried look. "He's not sick is he?"

"No, he's just been down lately," she answered, then took a long drink from the bottle.

"Honey, I know you're not asking for my advice, but it seems like he's been down a lot these last couple of months, just not himself. Do you think it might be time for him to see a doctor?"

"Oh, Mac, he's been to a psychiatrist if that's what you mean. The doctor prescribed an antidepressant, but Tom doesn't like taking it. He says the pills make him groggy and nauseated."

"Well, that can happen. I just, well, I worry about him. Sometimes a man can't pull himself up again if he sinks too low. Struggling against it just pulls him in deeper, like quicksand. I lost one of my soldiers to that."

"I know, but I don't know how to help him," she said, on the edge of tears, boxed in by frustration, the futility of her efforts, the irrelevance of her desire to help, however ardent.

Hearing the desperation in her voice, Mac offered to talk with Tom. Miriam gratefully accepted and Mac agreed to come over for lunch. Buoyed by the hope that Mac might be able to reach Tom when she couldn't, Miriam worked with Mac in the garden for another hour, then she gathered her things to go in, and Mac said he'd be over in fifteen minutes.

Tom was downstairs in the kitchen, making coffee, still wearing his pajamas, hair unbrushed and dark circles under his eyes. He mumbled that he was going to work on some copyediting for the journal. When Miriam said Mac was coming for lunch, Tom said he wasn't hungry but would sit with them. He got dressed and answered the door when Mac came with a bouquet of roses for Miriam. She thanked him and suggested that he and Tom relax in the sitting room while she finished the sandwiches. After a few minutes, she heard the low tones of their voices and a deep sigh from Tom. She dawdled over the plates until the voices ceased, then called them to the kitchen table. Neither looked happy, but Mac smiled, as if delighted with the turkey sandwiches, apple slices, potato salad, and Rosemary's snickerdoodle cookies.

"Looks like a feast," he said.

Tom sat with them, but barely touched his food, explaining that he'd just had breakfast, though she knew he'd had nothing but coffee. Usually, Tom made an effort to engage Mac in conversation, but today, Tom seemed lost in himself, quietly gazing at the table through most of the meal. Mac tried to draw him into talking about his classes, then about the baseball season, but got only perfunctory responses. She was relieved to clear the plates and told Mac she'd walk him back. Tom remained at the table, sipping another cup of coffee.

"I don't know," Mac said when they reached his front porch, "I think Tom's sunk pretty deep. He says he doesn't want to go to another doctor. Says he's just got to work through it on his own."

Miriam nodded. She'd heard the same. Disappointed, she realized how much she'd hoped Mac might be able to do more than she.

"I can ask around about a good doctor if you like. One of the active officers might know of someone." He didn't sound optimistic. Neither was she. She thanked him and returned home.

Tom remained in his study downstairs all afternoon, and Miriam in hers upstairs. At five-thirty, she went downstairs to find Tom behind his typewriter, surrounded by crumpled pages. He looked up at her and sighed.

"I thought I'd try to revise that paper that got rejected by the *Henry James Review,*" he said. Miriam glanced again at his desk, seeing no pages other than the crumpled ones.

"It hasn't gone very well," he said. Miriam massaged his shoulders.

"It'll come, you just have to keep trying."

He sighed heavily. "Do we really have to go to your parents' house for dinner tonight?"

"Yes, Tom, we can't just cancel. Mom's been cooking all day. She called me this afternoon to ask again about your favorite vegetables."

Tom frowned. "Okay, but I know your father is going to ask me about that article, and I don't feel like telling him it was rejected."

Relieved by Tom's acquiescence, Miriam said they'd better go upstairs and get ready.

"Is Mac coming?" Tom asked, hopeful.

"No, I wish he were, but I don't think they invited him this time."

On the way, Tom said maybe they could leave early, say that they both still had work to do that night. Miriam nodded, noncommittal.

Rosemary ushered them into the house, pleased with the bouquet of Mac's roses Miriam brought, but casting a worried glance at her behind Tom's back. She called William in from his study, and they sat in the living room for an uncomfortable half hour of appetizers and cocktails before adjourning to the dining room. Miriam and Rosemary went to the kitchen to put food in serving dishes while William and Tom engaged in the stilted conversation of two men who have little to say to each other. Miriam felt Tom's relief when they returned to the table with the dishes and sat down for the meal.

They'd barely finished passing the bowls of mashed potatoes, stewed tomatoes, and green beans before her father asked about Tom's paper. She inwardly winced as Tom mumbled that it had been rejected.

"I can't help you if you don't get a grip on yourself and start producing, Tom. I don't know what's wrong with you, but let me tell you, you have few supporters left in the department."

Tom stared at his plate, jaw clenched, food untouched. Miriam attempted to change the subject with extravagant praise of the meal. Her father abruptly stood, threw his napkin on the table, and left the room. Miriam glanced at her mother, who shrugged, her face troubled. They heard her father's rapid steps returning. He entered red-faced, holding his Smith & Wesson revolver and approaching Tom.

"Miriam tells her mother you're *depressed,*" William said, whining the word, "that you wish you were *dead.* So here. It's loaded." And he thrust the gun in Tom's face.

Tom stared at him, eyes wide, head back, like a horse who'd stumbled on a snake in the path. Miriam sprang from her chair, took Tom's hand, and jerked him to his feet.

"We're leaving," she said, half-dragging Tom to the door. Rosemary remained at the table, mouth open. Miriam sent her a withering look. What had her mother been thinking, telling her father that? She couldn't have thought he'd sympathize; should've known he'd take it as further evidence of Tom's weakness and ineptitude. Miriam slammed the door behind them, gently pushed Tom into the car, pulled out of the driveway and into the street. Tom put his face in his hands and sobbed.

All Miriam could say was, "I'm so sorry, so sorry."

At home, Tom went upstairs in silence and into the bedroom. She followed, not knowing what to say or do.

"Can I get you anything? A glass of water?" She approached and tried to put her arms around him, but he pushed her away, something he'd never done before.

"A glass of water? Yeah, that'll solve everything. Miriam, can't you see that it's toxic for us here? Don't you care?" His voice was rough, his mouth closed in a tight line, his eyes looked past her, refusing to meet hers.

She had no answer to that. She stood, stung and awkward, while he changed into pajamas, ignoring her, as if she weren't there, and got into bed.

"Tom, of course I care—I love you. Can we talk?"

"Why?" he said and rolled away from her when she sat on the bed next to him. Not knowing what to do, she went back downstairs, numb and disoriented. The phone rang. It was her mother.

"Miriam, I'm so sorry. I don't know why William did that. Maybe he thought he could shock Tom out of his depression."

"Maybe. I have to go now, Mom," she said and hung up with Rosemary still talking. Maybe they couldn't stay here. She should go up to Tom.

There was something else she should do. She crept up the stairs, looked in on Tom, listened to his deep, even breathing, whispered his name and got no response. Assured that he was asleep, she went back downstairs and into his office. She sat at the desk, retrieved the key to the drawer that held the revolver, opened it, and took out the gun case. She thought about the alternatives. She could take the key to the drawer, which would be easy to hide. But he might notice, and she didn't want to have that conversation. She took the gun case out of the drawer and opened it. If she took the whole case, he might notice that too. What if she took the gun out of the case and left the case there? If he opened it and found the gun missing, he'd have to explain why he was looking for it (and she would know he had been). If he opened the drawer just to check that the case was still there, it would be. She took the gun from the case, put the case back in the drawer with the bullets, locked it, and returned the key.

She needed to hide the gun somewhere he wouldn't look, which ruled out her dresser drawers and her office. As she passed the kitchen pantry, she thought, why not there? She did all the cooking and could avoid the things he might look for, like chips or cereal. The middle back shelf held dry goods—white rice, flour, sugar, baking soda, Rice-a-Roni, cake and muffin mixes, canned goods, and other things that wouldn't draw Tom's interest. She put the gun on the back edge of the shelf and carefully repositioned items in front of it.

She closed the pantry door and sat down heavily at the kitchen table, feeling the creeping misery cover and suffocate hope. How had they come to this dead end, after all the work, all the dedication? She stayed there, arms folded on the table, looking out at the dark night, shedding tears of hopelessness, sorrow, frustration, and anger. Her tears brought no relief. Instead, a rising panic suffused her, making it hard to breathe. She couldn't solve this, and Tom was sinking further, like Mac said. The tears gave way to fear in the face of her helplessness. She stayed there a long time, pinned by a desperate, frenzied searching that found no answers.

CHAPTER 8

DESPERATE HOPE

Tom and Miriam spent Christmas in Boston with Tom's parents, whose obvious excitement made Miriam feel guilty that she and Tom had visited so seldom during the three years they'd been married. Miriam's mother had been sorry they'd be gone for the holiday and had brought their gifts over and put them under the tree, where they remained, unopened. Miriam, still angry, had handed her mother the presents she had for them, then said she needed to get back to packing.

Tom and Miriam slept late on their first morning in the comfortable guest suite of his parents' condo in an upscale high-rise building in the heart of the city. Waking to the smell of bacon frying and muted voices in the kitchen, Miriam got up, opened the curtains, and took in the view. Fresh snow sparkled in the sunlight on the street far below, covering the dingy city buildings like grace.

Tom joined her by the window. "It's pretty, isn't it?" he said, putting his arm around her.

She nodded, smiling. "Yes, and dinner last night was nice—but I might have nodded off when we were talking afterward." They hadn't gotten in until nine, and Tom's parents had ordered the best Chinese food she'd ever had and served it with excellent wine. "Maybe your parents would like to visit us later this winter, when they get tired of the cold."

"Maybe, but it's hard to get my father away from his bank for long —my mother says it's like his third child."

Miriam pondered that as they dressed. She suspected that Tom's parents weren't especially fond of Louisiana. They'd looked perpetually wilted when they'd come for the July wedding, astonished that the suffocating heat and humidity persisted nearly unabated into the evening, so unlike the soft, pleasantly warm summer nights in Boston. Quietly refined New Englanders, Evelyn and Gerald Johnson, though unfailingly courteous, were reserved and even aloof in comparison with the warmth and casual familiarity of Louisiana natives. They hadn't mixed easily with the other guests and seemed taken aback at the frequent hugs, occasionally uninhibited humor, and lack of restraint with personal questions. But they seemed to enjoy the Cajun cuisine, except when they found it overly spicy, and sampled everything from chargrilled oysters and cedar-roasted redfish to fried soft-shelled crabs and seafood gumbo.

"It smells like my Mom has breakfast ready," Tom said, and they joined his parents in the sleek, modern kitchen. They sat on black leather barstools at the marble kitchen island and filled their plates from the platters of scrambled eggs, bacon, sausage, and muffins. After breakfast, Evelyn and Gerald took them to the Boston Museum of Art and then to lunch at Trident Booksellers & Café in the Back Bay ("in honor of the English professor," Gerald said, smiling at Tom). They returned in time for Evelyn to put a roast in the oven for dinner while Gerald chatted with Tom and Miriam.

"Well, Tom, how are things going in academia?" Gerald asked. "Are you enjoying your work on that *Southern Literary Journal?*"

Tom brightened and sat up straighter as he talked about the issue underway. Absent was any mention of his classes or research.

Tom's sister, Claire, arrived for her holiday visit in time for dinner.

She'd taken the train straight from her office in New York City and arrived wearing a Burberry coat over a designer suit and black leather high-heeled boots. Tall and slender, with shiny chestnut-brown hair that fell past her shoulders, Claire was attractive in a sharp-edged way. A successful literary agent, she carried herself with the confidence of one who excels in her profession and is sought-after in the city at the center of it.

"Tom's been telling us about his work as editor on that journal," Gerald said, looking pleased. "I think he's found his calling."

"Oh, uh, it's not a paying job," Tom said, "just an extra thing I do in the department—and I'm only a copy editor."

"But this Professor Rothschild seems pretty impressed with your ability," Gerald said. "Maybe you should consider editing as a career."

Claire nodded, unsurprised. Miriam realized that Tom's family had already thought about this, maybe discussed it. They probably also knew about his struggles in the department and worries about tenure. Gerald and Claire exchanged looks, excluding Miriam, who was now reduced to an awkward bystander.

"Oh, I don't know," Tom said. "I did go over to LSU Press and ask about a position there. I talked to the managing editor, who introduced me to the editor-in-chief. They were both complimentary— Herb Rothschild set up the appointment for me. The Press recently published his book on Melville."

What? Miriam hadn't heard about this. Or was it vaguely familiar? Had she been half listening to Tom, mentally picking at a knot in her research, or composing a comment on a student's thesis? Or maybe he hadn't told her, afraid that she'd consider any alternative to his tenure-track position a failure. Now she tried to appear knowing (calm smile of encouragement for Tom), but Claire's glance was penetrating, maybe smug.

"Unfortunately, they didn't have any openings," Tom said. "It's a small university press with only a few full-time editorial positions. They use freelance editors, and they said they'd put me on the list. But it would be hard to fit in a freelance job with the responsibilities I have in the department."

"Yes, I should think so," Gerald said. "You don't need a part-time job. You need a full-time job that makes the best use of your talents and interests."

Nodding in her superior way, Claire said, "Yes, and good editors are gold. But you have to be near the big publishers to have real opportunities."

Claire shifted her gaze to Miriam, eyes unfriendly. Did Claire blame her for Tom's unhappiness? Tom and Claire were close; he wrote and called her regularly. What had he told her?

Evelyn called them to dinner, and they sat down at an elegant table, set with china, silver, and crystal, and a centerpiece with thick red candles surrounded by holiday greenery. Gerald carved the roast while they passed heaping bowls of mashed potatoes, carrots, and peas. Miriam sprinkled salt and pepper liberally on the bland meat and potatoes. After the compliments on the dinner, Gerald cleared his throat, and Evelyn and Claire looked at him expectantly. Miriam waited, again aware that significant discussions had occurred without her.

"We wanted to talk with you about something that might be of interest," Gerald began, Evelyn, Claire, and Tom attentive. "The bank has worked for many years with one of the big publishing houses in New York. I have lunch every few weeks with a couple of their folks, and last time they were complaining about how hard it is to find good editors."

When Gerald glanced at her, Miriam attempted to appear interested rather than alarmed. Tom, she noticed, leaned forward eagerly. Did he know what was coming?

Gerald said, "I told them a little about Tom, and I just happened to have an issue of the *Southern Literary Journal* with his name on the masthead." He chuckled, and Miriam smiled politely through the anxiety clutching her gut. "They know Claire too, of course, since she's brought them some good authors." Tom grinned at Claire, who winked at him.

"Anyway, that little old Louisiana magazine apparently gets quite a bit of respect around the country. So, the upshot was that they'd love to meet with Tom while you're here—if it fits in your schedule, of course," Gerald added, looking at Miriam, the confident smile faltering a bit. Was her dismay showing?

Tom didn't hesitate. "That would be great, Dad! I'd love to show Miriam around New York City—she's never been."

"Really?" Evelyn blurted, looking wide-eyed at Miriam, as if she'd just emerged from the depths of the Amazon rain forest. Claire smirked, as if she'd guessed as much.

Being the businessman he was, Gerald moved quickly to close the deal, pulling a card from his pocket, turning it over to show Tom notes on the back. "Here's Alan Goldman's card—he's the managing editor. He's one of the fellows I talked with, and they said he'd be the best one to meet with you. We tentatively set the time for tomorrow afternoon at three, but, uh, of course, you can change it if you, uh, have other plans." Another quick glance Miriam's way. Claire's eyes locked on Miriam, daring her to refuse.

Tom turned to Miriam, eyebrows raised, clutching the card. "What do you think?"

Evelyn said, "Gerald and I made you a reservation for tomorrow night at the Plaza Hotel in case you wanted to stay for a show. Claire might have some tickets for you," she added, sly glance at her daughter, who smiled at Tom in that secret sibling way.

"I was able to get tickets to that show you wanted to see, Tom. In fact, that was the only night there were any good seats left—serendipity, right?"

So, it was decided—they would take the early train to New York tomorrow. Tom looked delighted. He thanked his family enthusiastically. Miriam smiled and nodded, forcing out a few words in response to Evelyn's offer to provide a list of places near the Plaza she might like to visit while Tom was interviewing.

"We arranged for early check-in so Miriam could set up camp there and have some time to walk in Central Park or shop while Tom goes to the publishing house," Gerald said. "You could try the Plaza's famous lobster salad for lunch."

Yes, they'd thought of everything. Well, except for Miriam's career prospects in New York. Sure, the city had great universities, but she doubted they'd have an opening just waiting for a young associate professor from a state university in Louisiana.

Back in their room, Tom asked, "Are you okay with going, Miriam?" The anxiety in his eyes excluded any answer but yes.

She busied herself with packing the overnight bag Evelyn had loaned them. Tom put his arms around her from behind and kissed her neck. When she turned to him, he looked at her in that way that made everything else fade into insignificance. It would be fine; she'd just enjoy the time with him in the city. It was too early to panic about the future. The overnight trip wasn't a commitment, and an interview wasn't a job offer.

ON THE TRAIN THE NEXT MORNING, TOM'S EYES DARTED RESTLESSLY, bright with a hectic excitement, and she knew he was nervous about the interview.

"I'm looking forward to seeing the famous Plaza Hotel and that lobster salad," she said, squeezing his hand. He smiled and put his arm around her.

"We can go to the Museum of Modern Art tomorrow morning," he said, "or the Metropolitan Museum if you'd rather."

They went straight to the Plaza Hotel when they arrived in New York and checked into their room, quite small in proportion to the rate she'd seen on the receipt at the desk. The view through the heavy damask curtains was the wall of the neighboring building. She hung their things in the closet (which barely accommodated the clothes for their overnight stay) and crowded a few toiletries wherever she could put them in the tiny bathroom. They went directly down to lunch; she knew Tom wanted to be finished well before his three o'clock interview. Back in their room, she chatted with Tom while he changed into his best suit, straightened his tie for him, and told him how handsome he looked. After he left, she bundled up in the heavy coat Evelyn had loaned her and attempted to walk in Central Park, but the freezing wind quickly deterred her. She proceeded to Bloomingdale's, shivering in the winds funneled between the tall buildings, hating the crowded sidewalks. Stunned by the store's prices, she quickly left, returned to the Plaza, and spent the rest of the afternoon reading the novel she'd brought.

Tom didn't get back until a quarter of six. She watched him closely, saw the old sadness in his face and the slump of his shoulders, ashamed that her relief outweighed her dismay. He sat beside her on the bed.

"Well, they were nice, but they said they don't have any openings right now. They probably met with me just to please Dad." He paused, and Miriam leaned over and put her arm around him. He slipped his arms around her, pulled her close, then straightened and met her eyes.

"Alan Goldman spent an hour with me talking about the business. I'd love to work there, Miriam." Unspoken question in his eyes. She remained silent, and he continued. "Alan said it's very competitive—we knew that."

Miriam nodded, waiting.

"He said I'd make an excellent addition to their staff, and they'll keep my CV on file. They'll let me know if something opens up. But he also said my chances would be better if we lived nearby. They have so many applicants in the City that they don't really need to look elsewhere."

Miriam's eyes slid away as she nodded again. Tom persevered.

"If we moved to New York, Alan said he would see that I got freelance work until they had an opening. They could get to know me better than if I just did freelance work through the mail. He said they work together closely as a team and knowing that a candidate would be a good fit is important." Tom's eyes searched hers. "It would give me higher priority when a position opens." She remained silent.

"If we moved here, we could stay with my parents until we both found jobs—Boston's close enough to look from there." Tom paused, then said, "Or we could sell the house in Baton Rouge and use the money to help us get set up here."

She was stunned—her treasured family home, the grand gift to them from her parents, her legacy. She saw the century-old live oaks arching over the street from both sides, leaves lit like stained glass in the sunlight, springtime extravagance of blooms on the azaleas and camellias clustered on wide green lawns, the home where they'd raise their children.

"It's our house free and clear—or yours, actually," Tom said. "You can do with it as you please."

Tom was right; it was her separate property. Her father had had the papers prepared to name her as the sole owner. She hadn't commented on that, and neither had Tom. She hadn't thought he'd noticed.

"I couldn't just sell that house," Miriam said. "I guess we could give it back to my parents if we moved. But it seems insane to leave our home and our positions at LSU to move to New York City without jobs."

Tom stood, defeated, and said, "We should get ready if you want to have dinner before the show." He went into the bathroom and closed the door, and she dressed, determined not to think about the conversation further that night. They had an excellent meal at Frankie and Johnnie's steakhouse within walking distance of the theater, captivated by the worn elegance of the old restaurant, the posters on the walls from decades of Broadway shows. They covertly watched couples and families, clearly well known to the waiters, seeing the prominence of this place in the long-time diners' lives and memories, a kind of home.

They watched *Cats* in a beautiful old theater, entranced, marveling at the talented cast. They walked through the Broadway blocks afterward, briskly in the cold, but still pausing to look at the posters and marquees on the theaters they passed. Back at the room, pleasantly exhausted, they went to bed, nestled together under crisp sheets and the plush duvet. Holding her close, Tom thanked her for making the trip and said he hoped she was enjoying it.

She murmured that she was, and he gave her a long, unhurried kiss, but when they made love, she felt an edge of desperation in him. He fell asleep afterward, spooning against her, oblivious to the city noises that kept her awake. She lay there, feeling the wakefulness of the city, still busy with traffic, remembering the press of nocturnal crowds on the sidewalk as they'd walked back, yearning for the evening peace of their quiet street, the occasional low hoot of an owl harmonizing with the night. No, she thought, I could never live here.

The next morning, they walked to Claire's nearby apartment. She was still in Boston and had given Tom a key so he could see it. "Claire's pretty proud of her new place," he said. "Apparently, it was quite a find in this location. We can leave our bag there, then go to the museum and have lunch before we head back."

The building lobby was small, but nice, and there was a doorman. They reached Claire's floor, entered the tiny apartment, and toured the rooms. It didn't take long.

"I don't think this is even six hundred square feet," Miriam said. They sat on the stylish white leather couch and looked out the living room's single large window at an impressive view of the city skyline.

"Maybe not—in New York, you pay for the location," Tom said. Then he told her how much Claire had paid.

Miriam gasped. "Tom, even if we sold the house, we couldn't afford a place here—even if we both had jobs. That is, I assume being an editor isn't a high-paying job, and I know being a professor isn't."

"No, we'd probably have to live farther out, not in Manhattan. Claire earns a very good income, but that's after working her way up in the business for ten years."

So, a lengthy daily commute. This just got better and better. How could Tom prefer this to their home ten minutes from campus?

They spent several hours in the Museum of Modern Art, Miriam nearly breathless at being within inches of so many masterpieces. They stopped for a late lunch in the museum coffee shop, and Miriam found herself wishing that they had another day to visit the Metropolitan Museum of Art. Tom assured her that they would on their next visit. Hope dawned in his eyes.

"I knew you'd like it—we could go to the museums every weekend if we lived here."

"Yes, I admit New York is a nice place to visit."

His face fell, but he said nothing more.

They returned to Boston that evening in time for dinner with Tom's parents and Claire. They settled around the table, and, after the anxiety of the last two days, Miriam didn't mind the bland food. Tom reported on his interview.

"It sounds like it went as well as could be expected," Gerald said, with artificial optimism. Or maybe he was sincere. She couldn't tell.

"It really does, Tom," Claire said. "I'll keep my ear to the ground for opportunities at other publishing houses too. But it would be so much better if you were here." She cast a sidelong glance at Miriam, who flicked her eyes away to look straight ahead.

"Yes, Alan mentioned that. But he also said they'd be in touch when something opened up," Tom said.

"Well, we all just have to be patient," Evelyn said. "It'll work out for the best. And you may hear from the LSU Press as well." Miriam looked up at her, startled. Could it be that one member of Tom's family thought Baton Rouge could compete with The City?

Claire huffed, not ready to let it go. "Yeah, and at LSU you won't get manuscripts worth pouring your heart into the way I know you will, Tom. If you were with a publisher here, I could steer some good things your way, authors that could make your career and would be worth your talent."

Miriam started to break in, to point out that LSU Press had published some excellent authors, though her overwrought mind refused to produce their names. Evelyn responded first.

"You know, I'm not completely convinced that moving to New York would be the best thing, even if Tom got that job."

Was Evelyn her ally? Gerald sat back in his chair, neither agreeing nor disagreeing, cautious, expression carefully blank, staying out of the crossfire.

"Why ever not, Mom?" Claire asked, astonished. "He's miserable in Baton Rouge." She glared at Miriam.

Evelyn said, "I'm just saying they have to consider the whole balance. Is a high-pressure job in the City what they want? If they want a family, Baton Rouge could be a much easier place to raise one." Evelyn cast a warning glance, first at Claire, then Gerald. Miriam looked at Tom for his response, but he only nodded noncommittally. Why didn't he say something, agree with his mother, defend their lives? She hazarded a glance and a small smile at Evelyn, who smiled back. In this tacit alliance, was Miriam offering a grandchild for their home? Would she? Would Tom?

Claire said, "It sounds more like Tom's hitting a brick wall there, with Miriam's father as his department chair." There it was. Tom had the decency to look stricken. He glanced at Miriam, his expression guilty and apologetic. She looked away. Claire pressed her point. "The literary scene here may be high pressure, but it's stimulating and rewarding too. Like I said, I could—"

Evelyn cut her off. "Claire, Tom and Miriam have to consider their future in the context of their lives, not yours, and I'm sure they'll make the right decision. Now, who wants dessert? I have lemon meringue pie."

Evelyn told Miriam to stay seated while she and Claire carried plates into the kitchen. Miriam listened to Tom tell his father about attending LSU baseball games and watching football on television with Mac.

"Those Southerners will make a sports fan out of you yet!" Gerald laughed.

Tom asked about the bank, and the ensuing discussion revealed that Tom, though uninterested in being a banker, knew a great deal about this particular bank. Miriam picked up the last of the dishes and headed to the kitchen. Hearing Evelyn and Claire talking, she paused outside the door.

"I'm just saying that Ms. Southern Belle isn't thinking about Tom at all. She should've married a good ole boy who'd think New Orleans is the big city," Claire said. Miriam retreated behind the door frame, out of sight from either room.

"Oh, Claire, you can hardly blame her," Evelyn said. "Miriam is apparently a rising star at the university, and their home is truly beautiful. It was like staying in one of those plantation bed and breakfasts when we visited last year, like something out of *Southern Living*."

"Mom, when have you ever opened *Southern Living*?" Both laughed.

"When I was there, actually—Miriam had one on the coffee table. Quite a nice magazine."

"Oh, jeez. But seriously, I'm worried about Tom. Do you think he's told her about what happened in high school?"

"I doubt it. That's all behind him now."

"Well, maybe you should talk to her, so she'll understand what he's dealing with."

"No, it's Tom's business and his decision whether he wants to share that."

"He hasn't always made the best decisions. I don't think failure is going to help him stay out of the sinkhole he fell into before."

"Claire, Tom doesn't thrive on competition and pressure like you do. When he gets too stressed, he retreats into himself—it can para-lyze him."

Tom nearly ran into Miriam as he rounded the corner from the dining room, carrying empty glasses.

"Hey, Miriam, I didn't see you there," he said, and she jumped forward into the kitchen. Claire and Evelyn turned around, startled, probably wondering how much she'd heard.

Miriam turned to Tom and said brightly, "Just thought I'd clear these off—you didn't have to interrupt your conversation with your father."

Tom looked at her, curious, wondering. "That's okay, we were done." They stacked the dishes on the counter and Evelyn suggested that they move into the living room for dessert and a nightcap.

The rest of the visit was uneventful. Miriam quickly went from admiring the beauty of the snow to tiring of the bitter cold and the difficulty of getting from one place to another. When they finally returned to Baton Rouge, she gratefully inhaled the evening air as they exited the airport—crisp and cool, not frozen. Back at home, as she unpacked, she felt herself relaxing, her mind unclenching and stretching in their spacious home with the grass and trees between them and the neighbors. The birds sang their twilight melodies, the setting sun lit up the oak leaves, and she was where she belonged. But Tom sank back into himself. He went straight to the mail each day when he came home and rifled through it, hoping for the letter that didn't come. She decided not to think about what she would do if it did, unless she had to. And she wondered how to ask Tom about what had happened in high school.

PART III
NOW

CHAPTER 9

FINDING A NEW PURPOSE

After Camille left for classes, Miriam read the newspaper in her recliner, then prowled around in the morning quiet, restless and at loose ends, looking for something to do, the unaccustomed idleness oppressive. Perhaps she could paint now, without being compelled to do more important things, like refining her lectures, mopping the kitchen floor to get the spots her cleaning service missed, or straightening and vacuuming her bedroom closet. But laying out her supplies, mixing the paints on the palette, and then cleaning up afterward seemed too hard. Maybe if she had a painting in progress, but she'd finished her last one shortly before the diagnosis, and the thought of beginning a new one, of facing a blank canvas, was overwhelming.

She wandered up the stairs and found herself continuing down the hall to the closed door of her office. Petey ran ahead; he'd always loved that room. Miriam opened the door and glanced around the sunny space, her desk and easel waiting for her. She opened the closet where she kept her paintings. Petey flopped down and stretched out on the rug in the sunny spot. She took out five of her favorites and put them on the display ledge Mac had installed midway up the room's walls, carefully notching it in his workshop, then painting it with white enamel to match the baseboards and crown molding.

"If you won't hang any of your paintings, this will at least be a way for you to let them out of that dark closet every once in a while," he'd said, smiling to lighten the words. Miriam sat in the comfortable chair in the corner opposite the ledge and leaned back with her feet on the ottoman, enjoying the paintings as if they were someone else's. She was startled to hear Camille coming in downstairs and checked her watch. Already noon. Well, she'd whiled away the morning with nothing to show for it. She closed the office door and went down to the kitchen, where Camille paused from mixing egg salad for lunch to greet Miriam with her usual (sometimes annoying) cheerfulness.

Miriam frowned at the two cans of tuna, bag of noodles, and can of mushroom soup on the black-and-white tile counter. Camille must be planning to make tuna-noodle casserole for dinner again. Miriam realized she hadn't struck quite the right balance last week between appropriate gratitude and subtle discouragement of a repeat performance.

"Oh, Camille, I meant to tell you this morning that I'm picking up vegetable beef soup for us to have tonight. Calandro's makes a fresh batch every Tuesday, and it's very good.

Camille looked disappointed that her "surprise" was spoiled, but said, "That sounds good. I bought some things, but we can save them for another night."

They could save them for the next decade; no fresh ingredients there. Camille must have purchased the groceries herself to avoid Miriam's consistent refusal to accept payment for what Camille termed "her half" of the groceries or meals, as if Miriam wanted or needed Camille's money. Just last night, she'd told her, in the tone reserved to freeze in mid-sentence a student speaking out of turn, to please cease offering her money. Perhaps she'd been a tad overbearing—Camille had looked hurt—but Miriam wasn't up to going around in circles about it. "Camille," she began again, the sternness in her voice causing the girl to look up from the bread she was toasting, "it's very good of you to go to the store and help with meals, but you mustn't spend your money on the supplies."

"Thank you, Miriam, but you aren't obligated to feed me."

"I know, but that goes for you, too. I'm still able to grocery shop, but that may not be true for much longer. I'd prefer that we agree that you are not to pay for items you purchase. I'll phone Calandro's and instruct them that you may put items on my tab there. This is for anything else." Miriam opened a kitchen drawer and took out an envelope labeled "Food and Supplies" that she'd stuffed with bills of varying denominations, holding it in front of Camille. "Please take money from this envelope to the store or deli, or repay yourself from it afterward."

Camille frowned and turned back to rinsing the bowl in the capacious white porcelain sink, then looked out the window at the baskets of bright pink flowering bougainvillea hanging from the porch rafters before saying, "I would prefer to pay for my half when I eat with you."

Miriam frowned, exasperated. This would never do. "Camille, I'm afraid I must insist. I cannot accept your paying for any of our meals. Let us please agree on that now," she finished with the finality she'd used to close the conversation with a student arguing about a grade.

Camille looked unhappy but nodded, a little sullen. What was the problem? Then Camille's face brightened. "I almost forgot!" she said, darting back to the foyer, returning with a bouquet of fresh flowers. She pulled a vase from the cabinet and said, "I got these at Calandro's. They'd just come in and were so fresh and pretty, I thought you'd like them." She gave Miriam her lovely smile.

Miriam noted the price tag as she discarded the cellophane but was undeniably pleased. It had been a very long time since anyone had brought her flowers. She thanked Camille, took a few bills out of the envelope, and thrust them toward her. "Now, please, accept this reimbursement."

Camille sorted through the bills and accepted two of them, returning the third to the envelope. "If you insist, as my *employer,* Miriam, I'll take the money for the groceries. But the flowers were a gift." Camille had a rather fine natural dignity as she made this statement that left no room for argument.

"I'm sorry, I didn't mean to offend you," Miriam said, humbled. "The flowers are beautiful, and I greatly appreciate them." She'd need to better observe the line Camille was drawing between employer and well, maybe, friend, though it seemed unlikely that this attractive young woman would want a dying old one as a friend.

Camille nodded, looking mollified, then took a bowl of assorted berries from the refrigerator. "I researched healthful foods, and berries are highly rated. So I thought we could have these with our sandwiches. And I bought some oatmeal for breakfast."

Oatmeal, ugh, Miriam had never been able to stomach the stuff.

Camille caught her expression and added, "Or if that doesn't sound good, I bought some eggs—they're on the list too."

Miriam vaguely remembered "the list," a sheet from Dr. Viator recommending various healthful foods (without specifically relating them to cancer) that she'd put on the kitchen bulletin board and promptly forgotten. Camille seemed to think she would be assuming oversight of Miriam's care rather than the more limited role Miriam had envisioned.

After Camille left for class, Miriam, forced to acknowledge her need to rest, reclined in her chair and closed her eyes, feeling the slant of the afternoon sun through the windows, wondering idly when Petey would join her. Her thoughts crept to what lay ahead. She'd done enough research to confirm her doctor's prediction of her decline— possibly little pain (unless the tumor changed its direction of growth); increasing fatigue (maybe gradual, maybe rapid); and probably a brief duration of the grimmest phase at the end (although that phase could commence sooner and last longer). She couldn't blame the doctor for the prevaricating and vagueness; her research had made that much plain.

She'd never handled uncertainty or helplessness well, and she'd never felt so alone. After Tom's death, she'd withdrawn from friends, except Herb and Emily, who'd persevered through her refusal to be comforted, never abandoning her. But after a few years, Miriam had been saddened, but not surprised, when they'd told her that Herb had accepted a prestigious professorship at a California university that had hired Emily as well. They'd stayed in touch for years, but gradually the correspondence slowed, defeated by distance. Herb and Emily had tried to maintain the connection, had even asked her to be the godmother of their firstborn, but she'd never answered that letter, and they hadn't pursued it. After Mac and her parents died, she'd found it easier to be alone than to build new relationships, living with her ghosts instead.

So what refuge or solace was left to her? Faith had not been part of her life for many years. She hadn't lost it in one cataclysmic break—she'd let it dry rot like her old hiking boots in the back of her closet. When she'd finally pulled them out for a walk on the levee, the soles had separated and flapped loose, disintegrated after being so long unused and neglected. Maybe she'd made an idol of her work, sacrificing too much on its altar, hoping for atonement. Well, she wasn't one to suddenly find religion when faced with death. Even if, as she barely admitted, she sometimes felt that pull, occasionally thought she heard the whisper of that still, small voice calling her, it was too late now.

Enough of this. For years, she'd disciplined her mind to exclude thoughts of what she'd lost and her culpability. Now she could suppress these new fears of imminent pain and loss of independence. The key was keeping her mind engaged and challenged. She could do further research; she'd kept a list of potential topics. Her computer made trips to libraries unnecessary. She considered some of the topics she recalled from the list, but they no longer intrigued her or sparked that passion that had once driven her. In fact, the topics now seemed more like esoteric self-indulgence than productive scholarly research.

She could still mentor the graduate students she'd handed off to other professors. The students could benefit from her experience, connections, and insights without worrying about the politics of pleasing her. But their new professors might consider her input meddlesome interference, a distraction from their own guidance, especially if they didn't agree with her advice. Probably better not to intrude on the studies of students she'd surrendered.

She missed teaching with a dull ache that surprised her. She wandered into Tom's study and spied a couple of Camille's textbooks on the desk—algebra and English composition. She flipped through a notebook and saw Camille's schedule in an inside pocket—chemistry and biology were the others, and Camille had noted the titles of those textbooks.

True, not her subjects. She leafed through the text for the composition class—grammar and some elementary writing instruction. Simple enough. She could certainly assist Camille with that subject. The algebra text was, of course, more foreign. Still, it wasn't rocket science. The biology and chemistry would be the same—all introductory courses.

She still had her intellect; the disease hadn't taken that, and it would be good to have a last student. All of the texts were from the same academic publisher, one she'd used for textbooks for her courses. She called her sales agent, explained her forced retirement and wish to assist her young caregiver with classes (shamelessly taking advantage of his sympathy and their long relationship). He promised to send her the teachers' edition of the texts—she wanted the answers to the exercises. She could figure them out, but it would be tedious.

WHEN CAMILLE RETURNED THAT EVENING, THE SOUND OF THE DOOR opening triggered a loud wailing from upstairs—Petey! Camille dropped her backpack in the foyer, shouted, "I'll see what's wrong," and bounded up the stairs before Miriam could move. Dammit, she'd left Petey in her office, the room she'd told Camille remained closed. Miriam stood up, calling out that she would get him, but of course it was too late; she heard the door open and Petey rushing out, indignantly meowing as if letting loose a string of kitty expletives. Miriam climbed the stairs, bending to stroke Petey apologetically as he strode past, ignoring her efforts. She continued to the office and found Camille inside, examining the paintings left on the display ledge.

"Miriam, these are incredible," Camille said, with seemingly genuine awe. "Are they yours?"

Miriam considered and rejected denying it. Who else's would they be? "Yes, remember, I told you painting was my hobby."

"Miriam, these are much more than a hobby," Camille said, "I've never seen anything like them."

"Well, I was an art history professor for thirty-eight years, so it's natural that I would dabble a bit myself. Let's go downstairs—Petey wants his dinner," Miriam said, attempting to shepherd Camille out of the room.

"Please let me look at them for just a few more minutes," Camille said, bent over the first in the series on the ledge. The focal point of each painting was a single rosebush, rendered in sharp detail, as if viewed through a camera lens focused on it, the surrounding azaleas, bridal wreath bushes, and camellias painted in a contrasting, blurred, Impressionistic style. Tom once said the surreal exaggerations of sunlight and shadows in the clouds above and among the blossoms and leaves gave the paintings a mystical quality.

Miriam had placed the paintings in temporal order. In the first, dewdrops sparkled in early morning light on a rosebush covered in blush-pink blossoms, and wispy pink clouds lingered in the fresh, pale blue sky. Camille gazed at it in wonder before moving on to the next. Miriam watched, pleased despite her discomfort—no one had viewed the paintings in years, not since Mac's death. At the next one, Camille's lips parted and she took a deep breath, as if she could smell the yellow roses opening in bright sunlight from a clear blue sky, the essence of summer.

When Camille stopped at the next painting, an overcast afternoon scene, shafts of light escaping thick clouds to illuminate siren red roses, she murmured, "Oh, Miriam, so beautiful." Miriam nodded, softened by Camille's obvious pleasure in the works, moving closer to her as she gazed at the next, in which a few golden rays pierced purple-gray storm clouds, lighting up pale lavender roses, the surrounding garden in storm-dark shadows. Camille shook her head, silent, as if overcome. The last painting was Miriam's only night scene: a bush with white roses, backed by a velvet sky with a low-hanging full moon and stars, the surrounding plants reduced to silhouettes.

"I could look at these for hours, Miriam. Have you ever shown them?"

"No. Like I said, it's just a hobby."

Camille looked at her, brows raised, clearly ready to pursue this further, but Petey's insistent meowing from the kitchen and Miriam's determined ushering her from the room silenced her. Miriam had a feeling the subject would arise again. Annoying, yet she had to admit that she'd been gratified by the girl's frank admiration.

MIRIAM FED THE STILL-MIFFED PETEY, WHO CONDESCENDED TO LICK his bowl clean. After dinner, when Camille returned from walking Hanks and released him into the backyard, Miriam reminded her that she needn't stay any later.

"Miriam, with the hours I'm taking off for my classes, it makes sense for me to stay later," Camille answered, as she had before. She glanced out the French door at Hanks, and Miriam guessed that she kept him inside at night. Well, tomorrow she'd order that large dog bed on the Orvis website, the one with the memory foam mattress. She'd tell Camille that Hanks could join them inside in the evenings, which were growing cooler. That is, he could once the dog bed arrived. She didn't want him on her furniture. Maybe she'd pay for express delivery.

Camille made tea, and they brought it into the sitting room. It occurred to Miriam that she knew little about Camille's background. She'd almost forgotten what it was like to be interested in another person's world beyond the academic boundaries. In response to Miriam's questions, Camille said she didn't remember much about her parents. Her grandparents had taken her in after her parents had died in a car accident when she was two. Her grandfather had been a fisherman in the small river town of Pierre Part before they'd moved to Baton Rouge, where her grandparents thought she'd have more opportunities. Her grandfather had found work as a housepainter. Her grandmother stayed home with Camille until she started school, then worked part-time as a hotel maid, arranging her hours to be home with Camille after school.

"They worked hard and were strict," Camille said, "but I always knew how much they loved me." Her voice cracked, and she blinked back tears. Hanks watched Camille through the French door, subdued, tail lowered.

Well, perhaps that explained the shadow of loneliness, as if Camille, too, knew what it was to go home to an empty house. Maybe

Camille really didn't mind staying a little later or sharing their evening meal. Miriam relaxed a notch; this vulnerability might make Camille more likely to accept her mentoring.

A FEW DAYS LATER, THE TEXTBOOKS AND TEACHERS' MANUALS arrived. Miriam smiled as she unpacked them, liking the feel of the new books in her hands as she flipped through the pages. Miriam sat down with the algebra text (not a particularly good subject for her, as she recalled) and perused it with Camille's notebook in hand to see how far she'd gotten. Not very far; they were moving slowly. The text must be for both semesters. That night, after Camille left, Miriam picked up the algebra text. Within two hours, she'd gone from the first page through the end of Camille's current chapter, including the problems. This wasn't terribly difficult at all.

But the problems didn't go far enough. Miriam went through the last ones again and added a further step to each that would force her student to conceptualize at a slightly higher level, to go beyond what the text had spoon-fed her. Perhaps what they said about the dumbing down of America's colleges was true after all. Miriam composed a couple more problems that would force Camille to think on her own. Afterward, she was pleasantly tired enough to dull the anxiety and worries. She slept better that night than she had in weeks.

MIRIAM REPEATED THE PROCESS THE NEXT MORNING WHILE CAMILLE was in class, studying the composition text with its ridiculously simple grammar and writing exercises. She looked up, surprised, when she heard Camille entering the foyer. Lunch time already, and she hadn't prepared a thing. She didn't think she could take another round of egg or tuna salad sandwiches. She hurriedly put the newspaper on top of the text and teachers' manual, heard the rustle of paper bags, and looked up to see Camille walk in smiling.

"I stopped at a deli on the way and got us some sandwiches and potato salad. I thought you might like some variety."

"That was very thoughtful, Camille, and much appreciated." Miriam walked to the kitchen, took out the cash envelope, and handed it to Camille, saying, "Now please reimburse yourself from the envelope, as we discussed."

Camille hesitated, then said, "Oh, all right, Miriam, I'll let you repay me for yours."

"No, Camille, I insist that you let me cover both." Miriam looked at her sternly. "I'm not giving in on this, and the alternative is that you cease doing me the favor of providing lunch and sharing it with me." She stopped, seeing that petulant look on Camille's face. She'd have to say more.

"Camille, I realize that it takes more time for you to make lunch or deliver food to my home and eat here than it would for you to stop for something on campus with your friends. Please allow me the dignity of at least accepting what I can give in return."

The petulance was replaced with comprehension. Camille gave her a bright smile and said, "Well, if you put it that way, I guess I have no choice." She took the bills, then added, "Next time I'm getting those chocolate chip cookies they have too." Looking guilty, she added, "uh, except that you really shouldn't have anything with that much sugar, and now that I think about it, they had a fruit cup that looked delicious."

"You get a cookie for yourself, please. You can take it with you for an afternoon snack if you like," Miriam said. She put the sandwiches—quite nice ones—on plates with the potato salad while Camille went out to see Hanks and throw his Frisbee a few times before joining her.

As they settled into their lunch, Miriam said, "After you walk Hanks tonight, I was thinking that perhaps I could work with you a bit on your studies."

Camille looked up from her potato salad (for such a slender young woman, she certainly could put it away), and said, "But, Miriam, I'm not taking the sort of classes you taught."

"Of course not, but I think I'm up to the task of assisting with the basic courses you have at this stage. Let's just give it a try, and if you don't see value in the time we spend, we can discontinue the sessions." She wasn't really giving Camille a choice, but sometimes students had to be led rather forcibly toward the light.

"Um, well, okay, Miriam, if you want, but I shouldn't take up too much of your time," Camille stumbled, her expression far short of grateful or eager. Was she reluctant to invest more time in her studies (hopefully not) or doubtful of Miriam's ability to make the investment worthwhile? Camille glanced at the clock, said she had to leave for her afternoon classes, gathered her backpack, waved to Hanks through the window (silly—the dog was asleep), and was gone.

The mail brought a couple of cards from fellow professors, as well as one signed by staff members, including student workers—apparently, word of her illness had spread through the department. Kind of them, especially since she'd done nothing to stay in touch with her colleagues. They'd had a small retirement party for her in the coffee room, despite her saying she didn't want one. When she left the department that day, she'd tossed the cards from the party in the recycling bin, and she hadn't kept her promises to call or have lunch. Not that anyone had called her either, but she knew how the retired receded from the minds of those who remained in the busy working world with its aura of purpose and importance, distractions and deadlines.

AFTER DINNER THAT NIGHT, AS SHE AND CAMILLE CLEANED UP IN the kitchen, Miriam said casually, "Have you completed the problems for your algebra class tomorrow?"

Camille paused from putting the dishes away, surprised, "Yes, I finished them at the library between classes this afternoon. Why?" Camille seemed almost suspicious.

"Well, I thought I might go over them with you," Miriam said, keeping her tone light.

Camille hesitated before answering. "If you like."

"Fine, then, why don't you take Hanks for his walk, and I'll set us up at the kitchen table?" Perhaps having their sessions in the study would have made more sense, but she preferred her bright kitchen.

After they left, Miriam went into the garage and dragged in the box with the dog bed that had arrived that morning. She wasn't above presenting the bed tonight to improve Camille's mood about the study session. She unpacked it and put it near the kitchen table.

Camille returned and was leading Hanks to the French door when Miriam called her into the kitchen and pointed out the bed. Delighted, Camille took Hanks' leash off and patted her hand on the bed. Hanks sniffed it, then carefully stepped onto it, watching Camille to be sure he wasn't committing some infraction. Camille gave him the "down" command, and he complied, then settled with a deep sigh, resting his big head on the bolster that surrounded the back and sides. Miriam was proud of herself, as if she'd accomplished something more than ordering an item online.

They went through the problems in the book quickly—Camille was indeed prepared. Then Miriam explained the additional step she'd added for the first problem in the text. Camille was initially confused but then grasped what Miriam was doing and they worked through those quickly as well. Next, Miriam handed Camille a copy of the first of the problems she'd prepared herself.

Miriam saw Camille glance at her watch, probably ready to put her to bed and go home.

"Camille, I know you've already prepared what was assigned, and you understand the basics covered in the chapter. But as a scholar, you need to push yourself beyond what comes easily to you."

"Miriam, I'm sorry, but I'm just trying to get through the prerequisites so I can go on to the nursing classes and clinics." Camille frowned, her habitual cheerfulness dampened in a way Miriam hadn't seen. "Before Duncan called me about this job, I was thinking about dropping out of the program."

Miriam was shocked. "What, why?"

"It was just so hard, working every night, taking classes in the daytime, then trying to fit in homework in between. And I missed my grandparents so much. I was always tired and my grades were starting to slip."

The sadness in Camille's eyes touched Miriam. She'd never had to struggle like that. "But you seem very committed to your studies now," Miriam said, hoping that was true.

"Working for you has made a big difference to me, but I still wonder sometimes if I can make it through the whole curriculum, especially if this job with you ends before I'm done with school. And now that I've worked here, going back to my old job seems even harder."

"Camille, you're so smart and talented. Please don't give up. Let me help you."

Camille nodded, but was still uncharacteristically quiet, dispirited even. Perhaps she'd been wrong about this student. No, she was going to trust her instincts as an educator, which had been mostly correct. Camille could do more. And she was a striver; Miriam could feel it. Yes, Camille had a double load with work and classes; yes, she was tired at the end of a long day. But she was young and tough, too.

"Camille, let's just give my methods a try—humor me. If you don't like what we're doing after a week, we can stop, and I'll go back to watching movies and you can go back to studying on your own."

Camille sighed again, but said, "Oh, all right, Miriam. You sound like my grandmother. She always told me the most important thing wasn't the grade but that I'd done my best." Camille picked up the page and said, "Let me read the problem again."

The next hour passed very quickly, at least for Miriam. After Camille solved the first problem, she closed her notebook and text. Miriam pretended not to notice as she produced and handed Camille the second, more difficult problem. Camille's lips pressed into a tight line, but she reopened her notebook. She'd struggled more with that one; then Miriam saw the triumph in her eyes as she solved it.

"Do you have another one, Miriam?" Camille asked, forgetting her earlier reluctance. They did one more, then Miriam said they should stop for the night. She thought Camille would be ready for more the next night.

"Thank you, Miriam," Camille said before she left. "You were very kind to spend the time writing those problems and tutoring me. And I do understand the material in a way I didn't before."

Miriam said they'd go on to her biology homework the next night.

Again, Camille seemed less than joyful at the prospect, but she didn't protest either.

After Camille left, Miriam settled in bed with Henry James's *Portrait of a Lady,* rereading it for the fourth or fifth time, loving the way the elegant sentences caressed her mind, and feeling satisfied with how well the tutoring had gone. She closed the book earlier than usual, welcoming the soft sleepiness enveloping her. Focusing on this new student shifted her thoughts from the uncertainty and old regrets that fueled her insomnia. And she saw now that Camille needed her. Miriam vowed to use her remaining strength to help Camille realize all that she could achieve. She turned out the light and slept, untroubled by dreams.

CHAPTER 10

Miriam stood in her quiet bedroom, alone after Camille had left for morning classes, trying to remember why she'd come upstairs. She'd already prepared for their study session that night. She thought of painting and dismissed it, though she yearned for the feel of the brushes, the spread of the paint on the canvas. But her hands were no longer steady for the fine detail work. She probably couldn't even sit on the stool in front of the easel for more than an hour or two. Better not to try.

She looked at the framed photograph of her and Tom on their wedding day, their faces shining with that naïve confidence of youth. She picked it up and wished with a force that shook her that Tom was with her now. And Rosie. Well, regret was easy; remorse futile; forgiveness unattainable and undeserved.

She thought of the two drawings not yet destroyed, went to her office, took them out of the drawer and sat at her desk with them, tracing a finger over the lines of each, the face of the infant, then the child, lingering until the lines blurred, then she returned them to the drawer. She wished now she hadn't destroyed the other drawings of the child, but why? They were only images on paper, not the life she had let slip away in her careless despair.

A wave of nausea rolled over her, and she went back to her bedroom and lay down, weak. Was the disease beginning its final encroachment sooner than expected? Dr. Viator liked to repeat the oncologist's mantra—every cancer is different—then summarize the possible variations. There must be better pain medications than what Coralee had, or, even if they were still relying on that old standby, morphine, better delivery systems. Surely no more peaks and valleys— an hour of blessed relief until the pain began to creep in through the haze, then came roaring back with a vengeance that made the last hour or two before the next dose interminable. Here, alone, she admitted her fear.

After dinner that night, Camille stopped on her way out to walk Hanks and said, "Oh, I noticed on the calendar you have a doctor's appointment Friday at three. I'll be sure to be back from campus by two-forty."

"What? Why? I can still drive myself." She'd told Camille the last time she'd offered to accompany her that it was unnecessary.

Camille said, "I know you said that last time. But to do my job right, I need to meet your doctor and hear about your medication regimen. It's important for a nurse to be familiar with that."

This was unexpected. Miriam knew, but had contemplated as little as possible, that eventually she would need assistance with her medical appointments, and possibly even more humiliating chores. But she'd expected to maintain her privacy a bit longer.

"I don't think that's necessary, Camille," she said, waving her hand in dismissal.

"I'm sorry, Miriam, but it's something I have to do. It would be irresponsible for me not to go with you."

"I suppose you expect to be paid an additional fee for the service." She instantly regretted the words.

Anger sparked in Camille's dark eyes but was quickly replaced by compassion that Miriam liked even less.

"Miriam, it's part of what you already pay me to do." Then Camille walked out with Hanks, closing the front door quietly behind her.

Miriam wasn't only concerned about the further erosion of her independence. She wasn't ready for Camille to learn of her cancer diagnosis or the brevity of her remaining time. However irrational, Miriam held that close, as if revealing the truth would give the cancer a further advantage. Preserving the fiction that she'd hired a caregiver only as a precaution against the possible worsening of unnamed "health issues" only postponed the inevitable. But she preferred to delay admitting her true status to Camille, however vain and foolish that was.

AFTER CAMILLE LEFT FOR THE NIGHT, MIRIAM LAY PROPPED UP IN bed with *Bleak House*, savoring the solitude, made more precious by its increasing scarcity. She'd met with Duncan that week, signed the power of attorney to enable him to oversee her financial affairs and arranged for his paralegal to coordinate with her accountant to handle the bill paying, sending Miriam a tidy monthly statement. Duncan, initially reluctant to take responsibility for these tasks, had agreed, more, she thought, from kindness than any desire for the monthly fees.

It was the first time she'd seen Duncan's new office in a renovated, elegant old building downtown, with large windows in the conference room overlooking the Mississippi River. He'd gone over the revisions to her will, including the bequest to the "Thomas Johnson Memorial Fund" that would support the research of young professors. She'd approved them, and they sat a moment watching a tugboat push a barge up the river. Maybe noticing her wistful expression, Duncan had asked if she still wanted to leave the bulk of her estate to her cousins, Pam and Jack Landry. Like Tom, Duncan was a listener, and he'd probably gathered from scattered comments over the years that she wasn't fond of the cousins, her closest relatives.

"You could make other charitable gifts like the one to the Memorial Fund," he said. "I know you give to animal welfare organizations. How about leaving something to one of them?"

Miriam liked the idea and wondered why she hadn't thought of it. Knowing that she liked to research for herself, Duncan gave her several websites that provided alternatives for charitable giving. Intrigued, she'd promised to look into the possibilities before their next meeting.

Well, she'd start on that tomorrow. She turned out the light, and Petey curled up next to her, his loud purring like a warm sound machine, smoothing the small rustlings of the night. She closed her eyes, ready for sleep. But the longer she lay there, the farther sleep retreated. Petey meowed in protest as she tossed about, flipped the pillow over, pushed the covers back, then pulled them up again. When her mind began wandering into the dark places, she switched the light back on and sat on the edge of the bed, considering what to do. She could start the research discussed with Duncan, but she didn't feel like thinking any more tonight about her impending death in the concrete terms of dividing her assets. She stroked Petey, scratched under his chin, then put on slippers and went downstairs to the study.

Camille had taken it over nicely. She'd pulled open the heavy drapes to let the sun in, and even now, the moonlight brightened the room in defiance of the dark wood paneling. On the desk was a framed photo of a diminutive woman, black hair fading to gray, and a lean, wiry man, maybe in their sixties, probably Camille's grandparents, sitting on a worn flowered couch. A smaller frame held a picture of Hanks, grinning obligingly for the camera. Miriam shamelessly rifled through Camille's books and notebooks on the desk until she came across the materials for the composition class. She flipped through Camille's notes from the class to assess progress (elementary). She paused to read words scrawled in the top margin—round script in purple ink said, "He's looking at u again! He's SO INTO U!!" Underneath, in Camille's black ink: "Shut up!!" Purple ink: "Ur blushing!" Black ink: "STOP IT!!"

Miriam smiled and took out a paper from the pocket of the notebook, a large "A" written at the top. She sat down at the desk and read it. Standards had certainly deteriorated. Or maybe this was representative of the lower expectations at the community college. She picked up a pen, and after an hour of intense editing, felt blessedly sleepy. She tucked the paper into a desk drawer beneath some folders.

. . .

WHEN CAMILLE ARRIVED THE NEXT MORNING, MIRIAM WAS IN THE sitting room looking out at the pansies she'd had planted for the fall. They were blooming brightly, clearly enjoying the cooler mornings, their painted faces seeming to glory in the early sun.

Camille stood beside her and followed her gaze.

"You should paint them, Miriam."

Yes, she missed the soul-satisfying pleasure when she captured the light illuminating the petals, but that was over now.

"I don't think I could. By the time I finished getting out the paints, I'd be tired. And even if I managed to paint a little, I'd be too tired to put it all away again." She hated the weakness in her voice, almost a whine.

"There might be a way," Camille said, "if you were willing to settle for something smaller or simpler than the paintings you've done before." Camille glanced at her watch and then at Hanks, asleep in his new bed by the fire.

"He can stay in with me for a while," Miriam said. Petey lay next to the big dog. Camille blew Hanks a kiss, said she'd be back with lunch from the deli, and dashed out the door.

It was funny, Miriam thought, you could tell yourself it was only a hobby, only an occasional indulgence, and when it's stripped away, you realize it was part of the lifeblood circulating through you. She sat looking at the pansies and mourning her lost art.

CAMILLE RETURNED AT NOON, LADEN WITH SEVERAL BAGS, MORE than lunch, and smiling like she'd just solved world hunger. Miriam hoped she hadn't done more than buy the chocolate chip cookies.

"Miriam, I have something for you." Camille put the other bags on the kitchen counter, then came into the sitting room with a sack Miriam instantly recognized as from an art supply store she'd frequented over the years. Camille reached in and pulled out two small canvases, one only eight by eight inches and the other ten by ten inches, and several tubes of paint.

"The lady at the art store said that a seasoned artist would know how to mix the exact shades needed from primary colors and white, so we chose these, but I can get more if you like." Pulling a jar of mineral spirits from the bag, Camille added, "She said you might need this too. And they had other small canvases, larger than these, or rectangular instead of square. I didn't get any brushes, but I can go back for whatever you want."

Miriam was speechless.

"The store lady asked me if you had an easel that would be the right height for smaller canvases, but I didn't know." Camille looked worried.

Miriam recovered herself enough to answer. "I do—Mac made me an adjustable easel. Camille, you shouldn't have—this was so kind of you. But I don't know if I can--."

Camille cut her off. "It's worth a try, Miriam. You can teach me how to set up the paints, and when you're finished, you can leave everything out for me to put away. You can show me how to clean the brushes and save your strength for the painting."

Miriam picked up each tube of paint, looking at the colors, then traced her fingers over the small canvases, loving the familiar feel. Camille set out their lunch, saying, "We can talk while we eat about which brushes and other stuff you want me to get out before I leave. It's warmed up outside, but I can pull out a sweater for you and some sweatpants if you have any." She smirked, presumably at the thought of Miriam in sweatpants.

Miriam said she had sweatpants (and she hoped she could find them). As they ate and talked about how to set up on the back porch, Miriam's excitement grew, and she finished her chicken noodle soup in record time. Camille brought out the fruit salad, but Miriam didn't have the patience to sit still any longer. For once not urging her to eat more, Camille put it back in the refrigerator and stashed a cookie in her backpack. Then she rushed upstairs to gather the easel and remaining supplies. Miriam followed more slowly to get a sweater and the old paint-stained sweatpants she hadn't worn since last February.

Camille looked at them with raised eyebrows and said, "I think I could find you some better ones at the Goodwill Store."

On the porch, Miriam showed Camille how to set up the paints and adjust the easel. Camille darted back inside for Miriam's phone.

"You told me you used to take photographs too. You could take some on your phone. Then we can put them up on your computer screen if you want to paint in your office."

An excellent idea—the light faded so fast this time of year. Camille left for classes, and Miriam sat in front of the easel, the afternoon sun warm on her face. She smiled as she picked up a brush for the first time since her diagnosis. Even knowing that her ability would be dulled, the same quiet joy bubbled up deep within her as she worked. She felt tears of gratitude spill over; she wiped them away and continued.

THE NEXT MORNING, MIRIAM WORKED ON CLEANING OUT THE shelves in her bedroom closet, telling herself that painting afterward would be her reward. After lunch, she painted on the porch while Hanks snoozed beside her on the porch rug. An hour passed, and she sat back and contemplated the work. The cluster of pansies with the light filtering through their petals seemed to bask in the sun, raising their leaves as if in worship. She'd painted them in a style looser than the rose bushes, but more detailed than the backgrounds of those paintings. She picked up the brush again, adjusting the colors of the petals, slightly exaggerating the sunlight illuminating them, pausing to consider, then leaning forward to refine a shadow or sharpen the edge of a petal. Startled to hear footsteps crossing the sitting room, she looked up, incredulous that Camille was already returning from her afternoon classes.

Camille joined her, looking at the canvas with wide-eyed admiration. "Miriam, it's incredible—I can't believe you did all of this today! Truly beautiful."

"Well, it's not finished yet—I'll probably work on it more tomorrow." She didn't acknowledge the praise, but it cheered her. Camille briskly began picking up the paints and brushes, pausing to regard Miriam's clothing with disapproval.

"You'd better go in while I put everything away," Camille said. "It's gotten chilly and you're not dressed warmly enough. You're probably more susceptible to colds now." Miriam went in meekly and sat in her recliner, closing her eyes as Petey settled in her lap. Camille popped in and lit the fire, then finished cleaning up.

Miriam roused herself, realizing that she'd failed to make any preparations for dinner. Between the fatigue and the dull pain in her belly and back that came and went, she no longer felt like shopping or cooking. Driving would soon be beyond her as well. Camille brought the painting things in and said she'd take Hanks for his walk and then heat up some soup they could have with toast and the fruit salad. Miriam nodded gratefully. Her own appetite was slight, but she'd have to arrange better for Camille if she wanted to continue their habit of eating together (and she'd grown accustomed to the company). While Camille walked, Miriam opened her laptop, found a meal service, and ordered meals to be delivered three nights the following week. If they worked out well, she'd increase it. She told Camille about it when she returned and regretted not doing it sooner when she saw Camille's surprised relief.

Miriam had put cash by Camille's place at the table.

"What's all this for, Miriam? Lunch wasn't nearly this much."

"The art supplies, of course—I forgot to repay you yesterday. Thank you again for buying them. The small canvases were a brilliant idea."

Camille reached over and gave Miriam's hand a squeeze.

"Miriam, don't you remember? It's your birthday. I was planning to wrap the supplies and give them to you today, but I was too excited to wait." Before Miriam could respond, Camille got up and pulled from a bag on the counter a small cake with cream cheese frosting coated with pecan pieces and a little carrot rendered in colored icing in the middle.

"They had these cute little cakes at Calandro's," Camille said, "just the right size for us. Happy birthday, Miriam. I'm so glad to be spending it with you."

Miriam had indeed forgotten her own birthday. At first, she wondered how Camille had known, then remembered she'd had to give Camille the date to pick up a prescription at the pharmacy. Camille cut the pretty little cake and served it. It was quite good. Miriam hadn't celebrated her birthday in years.

Camille beamed with pleasure when Miriam thanked her again, then offered, perhaps hopefully, that Miriam probably hadn't had time to prepare anything for their usual evening study session and must be tired after painting.

"Thank you, Camille, for your concern, and I am a bit tired, but fortunately, I've been running a chapter or two ahead of you in the algebra text and am ready for tonight."

"Oh, okay."

She could see Camille's doubt. Miriam still hoped to replace it with a dream that matched Camille's abilities and the confidence to pursue it. They went over an additional three problems Miriam had concocted. Camille did well, smiled at Miriam's rare words of praise, and gathered her things.

"Camille, I took the liberty of reviewing your work in the composition class, which we haven't yet considered." She handed Camille the paper, covered in editing marks and comments.

"Miriam, I'm sorry you spent time on that paper—it's already been turned in and graded." She looked at the essay and frowned, then at Miriam and said sharply, "Where did you get this? Were you going through my things?"

Miriam realized she should have foreseen this question, but she hadn't. "I, um, was in the office to clean out desk drawers when I ran across it, and—"

"Ran across it? Maybe I misunderstood, but when you said I could use the desk in the study, I thought you meant that it was my private space."

"I'm sorry, you're right. I didn't mean to pry, and I'll be more respectful in the future. But this is my house, after all, and I will require time in the study, when you're not using it, of course, to clean out items, such as those in the desk." Perhaps Camille had a legitimate complaint, but Miriam wasn't accustomed to anyone questioning her access to every corner of her home, nor was she prepared to surrender that.

"Maybe I should leave my books and notebooks in my car or backpack," Camille snapped, not at all mollified.

"Again, I apologize," Miriam repeated, now remembering the obviously private notes scrawled in the margins of the notebook where she'd found the essay. She rushed on. "Back to the essay. My aim was to begin by assessing your current mastery of the language, and--"

"My mastery of the language? My grandparents may have mixed Cajun French in their speech and lacked much education, but they saw to it that I worked hard in school."

Miriam tried a more placating tone. "I understand, Camille, and I was speaking in general terms, meaning your mastery of composition, of writing effectively."

Camille softened her tone, probably remembering that Miriam was her employer. "But I got an 'A' on that paper. The instructor even read parts of it to the class."

"Yes, but the goal is not to compare yourself to others, but to reach the highest level that you personally can achieve."

"I know biology, chemistry, and math are important for me, but I won't be writing essays as a nurse or publishing papers like you did as a professor."

"Camille, I can tell you from experience that developing skill in written communication will serve you well. Many nursing professionals have written articles helpful to both their peers and the doctors with whom they work. Some have written practice manuals for colleagues. Effective communication should never be underrated."

Camille looked at her silently, perhaps sullenly, then glanced at her watch. True, it was late, and Camille rose quite early. But Camille yielded, though her posture sagged, and she propped her chin up in her hand, no spark of interest in her eyes. They spent fifteen minutes going through Miriam's editing comments. Camille nodded as they did, finally becoming absorbed in what Miriam was showing her. Camille took out her laptop, placed the edited pages in front of her, and began working.

"You don't have to do it tonight," Miriam said. It was already eight.

"I may not finish it tonight, but I'd like to at least start making some notes on how I plan to revise while it's fresh in my mind. Do we have maybe half an hour before I help you get settled?"

Miriam assured her that they did and that Camille needn't help her, knowing that would be ignored. Well, to emphasize the point, she'd go upstairs and start getting ready for bed by herself. She did so, realizing as she moved about her bedroom how much easier it was when Camille was there, scooping up the clothes she took off to put in the hamper, laying out her nightgown, turning down the bed, running her bath. She'd barely noticed how those small steps had smoothed her way, but she did now. By the time she was finally in bed, she was exhausted, and the bathroom wasn't neat and dry like Camille always left it. The towel was wadded on the back of the toilet instead of hanging on the rack, the washcloth left in a sodden heap on the edge of the tub. She was getting out of bed to tidy up when Camille came in, having taken far more than the allotted thirty minutes.

"Miriam, I'm sorry, I was working on the essay and the time got away from me." Miriam looked at her, wondering whether that was truly the case or if Camille's actions had a passive-aggressive tone. But Camille's eyes were bright despite the circles beneath, and she looked pleased with herself. "I actually finished a revised draft, but I need to work on it more tomorrow before I show it to you."

As Camille talked, she moved about the bathroom, efficiently setting it to rights. Nine-thirty—Miriam told her to run along, no need to do anything further (not that there was anything left to do). Camille smiled, went downstairs, fussed about in the kitchen, then reappeared with a mug of herbal tea that she placed on the bedside table.

"Thank you, Miriam," she said softly as she turned on the lamp, flicked out the ceiling light, and closed the door halfway just like Miriam liked it. "I'll see you tomorrow."

Later, in a pathetic stab at self-reliance, Miriam took the empty tea mug downstairs to the kitchen to rinse. She passed the open office door on her way back upstairs and noticed the desktop was clear. She turned on the light and saw that Camille had removed all of her papers and notebooks from the office, away from Miriam's prying eyes. Now Miriam felt truly ashamed and, irrationally, hurt.

CHAPTER 11

FORMULATING A PLAN

Friday morning the weather remained sunny and pleasantly cool, so Camille set Miriam up on the porch to paint. Miriam asked her to bring out the pansy painting and the other small canvas.

"Are you going to work more on the pansy one? It's hard to imagine how you could improve it."

Miriam said she was, enjoying Camille's small, worried frown and protectiveness of the painting.

After Camille left, Miriam decided she needed paper and a pencil to sketch out an idea for her next painting before she forgot it. When she went into the study to get them, she saw a portable radio on the desk. She flipped it on idly to check the setting, expecting some variety of rock or pop, but it was a contemporary Christian music station. The purity of young voices singing with passionate conviction was charming, hopeful. She took pencil, paper, and Camille's radio back out to the porch with her. Surely Camille wouldn't consider that a further infringement on her treasured privacy. She'd enjoy having some music as she worked and was pleased to find that the station had no commercials. She sketched out some lines and notes for her next painting, then returned to the pansy painting.

Again, she fell into her art, seeing more that she could do. So much depended on when you decide a work is finished, whether it's a painting or a scholarly paper. Time evaporated, and she looked up to see Camille walking in with lunch. Miriam realized she still had the radio playing. She'd meant to put it back before Camille returned.

"I love that song," Camille said, coming out on the porch, singing along as the song ended, then saying, "The title, 'Priceless,' is perfect, don't you think?"

Miriam looked up and said, "Oh, I didn't notice." Why had she said that? It wasn't true. She'd heard every word as she painted, had even begun to hum along on the chorus.

"I love the whole idea that God doesn't see us as we are here, but as we are redeemed by Jesus—with all our sins washed away—clean and beautiful," Camille said.

"It's a nice thought," Miriam said noncommittally. What on earth would Camille have done that needed to be washed away anyhow? Perhaps a fleeting and quickly repressed resentment of the drudgery of her grandmother's care? Maybe letting a boy's hands stray too far on the second date? Please. Miriam, on the other hand, doubted that any redemption could wash away the ugly scars on her soul left by her many mistakes, deliberate and indeliberate. She could never see herself as clean and beautiful and didn't think God could either.

Camille came closer and stared at the painting, for once speechless. Her expression was that slack-jawed wonder Miriam had seen in students who suddenly comprehended the brilliance of a work, felt that current that sparked and flowed through art, whether it be music, dance, or a painting. The power that parted the musty veil woven of all that binds us to this earth to reveal a flash of the divine brilliance beyond.

"Miriam—it's—I can't believe—you've somehow put all the beauty of the sun and earth into this tiny painting. It makes me joyful." Camille's voice cracked, and she seemed to be blinking back tears.

Miriam flushed with pleasure, then got up from the stool, saying, "We'd better get on with lunch so you won't be late for class. I don't think I'll do more today—maybe tomorrow I'll start another. Do you think you might buy me more of the small canvases?" She wouldn't paint more today because of her doctor's appointment that afternoon, which she was still hoping Camille would forget.

"Of course, I can go this afternoon, right after lunch. I'll just clean up here and we can eat." Miriam went in to pull the soup and sandwiches out of bags and arrange them while Camille carefully cleaned the brushes and reverently carried the easel and painting inside to a corner of the sitting room.

CAMILLE HADN'T MENTIONED THE DOCTOR'S APPOINTMENT TODAY. Miriam waited at the living room window, car keys out, ready to slip away if Camille wasn't precisely on time, then thought, why wait? She hadn't asked Camille to come, had made it quite clear that accompanying her wasn't necessary or desired. On impulse, Miriam slipped out the side door into the garage and got in the black Ultra Luxury Lexus sedan she'd bought last year and pulled out to the street, elated. In the rearview mirror, she saw Camille pull into the driveway in her dull green, ancient Toyota Tercel. Miriam sped out of the neighborhood.

She hadn't factored in her new slowness, though. In the crowded parking lot, her space was far from the entrance. She was still making her way to the door when she heard a horn blast and turned to see Camille shouting out her car window for Miriam to wait for her. The old Miriam would have quickly outpaced Camille and entered the office without the unwanted escort, but Camille easily overtook her, leaping from the Tercel and sprinting to Miriam's side, face red, but not from exertion.

"Miriam, why did you leave without me? I told you I was coming to take you!"

"And I believe I told you that was unnecessary."

Camille stopped outside the door, arms crossed, not quite making a scene, but angry enough to make Miriam uncomfortable.

"Miriam, we have to agree right now that you will allow me to do my job. If you won't, then—"

The thought of being alone—or with the kind of caregiver she'd imagined before meeting Camille—prompted Miriam to quickly break in. "Oh, all right, if you insist." No apology offered.

Camille huffed and opened the door for her. They sat in the waiting room in frosty silence until the nurse called Miriam, when Camille stood to join her. Miriam had hoped, perhaps unrealistically, that Camille wouldn't accompany her to the examining room and considered telling her to remain in the waiting room. But realizing now that Camille wasn't above a public argument about it, she relented. Surely the doctor wouldn't specifically discuss her private health care information in front of Camille, or at least not the advanced stage of the cancer.

After Camille introduced herself as Miriam's caregiver, Dr. Viator didn't hesitate to discuss Miriam's case openly, and Miriam realized she'd been foolish to assume that he'd be any less forthcoming than he was when she was there alone. Of course, he'd assume that her caregiver was aware of her illness and its extent.

"The tumor is growing," Dr. Viator said, glancing through Miriam's file at her last round of tests and recent scan. "As we've discussed, Miriam, with your decision to forego chemotherapy, you'll continue to decline steadily in the months ahead. I'm sorry, but we knew this was coming."

Miriam glanced at Camille, who was staring at Dr. Viator, mouth half open, eyes wide with shock, leaning forward as if unsure that she'd heard correctly. Camille closed her eyes a moment, then began taking notes on her phone, fingers flying, as if capturing Dr. Viator's words would make them manageable. Miriam reminded herself to advise Camille of studies finding early arthritis in the thumb joints of young people, problematic for a medical professional.

Camille said, "Would chemotherapy be effective if Miriam decided to have it?"

"Miriam's decision regarding chemotherapy is completely understandable and a rational one," Dr. Viator said. "With late-stage pancreatic cancer, the results might well not be worth the, uh, rigor of the treatment. In addition, Miriam inherited her mother's weak heart, and chemo could accelerate those issues."

Miriam winced at the words, "late-stage pancreatic cancer." No more prevaricating or hiding the extent of her illness now. She saw Camille's mouth tighten into a thin line, sad eyes downcast, shoulders slumped. Then Camille looked back at her, mustered a tremulous smile, put an arm around Miriam's shoulders, and said, "Are you sure you don't want to consider the chemo, Miriam? I can go with you to the treatments."

Miriam tried to keep the sharpness out of her voice since, after all, the offer was kind. "Thank you, Camille, but no, as Dr. Viator said, that decision has been made."

"It would be better for Miriam not to be alone at night," Dr. Viator said, moving on. "Is anyone with her?" He directed the question to Camille, as if Miriam weren't there.

"I can stay with her," Camille answered without hesitation. Miriam didn't argue the point. She'd noticed Camille was spending more time at her home, but hadn't commented, had scarcely admitted to herself the comfort of it. Like a helpless child, she no longer savored the nightly solitude but was increasingly fearful of being alone.

Dr. Viator said, "We can talk more at the next appointment about when hospice care should begin and additional sitters should be employed for twenty-four-hour care. Your current arrangements are probably adequate for the next two or three months, but after that, Miriam might need both and possibly more active pain management."

Dr. Viator walked them out of the examining room, saying to call if Miriam needed to see him before the next scheduled appointment. The bleak prediction weighed on Miriam. Camille's dismay was evident in her downward gaze and slower steps, the rare absence of a smile, and the way she'd grown quiet. She grabbed Miriam's hand and held it as she walked Miriam to her car.

BACK AT MIRIAM'S HOUSE, CAMILLE SAID, "WHY DIDN'T YOU TELL

ME YOU HAD ADVANCED CANCER?" MIRIAM HEARD THE SHADE OF accusation in her voice, muffled by kindness, but still there.

"Well, that wasn't relevant to my retaining you. I believe I was quite specific about your duties and responsibilities here."

"Specific about everything but the duration of my employment here," Camille said, the accusation softening to sadness.

Miriam realized she'd thought only of how retaining Camille would affect her own life, not how it might affect Camille's. Of course, the length of her employment mattered to Camille. It made a big difference in her ability to continue her education. Camille had told her as much.

"I'm sorry, I should have thought more about how that would affect you," Miriam said, contrite.

"No, you're right, Miriam. You didn't mislead me. I just assumed we'd be together here for, uh, longer."

Miriam watched Camille go out on the porch to greet Hanks. She threw his frisbee, but without her characteristic energy and enthusiasm. Camille forgot to congratulate Hanks on his daring leap to grab the frisbee, appearing lost in her thoughts. Hanks sensed it. When he returned the frisbee, instead of running back out, anticipating another throw, he sat at Camille's feet, looking up at her, doleful, tail wagging slowly. She leaned over to stroke his back, scratched behind his ears, and came back in, Hanks still watching her.

Camille said she could begin staying the next night. She was her usual kind, efficient self, but Miriam felt something closed off now, that Camille had recognized a distance between them she hadn't before. Miriam thought of demurring, saying it wasn't necessary for Camille to stay here yet, or at least not every night, but found herself unwilling. Instead, she said in a small, shaky voice she barely recognized, "Thank you for staying with me." She'd have to further consider Camille's concerns. Because Miriam found she cared more than she'd realized. "I think Hanks could stay here, too."

Camille smiled at that and said, "Oh, I finished the rewrite of my essay, but I left it at home."

"Well, maybe we could go to Vinny's for an early dinner and then get it on the way back?" Miriam offered. "My treat, of course." A sharp look to silence any argument on that point, but Camille was smiling, a bit triumphant, perhaps understanding the tacit apology for Miriam's earlier behavior.

Camille left to take Hanks for a walk before dinner, and Miriam used the time to order another dog bed for the guest room and call Duncan about increasing Camille's pay. She was glad she'd have the diversion of the essay tonight, not wanting to dwell on the doctor's disheartening comments.

Miriam suggested that they take her car and handed Camille the keys without specifically admitting that driving hadn't been as effortless as remembered. They had a pleasant meal, neither mentioning Miriam's premature departure for the doctor's office that afternoon.

After dinner, Camille drove a couple of blocks beyond the turn into Miriam's neighborhood and into the narrow streets of hers. The houses here, small and crowded together, were in various states of disrepair, some abandoned, one with several partially dismantled vehicles in the yard. Camille's little house was relatively well-maintained. The yellow paint on the wood siding was peeling, but the yard was neatly cut, and a pot of petunias sat on a clean-swept porch by the front door.

"Do you, um, own his house, Camille?" Miriam asked, hoping not.

"Oh, no, after my grandmother died, the apartment where we'd lived was too much for me to keep by myself. Some old friends of my grandparents offered me this house for very low rent. They said they just wanted it occupied so they could keep it insured until they were ready to sell."

Miriam nodded. She could certainly see why they would want it occupied and insured, though putting a young woman there alone didn't seem like the best idea. She had a new appreciation for Hanks.

"They left an old push lawnmower in the garage, so I get a good workout cutting the grass on the weekends," Camille said, inclined, as usual, to see a burdensome task as beneficial. Perhaps she'd been read the story of Pollyanna at a too impressionable age. "Hanks likes to chase the lawnmower while I cut. I think he's afraid it might turn on me." She ran into the house and returned with her paper.

Back at home, Miriam said, "Camille, why don't you run along early tonight. It's been a long day, and that will give you a little time to pack some things for tomorrow. I'll read your essay and can get myself settled."

Camille hesitated but agreed and hurriedly completed the initial steps of Miriam's bedtime preparation, probably remembering the mess Miriam had made of it when left on her own. Even the young get tired, Miriam thought, and jotted a note to add more nights to the weekly meal service. Miriam finished getting ready, brought the essay upstairs, climbed into bed, and, with Petey settled in and purring on her lap, read. It was good. Really good, impressive even. She thought about the other work they'd done, including problems and exercises from next semester's sections of the textbooks. After only brief summaries of the intervening material, Camille completed them easily. Miriam had observed her progress with a mixture of satisfaction and growing anxiety that this student was not on the right path.

Miriam got up, suddenly energized, fetched her laptop from her office, and returned to bed. She researched the nursing programs and found quite a range, from Camille's two-year program at the community college to a five-year Bachelor of Science in Nursing at LSU that would qualify her to take the exam to be a registered nurse. Then she turned to the requirements for a pre-med college degree and medical school. Camille could handle these; Miriam was sure of it. And Camille had that rare combination of analytical intelligence, empathy, and unselfish compassion—she was a natural healer.

The challenge would be persuading Camille. Especially now that Camille realized that her position here was likely to be over in months rather than years. Camille hadn't considered medical school and rejected it; she'd been struggling to complete a two-year program, exhausted and alone as she'd been. And would be again. No wonder she'd been blind to the possibility of anything beyond that.

Miriam could do something about that. She could still change the trajectory of this last student. She put aside the laptop, turned out the light, stroked Petey as he snuggled next to her, and fell asleep constructing the approach she'd take with Camille.

. . .

THE NEXT MORNING, MIRIAM WATCHED CAMILLE HURRYING ABOUT after her morning walk with Hanks, her battered little suitcase still by the front door, waiting to be unpacked, the paper bag of supplies for Hanks on the kitchen counter.

"Miriam, if you don't mind, I'll unpack these things when I get back at lunch," Camille said, looking harried.

"No problem—do you have time for a cup of tea before you leave for school?"

Camille had glanced at her watch, looking nervous, but agreed. After they sat down, Miriam dove right in, eager to steer her student toward this new horizon.

"Camille, your rewritten essay was very good."

Camille looked a little startled at the unqualified praise and said nothing, as if waiting for the criticism to follow.

"It made me think more about your current curriculum."

Camille frowned and looked past Miriam out the window. Disregarding these signals, Miriam continued. "Have you ever considered anything beyond the nursing program at the community college?" She belatedly realized the condescending tone.

"No, the program has everything I need for the career I've chosen. Why?"

Undaunted, Miriam continued. "I think you could do more. You should consider the Bachelor of Science in nursing at LSU or even medical school. You could excel in either program." She looked at Camille, hoping for the breathless eagerness of her best students when she'd pronounced them worthy to pursue a doctorate.

Camille appeared not the least bit intrigued. "Miriam, thank you for your interest in my career, but nursing is what I want to do—it's been my dream since I was a child. And it hasn't been easy for me to come this far." Looking weary now, Camille put her mug down, preparing to leave. "I appreciate the salary you're paying me, along with the meals, and that's let me save for when I don't have this job anymore. That will help. I want to be a nurse. That will be enough."

Miriam watched as Camille took her mug into the kitchen without a backward glance. She returned with her backpack and said, "I'll be back with lunch. The doctor said smoothies would be good for you, so we could try those if you like. Oh, do you want me to set up your paints before I go?" Camille glanced at her watch again.

"No need this morning—I've got some homework to do myself. A smoothie sounds very nice, thank you."

Camille left quickly, forgetting to put Hanks out, acceptable since Miriam planned to let him right back in. She was still smarting from Camille's quashing of her suggestions. Camille hadn't even heard her out, had cut her off with finality. Maybe Camille was right. The end was coming fast for Miriam; she wouldn't be around to give Camille the support she'd need to tackle a big dream like medical school, or even a Bachelor of Science degree at LSU. Miriam wondered if she should give up on the idea, live out her remaining days peacefully painting and relaxing in her chair by the fire.

No. That wasn't her way. Never had been, never would be. But she needed to better prepare and choose her timing more carefully. She went to the study, pleased to find that in her haste, Camille hadn't completely cleared the desk. True, no notebooks remained, but she'd left the small pile that Miriam knew from past snooping included Camille's schedule and general material on her curriculum. She almost tripped on a new, stuffed backpack on the floor next to the desk. A quick (and cautious) peek confirmed that it held Camille's books and notebooks that she didn't need this morning. She'd probably intended to store it in her car, Miriam thought, briefly chastened, but undeterred from taking the curriculum materials upstairs to her office (vowing to return them to exactly the same place).

She carefully researched and compared the programs, prerequisites, and requirements for graduation. And the costs. Camille should easily qualify for the Louisiana state scholarship program, but she probably already knew that from her current studies. Yes, medical school tuition was quite expensive, and the years required were long. Camille's reluctance was understandable. But she couldn't possibly make the right decision without knowing the alternatives. Camille needed a mentor, a role Miriam knew well. That and the support she could offer.

She wasn't going to let Camille go back to scrubbing toilets and vacuuming offices at night, out of the question. Why not use some of her wealth to complete what she'd begun with Camille, to give the girl real choices that didn't require overwhelming sacrifice and hardship?

Overcoming Camille's resistance to accepting financial help was another issue. She'd talk with Duncan and think further herself. Making a plan and executing it would take time, and she didn't have much left. She'd been reconciled to that, but now she wanted to live long enough to help this one last student realize her full potential.

CHAPTER 12

ADVANCING THE PLAN

Camille's rental house concerned Miriam. Maybe she should leave Camille this house? No, she wouldn't want the burden of the house, nor would Miriam's cousins, who'd sell it the minute title cleared. The cousins wouldn't bother to sell the beautiful old antiques for what they were worth, either, wouldn't even recognize their value. They'd probably just have a big garage sale, the hand-tied silk Oriental rug in the dining room going for twenty-five dollars to the first person willing to haul it away. She couldn't bear to dwell on the fate of the beautiful paintings she and Tom had collected so lovingly.

But what if the house didn't have to be a burden while Camille was in school? She'd talk with Duncan about that as well.

After dinner that evening, as Camille was cleaning up and Miriam was retrieving her materials for the study session, she saw Camille pull her phone from her pocket, check the screen, then glance her way. Miriam went to the sitting room to give Camille some privacy (or at least the illusion of it) and heard Camille answer softly.

"Hello, Adelaide. Yes, I'm sorry. I've been busy."

Miriam sat in her chair on the other side of the wall, near enough to the kitchen door that she could hear.

"I know we have the algebra test next week." Pause. "That was nice of your mother to invite me, Adelaide, and I miss studying with you, too. I'll ask Miss Miriam if I can have time off that day."

Camille probably thought she'd gone upstairs to her office to gather her notes as she often did. Miriam stayed quiet, listening closely.

"No, she doesn't pay me extra for weekends. I'm making up time from being gone for classes during the week." Camille listened, then sighed loudly. "Look, we still have a week before the test. I'll check with Miss Miriam and call you back, okay?"

Miriam left her chair and was standing in the doorway when Camille put her phone back in her pocket and looked up, surprised to see her.

"Oh," Camille said, flustered, "I'm sorry, that was my friend, Adelaide, from school."

Miriam had never considered Camille's possible life outside this house. She mumbled a rare apology for monopolizing Camille's time and offered to arrange for someone else to help her a couple of days a week.

"No, Miriam, I like being here," Camille rushed to say, sounding sincere. "We'll get some other help as you need more, but right now, I don't have to do that much when I'm here. I just don't like leaving you alone."

Relief rushed over Miriam.

Camille plunged on, "It's just that Adelaide and I always studied together, and she may need us to meet before our algebra test next week. She hasn't been doing so well in that class."

"Well, do you think she might want to come here to study? She could come any afternoon or evening—you two could have the dining room table to yourselves or, if you like, I could quiz both of you for part of the time."

Camille smiled, possibly thinking that she might enjoy not being Miriam's sole focus. "That would be wonderful. Would Thursday after dinner be okay?"

"Sure, I'm two chapters ahead now, so I can be ready for you,"

Miriam said, returning to her chair. She heard Camille call Adelaide back and set the time for seven. A few minutes later, Camille's phone rang again, and Miriam heard her say, "Okay, Adelaide, thanks. Why don't you come a little earlier then, maybe five-thirty? Tell your mother thank you."

Camille came into the sitting room and said Adelaide's mother, Mrs. Doucet, was going to make chicken and andouille sausage gumbo and cornbread for Adelaide to bring over for dinner.

"Oh?" Miriam raised her eyebrows, surprised by this neighborly offer from someone she'd never met.

"I hope you don't mind, Miriam, but Mrs. Doucet loves to cook, and if you don't accept the gumbo, she may come over here and try to feed us herself."

"Well, far be it from me to refuse such a kind offer," Miriam said, hoping she sounded gracious. And why not? It would be the first time she'd had guests eating at the dining room table in years.

THE NEXT MORNING, MIRIAM PAINTED BUT TOLD CAMILLE SHE could put the paints away when she came home for lunch. After Camille left, Miriam spent a couple of hours refining her notes and problems, then went into the study hoping to check Camille's notebook to be sure she'd covered all the test material. The notebook was gone, but Miriam found a new framed photo on the desk. The picture, which she hadn't known Camille had taken, was of her on the back-porch swing, smiling at Hanks and scratching behind his ears. Miriam replaced the picture, noticing that it was next to the picture of Camille's grandparents. A knot in her chest loosened and her eyes grew misty. Really, the disease was making her far too sentimental.

THAT NIGHT, AS CAMILLE HELPED HER GET READY FOR BED, THE book on Miriam's bedside table caught her eye. "*The Golden Bowl*," she mused, picking it up and examining it. "Isn't Henry James one of your favorites?"

"I find it easier now to read old, familiar favorites than to try to concentrate on an unfamiliar plot or remember new characters." The now-constant pain—a dull throbbing in her upper abdomen that sometimes radiated out to her back—was still manageable in the daytime, but by evening the pain made her dyslexic, unable to focus or concentrate. The accompanying fear that worse was to come scattered her thoughts as well. She found herself testing the ache or stab of tonight's pain—was it worse than yesterday's, and if so, how much? Would the medications become ineffective? That, she feared.

Camille was watching her as if she could read these thoughts. She asked how Miriam was feeling, and she admitted that it hadn't been a good day.

Camille said, "My grandmother used to like me to read to her. I think it was easier than reading herself, and it soothed her. How about if I read to you for a little while before you sleep?"

Miriam was startled by the offer; Camille knew she had audiobooks on her phone. But Camille was right—the sound of someone in the room reading only to you was different from the disembodied voice coming through the earbuds, even if those readers were professionals.

"Yes, if you don't mind, Camille, that would be nice," Miriam said, then remembered she'd be infringing on Camille's study time and making an already long day longer. She glanced at Camille for signs of reluctance or even regret that her impulsive offer had been accepted but saw only a serene smile. The thought of leaning back on the pillows and letting the beautiful sentences cascade over her was too tempting to refuse. "Maybe for just a little while before you go back to your studies."

"I've never read most of the books you have, except maybe an excerpt in a high school class," Camille said with a pleasing interest in literature. "My grandfather used to say, 'You spend an hour watching TV, you waste an hour. You spend an hour reading a book, you gain something.'" She settled herself in the reading chair, feet on the ottoman, and turned on the lamp beside it.

Before Camille began reading, Miriam substituted *Portrait of a Lady* for *The Golden Bowl.* Both were excellent, but beginning with a simpler novel might lessen the chance that Camille wouldn't like the author—James wasn't for everyone.

Camille began reading, which she did beautifully. Miriam watched her face as she became engrossed in the novel, navigating the intricate sentences and detailed descriptions. Miriam closed her eyes, the sound of Camille's reading as comforting as a warm blanket fresh out of the dryer on a cold night. She slipped into sleep. Camille, under James's spell, hadn't noticed, and when Miriam woke to the sound of her turning off the lights and slipping out, an hour had passed. The next morning, Camille, sheepish, offered to repeat part of what she'd read, but Miriam assured her that she needn't.

"Adelaide will be here this afternoon to study, Miriam—do you still feel like having her? You don't have to tutor us if you don't feel up to it."

"I'm looking forward to it," Miriam said firmly, a slight exaggeration.

ADELAIDE RANG THE DOORBELL PROMPTLY AT FIVE-THIRTY. MIRIAM sat in the living room near the door, planning to answer it, but Camille rushed by, saying she'd help Adelaide bring everything in. Camille left the door ajar, and their voices drifted in from the driveway.

"I hope you did your homework, Adelaide," Camille teased.

"Don't worry, I'm ready for your lady. Glad we finally get to study together—she's been hogging all your time."

"Oh, come on. You're here now." Car doors slammed and footsteps clattered on the brick walk to the door.

"I know, I'm just saying. You think because that rich old lady buys your dog a bed and lets you bring him in the house that she's treating you like family." Adelaide wasn't ready to let it go. "You do realize, don't you, that she's getting a good deal—I bet she's not paying you for twenty-four hours a day."

"Sshhh, Adelaide, she's right inside the door."

"Ooops."

They came in, Adelaide looking only slightly abashed. Miriam had quickly picked up the newspaper and pretended to be engrossed in it and a little deaf. Most people assumed if you had gray hair that your hearing was impaired, especially if you were ill—which was useful.

"Oh, hello, girls," she said brightly. Adelaide looked relieved, Camille more cautious, as she introduced them. Adelaide was exceptionally beautiful—luminescent dark skin, arresting golden brown eyes, statuesque with a perfect figure, carefully styled hair falling past her shoulders. She knew how to dress and carried herself with confidence; Beyoncé had nothing on her (well, maybe the voice).

After putting the food away, Adelaide and Camille settled down to study at the kitchen table before dinner while Miriam read in her recliner. She listened as they worked together—Camille was clearly the stronger student, but based on Adelaide's conversational diversions, she was way ahead in social skills. After an hour, the girls put down the books to get the food ready. Miriam joined them for a pleasant dinner. Camille hadn't exaggerated about Mrs. Doucet's cooking.

In the kitchen after dinner, Adelaide took several storage containers from a bag, rolling her eyes. "Momma thought you'd like these for leftovers, so you'd have some dinners in the freezer. You know she's kind of a control freak when it comes to the kitchen."

Camille laughed, and Miriam said that would be lovely. She rarely helped with the meals anymore. Adelaide had a point about the number of hours Camille worked. Miriam had just given her a raise, but she'd call Duncan about giving her more. She might not have been completely honest with him about how much Camille was doing; it was hard to admit even to herself. No reason to be stingy at this point. It wasn't as if she'd outlive her resources.

They reconvened at the dining room table, and Miriam began the session with questions testing their grasp of the material, carefully explaining the more difficult sections, then questioning them again. Adelaide's eyes widened at Miriam's preparation, and initially, she fumbled with her answers. Although Miriam took an uncharitable satisfaction in flustering Adelaide, she knew nervous students didn't absorb the material well, and she softened her approach to put her at ease. Camille was holding back, watching Adelaide. As Miriam's questions pulled the pieces together for her, Adelaide's face lit up and her pace quickened as she absorbed the points she'd missed in class (probably texting from the back row instead of paying attention—or writing in Camille's notebook with the same purple pen she was using tonight). When they finished the test material, Miriam closed her notebook, thanked Adelaide again for the food, and told them goodnight. After she left the room, she heard Adelaide say, "She knows more than the professor!" Camille laughed and said, "I told you," maybe with a touch of pride.

After that, Adelaide began coming regularly, particularly when a test loomed. She always brought food from Mrs. Doucet, even when she came on a Saturday morning or afternoon and didn't share the meal. Miriam noticed that Mrs. Doucet seemed to know what she'd be able to eat. Recently, she'd begun sending chicken noodle soup delicately seasoned with herbs, finely chopped vegetables in savory beef broth, or mushroom soup in a light cream base, with sandwiches to supplement for Camille and Adelaide. Miriam usually tutored them, though some sessions were a bit shorter than she would have liked. It was fine to see the spark in their eyes as she worked with them, but she was tiring more quickly.

Miriam had gotten the Doucets' address from Adelaide, explaining that she'd like to send her mother a thank-you note for the meals. She'd also asked if she could contribute to the cost.

Horrified, Adelaide had said, "Oh, no, ma'am, Momma wouldn't like that at all. She cooks for folks all the time. She says it's her gift and her privilege to share it."

Not an unexpected answer. To express her gratitude in a more acceptable way, Miriam went online, ordered the best set of kitchen knives she could find, and had them gift-wrapped and delivered to Mrs. Doucet. Fine knives were apparently as expensive as jewelry. Well, they would be precision tools in Mrs. Doucet's able hands and would relieve Miriam of the uncomfortable feeling of being the recipient of unrequited kindness. Maybe she could listen and discover other kitchen items Mrs. Doucet might like.

The next time Adelaide came, she burst into the house and engulfed Miriam in an unexpected hug, saying, "Momma got your package in the mail today! She's been wanting knives like that forever —she always looks at them in that big kitchen store in the mall, but says they're way too dear for her kitchen. She almost cried when she opened the box!" Adelaide looked at Camille and said, "Momma said Miss Miriam shouldn't have, but no way was she going to give them back! She's trying to think of something special to make for next time."

"Everything your mother makes is special, Adelaide," Miriam said quietly, feeling unaccountably touched by Adelaide's gratitude.

ONE EVENING, AFTER ADELAIDE HAD DEPARTED FOLLOWING A particularly good study session, Miriam told Camille she'd like to chat about her education. Miriam figured she'd accumulated a little capital since that initial disastrous discussion. Camille sat down, not smiling, wary.

"Camille, I still think you should consider switching to pre-med at LSU." This time, Camille hesitated before rejecting the idea out of hand.

"I have thought about that more since we last talked. I'm just not sure it's right for me."

"Maybe you should talk with one of the advisors at LSU, or maybe one of your instructors at the community college?" Any educator would have to see the same potential in Camille that she did.

"Well, there is someone I've talked with about my future before."

"Good, who is it?"

"Actually, it's Mrs. Doucet, Adelaide's mother. She's a high school guidance counselor. She's helped me since my grandmother died."

Ah, the amazing Mrs. Doucet. Maybe she should meet this paragon. "That sounds like a good plan, Camille. I wonder if perhaps I could talk with her as well?" It would be prudent to be sure that Mrs. Doucet would reinforce her own advice to Camille.

"Why?" Camille asked, with unattractive suspicion.

"Oh, you know, two old educators might have a few things to chat about."

Camille looked doubtful, but she wrote down Mrs. Doucet's number for Miriam.

After Camille helped her get settled for the night, Miriam said, "It's late and we needn't read, but before you go back to your studies, let me just say one thing." Camille waited by the bedroom door.

"Consider your motives for decisions about your education. Don't reject medical school because you're afraid of it."

Camille's mouth opened, then closed, waiting.

"I learned many years ago that you cannot let fear be your motivator. Decisions based on fear are almost always wrong," Miriam said. "I don't mean small, practical decisions, like going back downstairs before bed to be sure you locked the doors." Camille nodded, attentive now. "I mean the big, life-changing decisions. Fear distorts how you see your alternatives. To see clearly and choose the right path, you must disregard fear of failure, fear of change, or other fears." Miriam paused, then added, "If you don't, you'll regret it."

Camille stayed still, as if unsure how to respond. "That's all," Miriam said, smiled, and told her goodnight. Camille was quiet downstairs, her usual rustling about silenced as if she might be doing more thinking than studying. Miriam drifted into a light sleep and woke again to hear Camille walking slowly upstairs, not at her usual brisk pace. Miriam smiled. The dream was taking root.

MIRIAM HAD PLANNED TO PAINT THE NEXT MORNING, BUT WHEN SHE sat in front of the easel, staring at the canvas, she was too restless. She returned to her sitting room and sat down with the notes she'd made the day before. No reason to delay. She called Duncan.

When she told Duncan what she wanted, he said, "I think helping Camille with her education would be a wonderful use of your funds."

"But can we do it in a way that would make it easier for her to accept the support? I'm also thinking of leaving her this house, but I don't want it to be a burden to her."

"I have some ideas," Duncan said. "Let me think them through and be back in touch with you."

Miriam agreed and hung up. Progress. And she didn't need to tell Duncan that the clock was ticking for her. He already knew.

Next, she called the inimitable Mrs. Doucet, who sounded surprised when Miriam invited her over to chat about their students, but graciously agreed to meet the following week. Satisfied to have moved beyond intentions to actions, Miriam put her notebook away, retrieved Camille's radio from the study (not having suffered any recriminations for that particular breach of privacy), and returned to her easel on the porch. Her mind cleared, she picked up her brush and welcomed the feeling of merging with her work as the world receded.

CAMILLE RETURNED FROM HER MORNING CLASSES AND POPPED OUT onto the porch, smiling at the song that was playing. Miriam, too, found the sentiment appealing. Fantasy or not, the idea of just letting go, no longer struggling to justify one's existence, and resting peacefully in the arms of a loving father had a universal appeal.

"I love that one, Miriam—how it reminds us that we don't have to cling so tightly to whatever we're struggling with every moment. After my grandmother died, I'd hear that song and just stop, sit down, and pray." She was quiet for a moment, then said, "Every time I did, every single time, I felt God's love running through me. And then I could wipe away my tears and go on."

If this radio station was going to prompt a sermonette every time Camille heard it, perhaps she should turn it off before lunchtime. Miriam nodded vaguely, as if uninterested, then felt ashamed. Camille had shared something from her heart and Miriam had ignored it. She searched for something to say, but before she could speak, Camille walked over to look at the canvas.

"Miriam, you're doing camellias now!" she cried with flattering excitement.

"Yes, they're blooming so beautifully, I thought I'd give them a try. I'm just getting started, though. Shall we have lunch?" Miriam could see that Camille was winding up for more praise, and her expression when she'd seen the new canvas was enough for now.

· · ·

That night, Camille said, "Miriam, how about if I read a little from the Bible before we do the other reading? My grandmother and I did that, and it always seemed like a good way to end the day."

Miriam nodded unenthusiastically.

"Don't worry," Camille said, "Only a few verses, and we can stop if you don't like it."

Miriam nodded again, noting that Camille was echoing her own offer when they'd begun the tutoring sessions, making it difficult to refuse the modest request.

"This is one of my favorites," Camille said by way of introduction, and read, "'I am the true vine, and my Father is the farmer. Every branch in me that doesn't bear fruit, he takes away. Every branch that bears fruit, he prunes, that it may bear more fruit.'"

Camille paused, and Miriam nodded, perhaps with more encouragement than intended, prompting Camille to comment. "I think about this verse when I'm going through a difficult time. You know, maybe I'm just being pruned."

"Yes, I suppose that makes sense," Miriam answered, and fluffed her pillow and resettled herself, hoping to signal that it was time to move on. Camille obliged, putting her Bible away and taking out *Portrait of a Lady.*

Miriam picked up a book from her bedside table and handed it to Camille. "I thought we'd take a little break from *Portrait of a Lady* for something different. Emily Dickinson is one of the only poets I truly love. Her poems don't have all those flowery flourishes, and they don't go on and on. She encapsulates the heart of her subject in a few short lines and simple words."

Camille examined the well-used volume with pages marked and notes in the margins.

"I've flagged my favorites. Let's see what you think."

Camille read through several poems, quickly engaged. She paused, absorbing the crystalline evocation of grief in "After great pain, a formal feeling comes." Next, she read "My life closed twice before its close," reading and then repeating the final observation: "Parting is all we know of heaven, and all we need of hell." Miriam saw that the poems sliced through the fragile padding of the months, exposing still-raw grief. Camille read, "I never lost as much but twice," in a shaky voice, glancing up to see if Miriam noticed, and Miriam quickly closed her eyes. Assuming she was asleep, Camille read the poem again, this time more slowly, "Twice have I stood a beggar/ Before the door of God!" Miriam heard Camille whisper, "It's so real."

CHAPTER 13

A MOTIVATING VISIT

Miriam awoke the next morning, grateful for sleep that had refreshed instead of being subsumed in unabated fatigue. Before sitting up, she surveyed that day's body. First, a cautious stretch, checking the level of abdominal pain or tenderness, nausea, that heavy feeling. Today might be good, one of those diminishing opportunities to accomplish carefully rationed tasks. Not that it couldn't all change within hours. She sat up and swung her legs to the side of the bed, sat a moment longer, stood, walked slowly to the bathroom, testing the movement of her joints and limbs. Still good. As she brushed her teeth and dressed, being quiet to avoid waking Camille this early, she considered minor tasks that were made complex or impossible on the bad days. She could trim her toenails! She could delay, a little longer, the humiliation of asking Camille for help because she no longer had the steadiness or dexterity she needed. She took out her clippers, a pumice stone, and file, and felt ridiculously proud when she'd completed her abbreviated pedicure. After breakfast, she could paint, and her heart lightened at the thought.

. . .

SHE'D PUT HER BRUSHES DOWN AFTER A SATISFYING SESSION AT THE easel and was washing up for lunch when she heard Camille answer the phone in the kitchen.

"She's here, but she's in the bathroom. I'm Camille, her caregiver—may I help you?"

A pause, then, "Oh, you didn't know she's been ill? Well, I should probably let her tell you about that herself." Another pause. "Okay, I'll let her know you called. Should she call you back? Okay, we'll see you later."

When Miriam entered the kitchen, Camille said, "That was your cousin, Jack. He seemed surprised to learn that you're ill." Camille clearly found it incomprehensible that Miriam hadn't informed her cousin of her terminal illness. Well, Camille hadn't met Jack and Pam. Miriam realized she should've known they'd appear before she was able to permanently avoid them.

Camille said, "I told Jack you would call, but, um, he said he and his sister, Pam, were on their way to Baton Rouge for the LSU game tomorrow, so they'd see you later this afternoon. I, uh, think Jack said they usually stay with you."

Damn. They'd just show up, tatty luggage in hand, expecting her to have guest rooms ready and waiting for them despite the lack of notice. Maybe they knew that, given the chance, she'd find a reason they couldn't stay. Fortunately, her cleaning service was coming today and could get the rooms ready. Now Camille looked worried; it was probably dawning on her that she didn't know the whole story.

"I'm sorry if I shouldn't have told them you were sick," Camille said.

"Well, probably best not to announce yourself as my caregiver without knowing to whom you are speaking." Camille winced, giving Miriam a moment of satisfaction. "Be prepared, they're probably going to just show up this evening."

"Should I go to the grocery?"

"No, we don't want to encourage them to stay, and they're usually out at LSU most of the time for tailgating and the game." Camille shot her a questioning look, but Miriam just said, "When you meet my cousins, you'll understand."

As expected, Jack and Pam knocked on the door that evening without even the courtesy of a preceding call. As usual, they were both wearing t-shirts and jeans, clothes Miriam thought better suited to college students than overweight, fifty-something adults. At least Pam's obnoxious husband, Billy, wasn't with them. They trooped into Miriam's house with their bags, untroubled by the lack of an invitation to stay. Camille offered to show them to the bedrooms, but Pam brusquely assured her that they knew the way to "their" rooms. Miriam hoped they'd remember that she didn't allow smoking in the house; she could hear Pam panting as she heaved her substantial girth up the stairs.

They returned and made themselves comfortable in the sitting room, doubtless waiting to be served something to drink, Jack commenting loudly about how bad the traffic had been on the drive in from Pascagoula.

"Mississippi roads are no picnic, but I think Louisiana has us beat for bad traffic," he complained. Maybe he should stay home. "Billy had to work overtime this weekend and couldn't come, but Pam still wanted to," Jack added, sounding put out. Billy had been his best friend since childhood.

"Yeah, well, it's about time I got a weekend off," Pam huffed as she went into the kitchen and opened the refrigerator. "Jack, should we bring in that beer and get it cooled down? It doesn't look like Miriam has any."

Jack frowned, as if she should have had it ready and waiting. Camille looked incredulous. Then Jack asked Camille, with hopeful geniality, "Well, what's for dinner?"

Miriam nipped that in the bud. "Jack, how kind of you to offer to take us to dinner." She paused, pleased at his obvious dismay, "but I'm afraid I should limit myself to the meals delivered by my service, and Camille usually just tosses herself a salad so she can help me with my dinner." Camille nodded, catching on quickly. Miriam could have easily enlarged the order, but she didn't care to do so.

Pam waddled in carrying a cooler, which she proceeded to unload into the refrigerator, then popped open two cans of Pabst Blue Ribbon and returned, handing one to Jack, who suggested that they order pizza.

After slurping from his beer, Jack said, "We was sorry to hear about your, uh, illness, Miriam. Pam and I talked about it on the way down and want you to know that we are ready and willing to help in any way we can."

They both looked at her with frank curiosity. Miriam supposed she should give them some information since they were her only family. Camille excused herself, and Miriam briefly summarized for them her diagnosis, explaining that Camille was now her in-home caregiver.

"Miriam, we're so sorry," Pam gushed, blinking rapidly, probably trying to work up some tears. Not that there was any reason she should be heartbroken. The families had never been close, and they knew that they stood to inherit from Miriam. Having her die sooner rather than later would be the best thing that ever happened to them.

They spent a little more time in desultory conversation, Pam producing pictures on her phone of her and Billy's two unattractive children, now teenagers, with dull, squinty eyes, soft pear-shaped bodies, and vacuous expressions. Jack rambled on about his possible promotion at the paper factory, a theme regularly repeated, the lack of change in the narrative suggesting that the promotion hadn't yet materialized. Thankfully, Miriam was able to slip away to her room when they busied themselves ordering the pizza, arguing over whether it should be from Papa John's or the less expensive Domino's, and then what toppings to have. She and Camille returned when they heard the pizza arrive, and Camille suggested that Pam and Jack eat in the dining room while she helped Miriam with her meal at the kitchen table. Pam and Jack agreed, and Camille put placemats under the fresh beers they'd brought to the table after wiping up the rings.

Camille returned to the kitchen as Miriam was pulling out the meal service food, and they warmed it and sat down. Regarding her with sympathy, Camille said, more loudly than necessary, "You look tired tonight, Miriam. Maybe we should get you to bed a little early this evening? I can help Pam and Jack get set up with a movie."

Miriam smiled and agreed. After Camille settled Pam and Jack with Netflix and the remote, she and Miriam went upstairs. When Miriam was propped up in bed with Petey on her lap, Camille lit one of the scented candles she'd bought to stave off the stale odor of illness that had begun to invade the room.

They finished *Portrait of a Lady,* and Miriam suggested they start Edith Wharton's lovely novel *The Age of Innocence.* Camille began reading with enthusiasm, but Miriam pretended to fall asleep after a few minutes, even though it was barely eight-thirty. When Camille turned out the light and closed the door, Miriam got out of bed and opened a window halfway, knowing Pam and Jack would sit on the porch below to smoke. Sure enough, she heard them go out and the crinkle of cigarette packages. The wicker rockers creaked, and smoke wafted up from under the porch roof.

"Well, looks like Miriam might be checkin' out sooner than we thought," Jack said.

"Yeah, she doesn't look so hot," Pam agreed, not very sympathetically. "I was thinking, maybe we should stay a few more days to see if we can help out."

"You mean to find out how soon she's really gonna die?" They both snickered. "I guess I could call in and say I need a few days off for a family medical leave. But what about your kids?"

"Oh, Billy can take care of them, not that they need that much. They're old enough now to get themselves to and from the bus stop and stick a frozen dinner in the microwave. How much do you think Miriam's got?"

"I don't know, but it's not like her family blew through everything the way our dear old dad did."

"Maybe a hundred thousand each?" Pam asked.

Miriam could almost see them salivating.

Jack snorted. "You kidding? No, I think she might have a million bucks."

"Really?" Pam squealed.

"Yeah, sure. She don't seem to spend that much—this house was prob'ly paid off years ago, and it's the same old furniture her parents had. She's got no kids and her husband kicked the bucket years ago."

"So maybe five hundred thousand *each?*" Pam asked again, as if barely able to comprehend such a sum.

"Yep, could be. I guess we shouldn't count our chickens before they're hatched, though. And it might be in that land, not cash, you know."

"Yeah, that land that pumps out checks every month. I'd be okay with that."

Jack said, "Maybe we should offer for one of us to stay with Miriam til she, uh, checks out, instead of that girl. Did you notice how buddy-buddy they're gettin'?"

"Yeah, you mean like she might leave all her money to the maid? But I don't really want to take care of her, do you?"

"No, but it would be more like supervising, you know. For what she's paying that girl to live here, we could get a sitter service to come in during the day. She shouldn't need a sitter at night when she's sleeping. The sitter could be sure she has a meal when she gets here, clean her up, put her back to bed, and leave somethin' for her in the oven."

"Yeah, she'd prob'ly like having family here instead of just hired help."

"I'd do it. Maybe ask her to pay me what I'd be losing from work."

"She might rather have me. You know, have another woman."

"Well," Jack said, considering, "Maybe you and I could spell each other, especially if it takes longer than we expect."

"You know," Pam said, "It's possible she might not leave us anything. Her father, the *Professor*, always thought we was white trash, and Miriam is kind of a hard ass herself."

"I guess it's possible," Jack said. "Remember how Mom used to say the Professor prob'ly made Miriam's husband—wasn't his name Tom? —feel like dirt because he wasn't a big hotshot at the college like him. Maybe Miriam did too—she and her Dad was a lot alike."

Having heard enough, Miriam was easing the window down when Jack spoke again.

"Nah, I take that back. Miriam was like a zombie after Tom died, remember? You could tell she was all tore up about it. Tom was an okay dude, at least for an egghead type."

Miriam closed the window as Pam and Jack were moving on to who they'd see tailgating tomorrow and what they'd eat and drink. Tom had met them when they'd stayed here for an LSU game. He'd been surprisingly good with them, maybe because he knew her father's low opinion of the cousins. He'd gotten Jack talking about the Tigers, his job at the paper mill, and fishing while they grilled burgers in the backyard. Jack had been wary at first, though she could tell he was flattered by Tom's sincere interest in his life. It was the most she'd ever seen Jack laugh.

The darkness of the room seemed to close in on her, suffocatingly dense. She felt tears leaking through and stifled a sob. Sick, alone, dying. How would she get through these next few months? Petey jumped on the bed, and she rolled over on her side and hugged him to her, like a child with a teddy bear, feeling the comforting vibration of his purr.

She'd have to head off their plans to stay with her, and that wouldn't be pleasant. She was drifting off when she remembered that they'd guessed her estate at a million and had been quite pleased with that. It was five times as much, but knowing their lower expectations was liberating. With all their flaws, they were still family, and they expected to be her only heirs. Maybe she shouldn't feel obligated to leave them anything, but here in Louisiana, keeping family wealth in the family—especially mineral property—was close to a moral imperative.

ON SUNDAY MORNING, PAM AND JACK SLEPT LATE AFTER THEIR strenuous day and night of tailgating, drinking, and watching the game. They went to McDonalds for the "big breakfast," correctly guessing that no such feast awaited them at Miriam's house. They returned after Camille had left to walk Hanks and cornered Miriam in the sitting room. They sat on the couch beside her chair, Jack with his greasy smile and Pam with her fake sympathy, and presented their offers to stay with her, obviously expecting her to be overcome with gratitude.

"Thank you both for your kindness," Miriam said tersely, "But I'm doing fine with my arrangements here. I certainly wouldn't want to be a burden to you."

Pam scowled and said, "You mean you'd rather have your hired help take care of you than your own family?"

"I don't consider Camille merely 'hired help,'" she said, without thinking.

"Yeah, well about that," Jack broke in, "What do you consider her? You know people like her can take advantage of an old person who's sick, get their trust, then rob them blind."

What exactly did "people like her" mean, and since when was she reduced to being a sick old lady? They were both looking at her with obstinate resentment, and maybe fear behind it, of being disenfranchised from "their" family share of her estate.

"Thank you for your concern for my welfare," she said icily, "but I am still quite capable of judging the motives and aspirations of those around me." She paused, shooting pointed looks at them. They had the decency to lower their eyes.

"We didn't mean it that way," Jack said. "We're just worried, that's all. Camille seems nice, but you never know, especially in a tempting situation."

Miriam sat silent.

"And we really do want to help," Pam said. "We're your family, and this is what family is for—helping each other. I could bring the kids with me once summer break starts, and we could all be together."

Miriam couldn't imagine a more nightmarish scenario for her final days. She said, "I appreciate your offer, but this is my home, and I will decide what I want and need for my remaining days." She said it with finality, leaving no room (she hoped) for further argument.

"No need to get all hoity-toity about it," Jack said, sullen. "Pam's just trying to be a good cousin, and so am I. We don't see why you'd rather have some girl you hired without even knowing her instead of your own family. Even if you don't think she'd take advantage of you, she's never going to care about you like your own flesh and blood." His face reddened, and he looked honestly hurt. But she wasn't going to give in to their plans and surrender her little remaining time to assuage their feelings.

"Again, I do appreciate your concern," Miriam said, "and I will certainly keep your offer in mind if I need further support from my family." Here she managed a sniff and dabbed at her (dry) eyes, hoping to shame them into silence. "I must, however, follow my own instincts about what will best serve me during this difficult time. To put your mind at rest, I can tell you that my attorney and his assistant are controlling all bill paying and overseeing my financial accounts each month—Camille has no access to my funds."

She paused, observing the look that passed between them and a slight nod from Jack, who said, "Well, uh, I'm glad you're being careful, Miriam, that's all I meant. If you'd like a family member to help instead of paying big fees to your attorney, I'd be glad to help with your bills, too."

I bet you would, she thought.

"Thank you again, Jack. I'll keep that in mind, but I'm very tired now. Perhaps it would be best for you to leave." Petey, apparently sensing a threat, sat up in Miriam's lap and hissed loudly in their direction, making Pam jump, and Jack shout, "Shit!" Miriam suppressed a smile and covertly stroked Petey.

Jack and Pam rose, and Miriam braced herself, expecting them to leave in an unpleasant snit, complete with door slamming and foot stomping.

Jack said gruffly, "Well, before we go, do you need anything done around the house? I mean, as long as we're here, I might as well take care of anything like that."

Startled at the unexpected generosity, she was at a loss and glanced at Camille, who'd just returned with Hanks.

Camille said, "Actually, Jack, the faucet in the kitchen keeps dripping. Do you have time to take a look?"

Jack went out to his truck for his tools. He fixed the faucet handily, looking satisfied with himself. While he was occupied with that, she heard Pam bumbling around upstairs, and she reappeared to say that she'd changed the sheets in both guest rooms and loaded the ones they'd used in the washer—something she'd never done before.

Miriam thanked them both sincerely, thrusting cash into Jack's hand for gas and maybe a stop for dinner. Unlike Camille, he took it easily.

When the door closed behind them, Camille said, "Next time they call, I'll tell them you're not taking visitors—assuming that's what you want?"

Miriam nodded and said, "It's not all their fault that they're the way they are. Their father was my father's younger brother, and he was always trouble. He was a gambler and an alcoholic until he drank himself to death, and he gradually sold off their family's half of the mineral property, so they don't have much."

"Growing up without good parents is hard."

"Yes. After their father died, Jack dropped out of high school and took a job at the paper mill to help his mother get by. My father used to send them money, but I think that just made them resent him more. And when our families did get together, my father made it pretty clear what he thought of them."

"Did Jack ever marry?"

"No, and he never did anything about completing his education, so he's been stuck in the same dead-end job. I can't say he's had much in life to make him happy."

Miriam paused, then added, "I haven't been much of a cousin. I try to remember their birthdays and send cards and checks, but that's about it." Not that they ever remembered hers.

THE COUSINS' VISIT GAVE MIRIAM FRESH MOTIVATION TO PROCEED with her planning, and she was glad when Duncan called and offered to meet at her house. He arrived shortly after Camille left for school, and Miriam brought him to the dining room table, where she'd laid out her well-organized notes.

"It's become quite clear to me that I do not wish to leave my cousins the bulk of my estate. As we've discussed, I would like to leave more to charity, specifically the endowment you helped me set up for organizations helping homeless animals." She paused and Duncan nodded, listening with his usual attention. "And, as I mentioned to you, I'd like to enable Camille to pursue her education through medical school, if that's what she chooses, without facing financial hardship or being distracted by the need to support herself."

Duncan said, "I've been thinking about it. We could meet both of your objectives by leaving a substantial amount in trust to pay for Camille's education and support while she's in school, then have the remainder pass to your animal fund when she's finished. How does that sound?"

"That sounds quite satisfactory, and I'd still have enough left to leave my cousins a substantial bequest."

"Aside from your wishes, it might discourage them from challenging the will if you leave them enough. I can add what we call an *in terrorem* clause, saying that the bequest of anyone who challenges the will is null and void. Those clauses have been held valid in Louisiana and can be an effective deterrent."

"Let's leave them a million to split between them. That should be substantial enough, don't you think?"

Duncan nodded and made a note. "Do you want it to be in cash?"

"No, they'd only spend it. Or maybe some cash, but the rest in the mineral property, so they'll have an ongoing income stream."

"That's a good idea, Miriam. I'll have a draft ready for you to review next week. Did you think any more about the ethical will we discussed?" He'd explained the document in their prior meeting, and though she'd been intrigued by the long history of the ethical will, dating back to biblical times, she'd been far less interested in actually writing a personal statement about her values and intentions for her estate and the reasons behind her bequests. It all seemed too personal. But she saw that he wasn't going to give up on the idea, though he knew that soul-baring wasn't her style.

"Do you really think it's necessary?" she asked.

"In your case, Miriam, it could be significant for two reasons. One, it would give your trustee and the administrators of the animal fund details about exactly what you want to accomplish when you're not there to explain. Two, if your cousins challenge the will, it would provide me with excellent evidence of your intentions and your competency. Courts have respected ethical wills and have weighed them heavily in deciding will challenges."

Miriam sighed but saw the wisdom of discouraging a protracted court battle over her estate, and she promised to work on it. After he left, she remained at the dining room table, staring at her notes, thinking about the ethical will, feeling the aloneness creeping up on her again. Then she stood, returned her notes to their respective folders, and carried them upstairs. Still an hour before lunch. Fine, she'd get started on the damned ethical will.

As she trudged up the stairs, though, her mood lightened. She'd made the first step in implementing her plan for Camille. She could do this, she knew it. She just had to keep going, had to finish it before her time was gone.

PART IV
THEN

CHAPTER 14

THE BEST THING FOR THEM

As 1982 began, Tom's hopes for a New York editing position faded, and Miriam watched with anxiety and helpless frustration as he slumped back into the depression that had dogged him through the fall. His pain touched her, and she sympathized, but he'd already missed his department's faculty meeting for the new semester, frowned upon to say the least. She struggled to comprehend how a person could lack the will to get out of bed.

This week, he'd abruptly switched from sleeping too much to insomnia accompanied by bursts of frantic energy. The first time she woke in the night to find his side of the bed empty, he'd been in his office hunched over a manuscript. He'd barely looked up when she asked if he was all right, wanted to talk, or whether she could bring him anything. He said he couldn't sleep and was going to do some editing. He didn't need anything. Sometimes he'd stay up all night editing manuscripts, working almost in a frenzy, then burst into the kitchen when she came down, bombarding her with nonstop talk about the article he was editing, barely pausing for breath. Other mornings, he might be back beside her in bed, leaving his desk covered with marked-up manuscripts or crumpled wads of paper from his own work, beginning the day haggard and exhausted.

Tonight, he'd drifted off soon after they'd turned out the light; maybe he'd taken one of the sleeping pills his doctor had prescribed. She lay awake, itchy and restless, unfairly resenting Tom's light snoring, weighing their choices. Move to New York like he wanted? Leave their home, LSU, colleagues, her graduate students—all precious to her, but not to him. She was building a reputation on hours of research and writing, tracking down obscure references, reading until the words blurred on the page, and her stomach soured from coffee. She flipped her pillow over and flopped to her other side, not being quiet about it, hoping he would wake so they could talk, and guilty for not guarding the elusive sleep he needed.

Was she being blind to the possibility that life in New York could be better? What if Tom greeted the mornings with anticipation, shared his triumphs with her in the evening, instead of being strangled by the creeping defeats? Might they both be happier, even deducting her sacrifices? Would her award of early tenure here transfer to another university? If it didn't, she'd still start a new tenure review process backed by a list of significant publications. She sighed. Any optimism she tried to muster about beginning again crumpled against her desire to stay. She couldn't truly believe in a brighter future in New York, lacked the conviction that it was likely or even possible. But she was watching Tom diminishing, fading away. Given that, she'd have to honestly consider going, discuss it with him as a real option. Finally, she slept.

IN THE MORNING, MOVING TO NEW YORK SEEMED CRAZY. SHE thought about it as she washed the breakfast dishes. Maybe they could find a new doctor, or Tom could take a less demanding position at a smaller college, even the community college in Baton Rouge. Or if nothing would satisfy Tom but the New York publishing world, maybe he could go without her to look for a position. But she dreaded the prospect of an extended separation. She imagined the solitary dinners

AT THE KITCHEN TABLE WITHOUT HIM, INSUFFICIENT PHONE CALLS, lonely nights, and sad, gray mornings.

She left the house and drove to the university in a fog, almost running a stop sign. She parked, then paused. Tom's mother had said Baton Rouge was a better place to raise a family. That look that had passed between her and Evelyn, the tacit pledge of support. Wouldn't Tom forget his sadness in the joy of their baby? Surely, he would—they'd talked about wanting children. But could they face the tsunami of a child's needs now? In Baton Rouge, Rosemary would gladly step in to help as needed. But in New York, even if Evelyn wanted to help, Boston was too far away for her to give daily or even frequent (or last-minute) assistance.

AT HOME THAT EVENING, SHE WATCHED THROUGH THE LIVING ROOM window as Tom pulled into the driveway and trudged up the walk. She swung the door open to greet him and suggested that they have dinner at Vinny's.

When they entered Vinny's, Tom's shoulders loosened in the warmth of the atmosphere, where the bartender welcomed them and said to pick their table. Tom greeted their server by name and asked how her law school applications were going as she lit the candle at their table.

After they'd ordered, Miriam said she wanted to talk about their future. Tom nodded, pensive, studying the red-checked tablecloth. They discussed the possibility of his teaching at a smaller college (he rejected that) and freelancing at LSU Press (possible), then paused when their meals arrived.

After the initial attention to their food, Miriam asked, with studied casualness, "Should we sell the house and move?" Neither had mentioned it since Tom had raised the possibility in New York.

Tom stopped with his fork poised above his spaghetti, then put it down, staring at her. "Seriously?"

"Yes. If you really want that." She was proud of keeping the tremor from her voice, hoping she'd kept the anxiety from her face. It had to be a real offer; she suppressed her own doubt that it was.

Tom paused, as if tempted—panic seized her—but he shook his head, took her hand, and said, "No, I can't ask you to leave everything here, not without having something lined up there."

He stroked the top of her hand with his thumb, smiled at her, then released it, and they ate in silence. Anxiety chased her initial relief as his silence lengthened. Tom concentrated on twirling his spaghetti around his fork; she ate her lasagna. The restaurant buzzed around them, loud laughter from two tables away, their server flirting with the bartender.

Miriam sipped her iced tea, cleared her throat, and said, "You could go up and look around without me. I could join you later, when you've found something."

Tom looked up from his plate, startled. Miriam tore off a piece of garlic bread, keeping her expression neutral. She hazarded a glance at Tom, now staring at the television mounted on the wall across the room, tuned to a basketball game with the sound off. She put the bread down and waited.

He squeezed her hand again and said, "Thank you for that. We'll see."

Maybe she should encourage him, but she couldn't because she didn't want him to leave her, even temporarily.

"I mean, I've been sending out letters and can see if I get any positive responses."

What? Why hadn't he told her, shown her the letters?

"I could stay with my parents while I talked to whatever publishers would let me in the door. Maybe go for two or three months in the summer between semesters."

She choked out a few words of agreement, not really seeing a choice. Chilled by the specter of his leaving, of his finding a position. Of the returning threat of leaving her home, of knowing that he still clung to that dream.

They ate and talked of inconsequential things—a movie they wanted to see, what flowers to plant for the spring, a possible trip to Florida over Easter. She didn't want to broach the topic of a baby in the crowded restaurant. She was more nervous about his reaction now than she'd been that morning.

Back at home, they settled on the couch in the sitting room. When Tom reached for the remote, she put her hand on his arm and suggested having a glass of wine and talking a little more. He didn't look pleased but went to the kitchen for glasses and a bottle. The lasagna was a lump in her stomach.

He poured merlot in their glasses and sat down stiffly, wearily, as if worn out with talking. "Okay," he said, nodding at her to start.

"You know how we've always said we wanted children?" She paused, tentative smile, hoping for an answering smile, a spark of interest.

"And?" he said, his tone almost hostile, accusatory, face flat.

"My doctor said we shouldn't wait much longer, that this would be a good time for us to try," she said, as if it were a medical directive.

No glimmer of joy or anticipation. She realized her idiocy in thinking this would cure everything, like a television-movie solution.

"Don't you think that's a decision for us, not your *doctor*?" His voice was hard.

"Of course," she agreed quickly, still hopeful. "That's why I wanted to talk to you about it." She reached out and took his hand—he didn't wrap his around hers, but withdrew it and shifted on the couch, sitting up straighter.

"I don't know why you think this would be a good time for us to have a baby," he said, his voice harsh, no trace of the tenderness she'd envisioned. "Or are you suggesting it to make sure we stay here? Because of what my mother said?" His lips tightened in a straight line, unyielding.

Her cheeks burned, and she blinked back tears. He'd never spoken to her like this; she felt small and defensive. Maybe he didn't want a family with her, maybe he wasn't sure that he still loved her. When had he last said it?

"Don't you want to—," she started, but her voice cracked, and she struggled to compose herself, cover the fear seeping through. She'd miscalculated badly.

Tom didn't take her in his arms; he stayed on his side of the couch, a yard away. "Miriam, I'm barely making it. I may not even have a job much longer. Having a baby isn't going to turn our lives into happily-ever-after."

She tried again: "If we had a baby, maybe you could stay home and do freelance editing."

His face darkened still more. "Assuming that I don't get tenure, you mean."

Like the thought was a betrayal. They both knew it was all but certain that he wouldn't.

"I could be the stay-at-home dad who can't hold a job? Thanks, Miriam."

"I didn't mean it that way." She scooted over and put her arms around him, but he stiffened and leaned away. Breaking her hold, he got up, said he was going to bed, and took his wine glass to the kitchen.

He came back and stood in the doorway, and she turned, hoping he'd softened. But he said, "Let's wait a year. Give me time to get myself in a better place." Then he turned to go up to bed, leaving her there.

She tried to derive comfort from his saying to wait a year, like he assumed they'd still be together. She swirled the wine in her glass, listening to the shower starting upstairs. The thought that he might have lost that certainty they'd shared of a future together terrified her. When he'd first said he loved her, looking into her eyes with the awe of an astronomer discovering a new planet, she'd said it back with permanence in every syllable.

Was that over? She imagined Tom explaining gently—even now he would do it gently—that it wasn't her fault, they'd just grown apart, wanted different things, and sometimes love didn't last. Apologetic, but final in his decision. And she would be devastated. Or might she feel she'd be less alone without him than with him?

No, she still wanted him—wanted them. Still believed that they were part of each other. But she yearned for the easy closeness she'd taken for granted. Now their connection faded in and out like faulty electrical wiring. She heard Tom come out of the bathroom and get into bed. She rinsed her wine glass, went upstairs and quietly changed into her nightgown in the bathroom. When she slid in beside him, he didn't move, and she lay awake a long time, wondering, worrying, frightened.

. . .

THE NEXT MORNING, TOM LEFT EARLY TO WORK ON JOURNAL articles with Herb. She moved through her morning routine feeling hopeless. She didn't believe that moving would be a panacea. She thought it more likely that his mother was right that he wouldn't thrive in a "pressure cooker" like the city. In the bathroom, she pulled her birth control pills out of the medicine cabinet and sat down on the edge of the tub, looking at the pill pack. He'd said to wait a year. But where would they be in a year, and how would a baby fit with moving to New York?

Wouldn't having a child's hands reach out to him, seeing the adoration in a little face, having a toddler follow him around—wouldn't that validate his worth in a way she couldn't? If they had a child, Tom's father would quit dangling New York as the solution to Tom's stalled career. She could imagine Tom laughing with the child in his arms, the pride on his face, the way he would lean into being a father, a family man.

She tossed the pill pack into the wastebasket. Then took it out. He'd see it there. She punched out the day's pill and returned the pack to the medicine chest. Then she put the pill in a Kleenex and crumpled it up to take downstairs and throw in the garbage. She'd tell Tom that she'd quit taking the pills. Eventually. Maybe. He might leave her if he found out she'd stopped without telling him. But he wouldn't leave her if she told him she was pregnant; it wasn't in him to do that. If he checked the pack, he'd see that the pills had been punched out in order. Nothing was 100% effective.

The decision wasn't irrevocable, at least not yet. She could still start taking the pills again. She could tell Tom how important having a baby was to her (but was it?), and that he was wrong to say it was only a way to anchor them here (but was it?). She looked at herself in the bathroom mirror. This was the best thing for both of them. To be a family.

CHAPTER 15

WANTING TO BELIEVE

They'd ceased talking about Tom's progress toward tenure, and neither had mentioned his possible trip to Boston for the summer again. Certainly, they hadn't returned to the possibility of a baby. Miriam continued throwing away her pill each morning, mechanically, as if it were a rote habit not requiring thought, like rinsing the dishes after dinner.

That March morning, Miriam came home after her seven-thirty class to spend a few hours revising a paper on Berthe Morisot's revolutionary use of color and depiction of light, which she planned to submit by the end of the month. Maybe she and Tom could even squeeze in a quick lunch.

She frowned as she put her key in the lock, remembering how the night before Tom had tossed and turned, eventually getting out of bed and whispering that he didn't want to keep waking her. She'd lain there, listening to him pad around downstairs. Then the porch swing had creaked, and she'd pictured him sitting out there alone in the dark. She'd almost gone down, but when she checked the clock—two-thirty

—she thought about how she had to be up in a few hours. She'd rolled over, grateful to feel sleep creeping back over her.

By morning, Tom was beside her again. He was still in bed when she left for her seven-thirty class.

She turned to go upstairs to her office and nearly tripped over Tom's briefcase, still by the staircase where he'd left it last night. She called up the stairs, not hiding her annoyance, "Tom, I'm home—are you still here?"

No answer. She went upstairs and found him still in bed. He stirred as she entered and looked up at her, dark shadows under hopeless eyes.

"Did you stay home again? Did you even call to cancel your class?"

"I'm drowning," he said. "It hurts. So much."

"Tom, we can't go on like this," she said resolutely, as if they could solve it by will. "Did you call the doctor Mac recommended?"

"Yes," he said softly, almost regretfully. "He saw me yesterday. He said he really specializes in treating soldiers suffering from PTSD. He looked at my prescription from the other doctor and said that's the best they have to offer. He gave me a different prescription, but he didn't think it would be any better."

Had the doctor really said that? Tom's original doctor said there were other alternatives, and he might have to try several medications before finding the best one for him. "Let's go back to your first doctor and ask him to try something else," she said. "You've got to get some help."

"I don't believe there's any help for me. I can't give you the life you want, that anyone would want. I'm dragging you down."

"Let's talk." Frightened by his despair, she sat down on the bed next to him and took his hand.

Tom pushed himself up to sit next to her and said, "Baby, don't you think things could be different for us if we lived somewhere else, away from here, really on our own?" Voice hoarse, without conviction, more as if trying to believe it himself.

"Why would that make any difference? We'd be the same people here or somewhere else." She tried to catch his eye, but he kept his face averted, then dropped his head in his hands. She reached for him and they held each other, but she felt no warmth or comfort and knew he didn't either.

She leaned back and stroked the side of his face, desperately missing the man under this crushing despair.

"It'll be okay, Miriam. I love you. Just give me time."

"Will you be all right if I go back for my office hours?"

"Sure."

Her office hours weren't until afternoon, and she knew she shouldn't leave him now, shouldn't desert him, but she didn't know what else to say. The suffocating weight of his hopelessness and her absolute inability to pull him from it filled her with an overwhelming need to leave, to escape for a few hours.

"Before I go, let's call your first doctor and make an appointment. I'll go with you."

"No, I can do that. I'll do it as soon as I get dressed. Then I'll go into the journal office for a few hours. See you back here tonight."

She heard his voice crack, saw how the effort strained him, but he was trying. That was good. Maybe he was learning to pull himself out of the dark hours, to reckon with his demons. She offered again to wait until he called the doctor so they could coordinate the scheduling, but he promised he'd take care of it. She didn't think she could push further without angering him, and she remembered that this doctor had emphasized that Tom had to make the appointments himself. So she kissed him goodbye and left for campus.

She called the house at eleven about meeting for lunch. When the phone rang, unanswered, she tried the journal office. Herb said Tom had just left after picking up some articles to work on at home. Herb was his usual genial self, no indication that he'd seen anything amiss. Encouraged, she decided to leave Tom to work on the articles, bought a ham sandwich at the cafeteria, ate it at her desk, and counseled several students during her office hours. She called home at three, and he answered, sounding fine, happy with his progress on the articles. She drove home at six.

She opened the door, nervous, dreading his continuing sadness that she couldn't assuage, their circular descent into his despair. A Chick Corea jazz album was playing softly and light came from the dining room. The table was set, candles waiting to be lit. Tom emerged from the kitchen, showered, shaved, and dressed in a pressed oxford cloth shirt, tucked into khaki pants, holding a bottle of wine.

"I thought you might like a nice dinner at home," he said. "You know I'm no cook, but even I can get takeout from Vinny's. I have lasagna, garlic bread, and Italian salad with anchovies."

She felt disoriented, as if she'd suddenly been transported back in time to their early married days. She followed him into the kitchen, smelling the lasagna warming in the oven, and he turned and took her in his arms. She held him, smelling the familiar scent of his Givenchy Gentleman cologne. He told her to go change clothes, and he'd have dinner on the table in ten minutes.

She went upstairs, wondering at the transformation. Maybe leaving him alone today, letting him find his own way back, had helped? She wanted to believe it, and why shouldn't she? Tom was smart, capable, still everything he had been. She kicked off her heels and hung up her gray skirt and jacket, slipped into jeans and a soft knit top and went back down.

Dinner was good. Tom served her, imitating Clint, the bartender and sometimes-waiter at Vinny's, when he poured the wine and brought in their plates from the kitchen. He asked thoughtful, perceptive questions about her paper, walking her through a possible solution to a revision she'd been struggling with.

When their plates were empty, Tom said, "Why don't I clean up and you work on the revisions we talked about while they're fresh in your mind?" She was tempted—their talk had opened a new path in her thinking, the way talking with him had so often in the past, and she yearned to get it down on paper. At the same time, she didn't want to leave this moment with him, the sweetness of his presence tonight. But he urged her to go, saying he had nothing due the next day, nothing that needed to be done tonight.

In her office, she worked well, the words falling into place, two hours passing before she realized it. Then, clattering from the kitchen broke through her immersion. A fragrance wafted up, rich and sweet. Tom's steps on the stairs.

He entered, smiling, holding a plate with a thick wedge of chocolate cake, her favorite.

"Surprise—I actually baked a cake for you, to help you power through your paper. Thought I might be able to lure you back downstairs to have some."

She was stunned and touched. Tom never cooked or baked anything and generally avoided the kitchen except to eat or help clean up. She followed him downstairs to the kitchen table, where he'd set places for them with mugs of tea. If she worked another hour, she could finish this draft, and he was right—the cake would do it.

"I asked this nice lady I met this afternoon in the cake mix aisle which one was the easiest." She could picture him doing it, charming the motherly type with his earnest effort to surprise his wife. "She showed me this one and told me what else to get, including this." He reached into the trash can and pulled out an empty container of Pillsbury chocolate fudge frosting. "Hope you don't mind, but making the icing was beyond me."

"It looks delicious."

"Red wine goes well with chocolate too, and we have enough for a glass each if you'd rather have that than tea."

She could get up early to finish the paper. They had the wine with the cake, Tom entertaining her with his description of making the cake, splattering the mix on the walls when he used the blender for the first time, rushing to clean it all up before she came down and saw it.

They rinsed the dishes, put the remaining cake away, and went upstairs. She went into the bathroom, feeling as giddy as a newlywed, brushed her hair, put on the translucent aqua gown that she knew he liked, and came out to find him waiting in bed. She got in, and they lay there, under the covers, facing each other.

"Miriam, you're so beautiful," Tom said, stroking her hair back from her face, running his hand down her arm, tracing the curve of her hip, eyes never leaving hers until he leaned forward and pulled her into a kiss. "I love you so much," he said, eyes soft, lingering. Reminding her that he'd been the only one to reach through to that inner part of her she'd always kept to herself, how he'd refused to acknowledge the barriers she'd erected, had overcome her fearful resistance. Because he'd blended himself with her, and within what they'd created, they were safe, self-sufficient, and, above all, true to each other.

"You're going to be all right, Miriam. You'll fly, nothing will hold you back."

The words prickled. "You mean, we're going to be all right? Us?"

He stroked her hair again, kissed her forehead, and said, "Yes, I'll be all right too."

That wasn't what she'd asked, but before she could formulate how to clarify, he put his arms around her and pulled her to him. He leaned back for a moment, studying her face, and said, "Please, always know how much I've loved you."

Loved? Or love? "I've loved" wasn't really past tense, was it? But she didn't want to interrupt this, to question, doubt. She nestled against him, murmuring her love back to him, thrilled by the touch she remembered, his soft smile, untroubled eyes. It was true. They could get through this, have it all back. Afterward, she curled against him and he pulled her close, spooning, warm, sheltered. She fell asleep, safe, hopeful, happy.

THE NEXT MORNING, HE WAS ALREADY UP WHEN SHE WOKE, AND SHE met him in the kitchen, making coffee. He said apologetically that his newfound cooking skill didn't extend to breakfast, but he'd set the table with her cereal bowl ready and waiting. He was showered and dressed, so the change wasn't a one-night thing. He was pulling himself through, just as she'd known he could. He said he was going to work at home for the morning on journal articles, then bring them into the office. She ate, rinsed her bowl, dressed, kissed him and left for her class.

She was humming as she drove, chuckling to herself as she turned into her parking place on campus, remembering Tom's story about choosing the easiest cake mix. She sat for a moment in her car, savoring the memory of the unexpected cake, seeing the blue box in the trash—Pillsbury Moist Supreme Devil's Food, pudgy Pillsbury dough boy lounging beside a giant wedge of chocolate cake. Actually, the same kind she'd already had in the pantry; he must not have looked first.

Her smile disappeared; cold dread suffused her. He'd found the gun she'd hidden in the pantry behind the dry goods. She turned the key and screeched out of the parking lot, barely noticing students jumping back in the crosswalk. Why hadn't she seen it, his sudden peace, the lifting of despair, the outpouring of love? Saying goodbye. She left campus, ran a red light, raced into her neighborhood, and pulled into her driveway. As she did, she heard it. A gunshot. She bolted past Mac, who'd been weeding his side garden. He rose to his feet and called out to her. She ignored him and rushed inside. She ran down the hall, through the sitting room, out the French door, and stopped short. She fell to her knees beside Tom on the gray porch floorboards, blood spreading from the back of his head into a red halo. She stared in uncomprehending horror, leaned over him, her hands slipping in his blood.

Mac burst through the back fence gate, still holding his trowel, running across the yard, up the stairs to the porch, stumbling to a stop in front of where Tom lay. Mac paused only a moment, then pulled Miriam up and half-dragged her inside. She fought him, struggling to stay next to Tom, but he was stronger. He gently pushed her down on the couch in the sitting room, sat beside her, and reached for the phone.

"There's been a gun accident at my neighbor's house," Mac said. "I'm with the wife of the man who's been shot, and I'll stay until help comes. I don't think the man is alive, and his wife needs medical attention for shock."

Miriam bolted for the French door, and Mac slammed down the phone and caught her.

"We have to help him," she cried, trying to wrench her arm free.

"Honey, he's beyond help. Come on, let's sit down."

"How do you know? He needs us!"

Mac looked at her, eyes brimming, firmly pushed her back to the couch, and said he would check, but she had to stay there. She watched him go out, kneel beside Tom, put his hand on Tom's throat, checking for a pulse. He stood slowly and came back in.

"I'm sorry, honey, he's gone."

THAT AFTERNOON, MIRIAM WOKE IN THE GUEST ROOM AT HER parents' house, still groggy from the sedative the paramedic had administered to calm her hysteria. Her mother was sitting beside the bed, watching her and holding her hand. When she saw Miriam's eyes open, her mother gave her a pill from a prescription bottle she said had been called in by their doctor. The next time she awoke, Rosemary brought her soup and another pill. Miriam slept the rest of the day and the following night, vaguely aware of her parents coming in and out of the room at intervals.

The next morning, Miriam stood silently in the guestroom, listening intently as her father told her mother goodbye and left for work. Miriam waited a few minutes more and heard her mother leave too, closing the door softly behind her. She came out then and found her mother's note on the kitchen counter, saying she'd gone to the grocery store and would be back soon. Miriam returned to the bedroom, dressed quickly in the pants and blouse her mother had left out for her, found her purse, and walked the two blocks to her house. She went into the sitting room and looked out the window to the back porch. Someone had made a first pass at cleaning the gray floorboards, though a large stain remained. Probably Mac. She walked to the dining room and peered through the curtains. Mac was in his driveway, bending over a bucket, preparing to come back and finish the job.

She crept upstairs to her office, stealthy in the empty house, as if she could evade the grief lurking in every corner. A note in Tom's handwriting was taped to the middle of her desk, its placement an accusation?

Miriam, I'm sorry. Please forgive me, but I just can't come out of this, and I'm pulling you down with me. There's nowhere for me to go, and I can't face another day, even with you. I love you, Tom.

She read the note, sank into her chair, then read it again and again, as if she could pull more meaning from it with repetition. She felt the tears on her cheeks and struggled to rein them in. She needed to walk back to her parents' house before her mother returned. She folded the note into a small square and put it in her top desk drawer.

She swiped at her eyes and swallowed hard, went to the bedroom, pulled out a small suitcase, yanked pajamas, socks, underwear, t-shirts, and sweatpants from her dresser, threw them in, then realized she needed clothes to wear out of the house too. She pulled out pants and sweaters, noticing as she closed the suitcase, but not caring, that they didn't match. She carried the suitcase into the garage and put it in the trunk of her silver Honda Accord.

She opened the car door to leave, then stopped, fixated on Tom's old Toyota Corona, its faded, dull yellow paint glowing ghost-like in the dim garage. He'd had that car the whole time they'd known each other. They'd taken it to Florida on their honeymoon when they'd decided to drive on the coastal roads along the Gulf side of the state. Miriam ran her fingers along the side of the old car, thinking of how they'd stopped at small beach towns whenever they felt like it, staying one night or three at the ones they liked. She remembered fried grouper sandwiches and cold beer on the deck of a seaside café where the fishermen tied up after being out all morning. The pleasant lethargy after long morning walks on the beach, the sun on her face and the salty breeze, the anticipation of another lazy afternoon with Tom. He'd promised they'd come back for their fifth anniversary if not before. That would never happen now.

She got in her car and pulled out of the garage, relieved not to see Mac, not wanting to talk to him or ignore him. She parked in front of her parents' house, pulled her suitcase out of the trunk, and went in. Her mother came out of the kitchen to greet her, clearly relieved, and Miriam felt guilty for worrying her. She explained that she'd gone by her house to get clothes and her car, saying nothing about the note. Her mother said she'd fix Miriam some eggs and toast.

Miriam sat at the kitchen table, aware of her mother's steady stream of small, comforting patter only as background noise. The smell of scrambled eggs nauseated her, but she forced down a few forkfuls and a bite of toast to avoid her mother's watching eyes. Miriam knew her mother wanted to talk, but couldn't face formulating words about Tom's death, could barely comprehend the loss. She mumbled that she would go back to bed. Rosemary nodded and handed her a glass of ice water.

As Miriam was leaving the kitchen, her mother said Tom's family would be coming in for the funeral. Miriam realized with a wave of self-loathing that she hadn't thought of them at all.

"I spoke with Evelyn last night while you were sleeping," her mother said. "Of course, they're devastated. Evelyn asked about you and how you were doing. I told her that, as she'd expect, Tom's death was a terrible blow and that you were pretty much destroyed."

Miriam thanked her mother for calling Tom's parents, grateful that she'd handled that. Miriam didn't think she could've done it herself. She backed out of the kitchen, pulled her suitcase to the guest room, changed into sweatpants and a t-shirt, and burrowed under the covers. Maybe she should try to pray. Or was God like an old friend who'd been forgotten and ignored until suddenly needed and was then understandably cool and distant. She'd done nothing to strengthen or even maintain a relationship with the Lord, so who was she to turn to him now? Still, she closed her eyes and bent her head, searching for the words. But before she found any, she heard the gun again and saw Tom lying on the porch. The words in his note replayed, echoing all the anguish he'd hidden from her that last night. She put her face under the covers like a child, as if she could hide from her failure to see it, her reckless willingness to believe that he was (miraculously, implausibly) healed. Her absolute certainty that Tom would have forgiven her only made it worse.

CHAPTER 16

In the reception room of the church where she and Tom had been married, Miriam watched her mother overseeing placement of the catered meats, cheeses, and breads, urns of coffee and hot water for tea, and the homemade biscuits and desserts brought by friends and neighbors. Miriam stood with her father, silent, her mind repeating on a loop the words of Gerard Manley Hopkins, "No worst, there is none" and "pitched past pitch of grief." Tom had shown her the poem, saying that Hopkins and Emily Dickinson had described grief more eloquently than any other. Now, with her father, she watched, with dread, for Tom's family. When they arrived, Evelyn and Gerald embraced her, but Claire stepped back, avoiding contact. Miriam was stung by her coldness but not surprised. Rosemary joined them in line to accept condolences and introduce the Johnsons ("this is Tom's mother, Evelyn"—pained smile and limp handshake; "this is Tom's father, Gerald"—forced polite smile, nod, and firm handshake; "this is Tom's sister, Claire"—slight nod, no smile, hands clasped in front of her).

Herb Rothschild arrived looking bedraggled and sad, Emily holding his hand, her usual effervescent nature subdued. Herb took both of Miriam's hands in his, brown eyes earnest behind steel-rimmed glasses, and said, "Tom was a rare one. Such a loss, irreplaceable—his friendship and his work." Herb leaned over to embrace her, then took her hands again and said, "I always thought he'd take over one day as editor-in-chief. Wish he'd had the chance to spread his wings, become the brilliant editor he was meant to be." He squeezed her hands and released her to Emily, who hugged Miriam and told her to please call any time she wanted to talk. Miriam watched them move on to her parents, knowing Herb wouldn't suspect how his words had scalded her. Yes. Tom would have. Been brilliant. If only his wife hadn't selfishly held him here, in this wasteland of opportunity.

As the parade of condolences continued, Miriam panicked that her fragile composure would dissolve into tears or screaming. Heat radiated through her; perspiration trickled between her breasts and over her belly, and nausea washed over her. Finally, her mother said it was time to go into the sanctuary. The Johnsons joined them. Miriam read the pressure of grief in their faces and the relief of escaping the cloying sympathy of well-meaning strangers.

They sat in the front pew reserved for them, the Johnsons at one end and Miriam's family at the other. As people filed into the sanctuary, the church organist played an old hymn Miriam half-recognized but couldn't name. The Johnsons whispered together at their end of the pew. Mac approached, and her mother asked him to sit with them. He sat next to Miriam and took her hand in his large one.

"How are you holding up, honey?" he asked, red-rimmed eyes searching her face. She nodded and squeezed his hand, knowing she didn't have to force a more coherent response with him, glad he was there. Her mother took her other hand, and her father leaned forward and covered their hands with his, giving her a lopsided, awkward smile meant to be encouraging. The minutes dragged.

The pastor began the service. Miriam tried to focus, but his words blurred together—phrases about the dark power of despair in a broken world, redeeming grace, and a mansion with many rooms. She kept seeing Tom's face—his miserable hopelessness of the morning, followed by his tender calm of the last evening.

A soloist sang "What a Friend We Have in Jesus." Herb and Mac both stood to speak of Tom, Herb praising his diligence and dedication in his work on the journal and Mac remembering Tom's kindness in the wake of Coralee's death, both expressing how greatly he'd be missed.

When the service ended, Mac stood with the rest of the pallbearers to take the casket from the sanctuary to the waiting hearse that would return it to the funeral home for cremation. After the last of the mourners filed out of the sanctuary, the two families were left, standing by the front pew, sad and awkward. Miriam's father shook hands with Gerald and Evelyn hugged Miriam and her mother. But Claire wasn't ready to let the service end with grace. Instead, she looked at Miriam, who inwardly cringed from the anger in Claire's eyes, wishing she could escape the fury she knew was coming.

"Tom was too good for you," Claire growled, her voice rough and harsh. Rosemary gasped, William's face reddened, and Evelyn put a hand on Claire's shoulder, which she shook off. "Tom was a true giver, and you let him give too much. As long as you kept taking, he kept giving. Until he had nothing left."

Miriam could only stand mute, tears streaking her face, letting the cruel words she'd never forget wound and scar her.

"Unlike you, Tom never put his own needs first, no matter what it cost him," Claire said, glaring, her voice rising.

Glancing at William's scarlet face, Gerald stepped forward before William could and put an arm around his daughter's waist. He said, "Claire, that's enough. We're all hurting. Let's go now."

Claire refused to budge. Rosemary tried to steer Miriam away, but she too stood fast, immobilized by Claire's eyes, tortured by the truth she heard in Claire's assertions. Miriam's heart pounded, her breathing came quick and shallow. She felt faint, but she stayed, facing Claire.

"One more thing," Claire snarled. "Where did Tom get a gun? I know it wasn't his. He hated guns." Claire folded her arms, radiating rage, demanding an answer.

"It was mine," Miriam said, her voice soft, nearly a whisper. "My father gave it to me years ago."

"Right. And who taught Tom how to use it?" Claire said, accusing more than asking.

"I did," Miriam choked out. "We went—"

"You knew he was suffering from severe depression, so you gave him a gun. Did you have a death wish for him?" Claire's voice rose again, nearly shouting now.

Both sets of parents started to speak at once. William, being the loudest, prevailed.

"Don't try to blame Miriam for Tom's cowardly choice to shoot himself instead of dealing with his problems. And leaving Miriam to suffer the consequences."

Gerald broke in then. "Wait a minute. We're saying things now we'll all regret. What happened was no one's fault. Tom suffered from clinical depression. He was no coward."

Rosemary said, "Gerald is right. We're all grieving, and we all loved Tom. Turning on each other doesn't help anyone."

Claire snorted, contemptuous, and said, "I'm still waiting for Miriam to tell us why she kept a gun in the house when she knew Tom was suicidal."

"How could Miriam know Tom was suicidal?" Rosemary asked, angry now.

"Well, maybe I would've known if you'd told me what happened in high school," Miriam said, roused from the paralysis of her guilt. "He tried it then, didn't he?" She hadn't been sure of it until now. She trembled with mixed anger and grief, her face hot, stomach twisting. Claire, brows lowered, eyes narrowed, turned to Evelyn, who shrank from her gaze. Miriam remembered overhearing Claire urge her mother to tell Miriam about the high school episode.

"What?" William bellowed, "Tom tried in high school, and no one told Miriam? Why the hell not?"

"Don't try to turn this on us," Claire said, raising her voice to match William's. "Tom was way past all that until he moved down here. Miriam knew he was miserable. So she put a gun in his hands."

Miriam had no defense. Still trembling, she stepped back from Claire's wrath, wanting to run from the church, run until she dropped from exhaustion, as if she could escape Claire's words.

William glared at Claire and said, with cold fury, "Access to a gun is hardly an invitation to shoot yourself."

"No," Claire hissed, "but it sure makes it easier, doesn't it?"

Evelyn, face pale, in a shaky voice, looked at Miriam and said, "You're right that we should have told you. Tom struggled with depression since high school. You couldn't have stopped what happened."

Claire opened her mouth to protest, but Evelyn stopped her with a warning look, and said, "I'm sorry for anything said that made you feel blame, Miriam. We all wanted to believe Tom had overcome what he'd suffered as a teenager." She gave Claire another look and said, "Claire shouldn't have said those things. She and Tom were very close, and she's devastated."

William looked like he wanted to say more, but Rosemary held out her hand and he took it. He put his other arm around Miriam, and she leaned against him, wobbly and numb. They walked out of the sanctuary together, followed by the Johnsons.

THE NEXT MORNING, MIRIAM RETURNED HOME DESPITE HER parents' strenuous efforts to persuade her to wait a few more days. She had to go back, though the memories embedded in the house evoked a sharp-edged despair that scraped and hollowed her out. She'd refused her mother's offer to help pack Tom's things. She wanted to be alone to touch and smell them, the thick fisherman's sweater he'd brought from Boston, his old corduroy pants worn thin in the seat, the plaid flannel robe she'd given him for Christmas. Her wildest mourning was too intimate to share.

She paced the rooms and made aimless trips upstairs and down. She felt as if the atoms of her body were dispersing and she would dissolve. She directed her attention to removing Tom's things because seeing them was unbearable. She fetched a garbage bag from the kitchen and started with their bathroom. She snatched up Tom's hairbrush, comb, razor, shaving cream, shampoo, deodorant, all of it, and tossed them into the bag quickly, as if they were burning her hands. She went to the bedroom next, tossing in the issues of *Time* magazine on his bedside table and his slippers beside the bed, then threw the bag into the garbage can outside.

She'd pack up the clothes in shopping bags and donate them to the Salvation Army thrift store. She paused in front of the long teak dresser they'd bought together. Tom had chosen the Scandinavian bedroom furniture. She'd appreciated the economy of the sleek, spare pieces and the beautiful teak, but told him they wouldn't harmonize well with the rest of the house. True, he'd said with his foxy smile, the other pieces are at least a century older. They'd bought the set anyway, and she'd surprised herself by loving it.

She pulled open the top dresser drawer on his side and looked at the neatly folded shirts. She pulled out the old denim one and buried her face in it. He'd worn it when they planted flowers in the backyard or whiled away a winter Sunday afternoon snug in front of the fireplace, watching a rerun of *Wuthering Heights*. She'd keep the shirt. She hung it in the back of the closet, running her hands down the sleeves, pressing the front of it against the tears rolling down her face. She emptied the dresser and closet of Tom's remaining clothes quickly, as if racing to outrun the avalanche of grief before it buried her.

She carried the bulging bags downstairs in several trips, breathing heavily by the time she put the last one in the trunk of her car to take to the thrift store. When she returned to the bedroom, the emptiness where his things had been almost sent her back to the garage to retrieve the bags and put everything back. She sat down on the bed heavily, thought about moving her things to a different bedroom instead of staying in this one, but she was too tired. She dragged herself back down to the kitchen; maybe she could eat something for lunch.

She looked out the window over the sink, at the indifferent brightness of the sun lighting up the potted bougainvillea hanging from the porch rafter and the petunias in pots on the porch stairs. She froze, seeing the faint stain on the boards in front of the porch swing, where it had been bright red. She heard the backyard gate opening, and Mac entered with a can of paint and a brush. She couldn't face his concerned kindness, so she backed away from the window and fled upstairs before he saw her.

She went straight to the bedroom walk-in closet, entered it, and closed the door without turning on the light. Then she lay down on the polished hardwood floor between the rows of shoes and hanging clothes. She squeezed her eyes shut and rolled onto her side, legs drawn up, head resting on one arm, hearing again the ragged hope in Tom's question that morning: *Baby, don't you think things could be different for us if we lived somewhere else, away from here, really on our own?* And her response: *Why would that make any difference? We'd be the same people here or somewhere else.*

What if she'd said yes? He hadn't returned to his plan to spend the summer in the city looking for an editing position. She hadn't either because she didn't want him to go.

So instead of nurturing that fragile seedling of hope, she'd ripped it out by the roots. What if she'd told him that morning that he could leave in two months, drawn him back with details of arrangements for his trip, making his dream real? They might be together now, Tom with the light back in his eyes, quick and agile with anticipation, excitement. Or he might have gone and realized his dream wasn't there, come back with a new appreciation for their life here, determined to make it work.

Was Claire right that Tom wouldn't have done it without the gun? Why hadn't she gotten rid of it? She hated the Johnsons for not telling her about high school. But would knowing have changed anything? In the quiet darkness, on the cool floor, she shrank from all the days ahead without him, heavy tears falling. Then, a creeping thought that maybe her life would be easier now, quickly stifled by shame. The anger roared back, her face growing hot and her hands trembling. He'd deceived her that last night, pretended that all was well, and robbed her of the chance to change his mind. That was wrong. She whimpered and beat a fist against the floor, hating him for leaving her, then got up, felt for his denim shirt at the back of the closet, tore it off the hanger and ripped the well-worn fabric down one seam. She threw it in the corner and lay on her back on the floor, staring into the darkness.

No, he'd been plain with her: *I can't give you the life you want, that anyone would want.* She could have heard it in his words that last night: *You'll fly, nothing will hold you back.* Not deceptive. He'd just allowed her to ignore the message, to lose herself in the sweetness of that night. And she had. Or had she known he was saying goodbye and let him go? Knowing that without the constant drag of his despair, the weight of his depression, she could fly.

No. She shoved the thought deep inside her. No. She would've never let him go.

When she heard Mac's heavy tread descending the porch stairs and the back gate squeaking and closing behind him, she went downstairs. She closed the door to Tom's study. She'd have to go through the desk drawers, throw away his never-published manuscripts, but not today. She had a sudden vision of herself ripping them to shreds in a fit of fury, the confetti of his futile efforts flying around her.

At six, her mother called to invite her to dinner. Miriam declined, guilty about her mother's worrying, but explaining she needed time alone. She warmed a can of tomato soup and ate it while she watched the news. That is, she gazed at the screen and heard a jumble of words, but comprehended little, not even the weather report. Afterward, she tried to prepare her next lecture, but couldn't put the ideas together, then tried to read, but couldn't grasp the words that slipped through her mind like slimy, wriggling fish. She went to bed but didn't sleep until the dark turned gray.

THE FOLLOWING WEEK, MIRIAM RETURNED TO HER CLASSES. Desperate to escape her solitary thoughts, she'd declined the department chair's offer to have someone else fill in for another week, a month, or the rest of the semester.

Once back, though, she stumbled through her lectures and spent half the time in her office staring blankly at the wall. Friends and colleagues left sympathy cards in her mailbox or stopped by her office, well-meaning but awkward, almost shame-faced, as if they shared her guilt. She suffered through their condolences, their assurances that things would get better with time, avoiding their eyes.

She declined the first two dinner invitations from Herb and Emily, then accepted the third, gratified and irritated by their persistence. She arrived, feeling gawky and clumsy on the doorstep, as if her clothes were on backwards. Emily welcomed her with quiet kindness, and Herb emerged from his study to greet her. They sat together around the kitchen island with the chilled bottle of Pinot Grigio Miriam had brought and slices of aged Gouda and goat cheese spread on crackers.

"How have you been?" Emily asked, leaning forward, rubbing a hand on Miriam's back, watching her face, wanting an honest answer.

Miriam faltered, "Well, I. Well, you know, uh." She paused, their sympathy melting her ability to respond, liquefying coherence into tears that blurred her eyes, that she blinked back, feeling naked in her grief.

Herb said, "Of course, we know you're going through an unimaginably difficult time. What we mean is, we're here for you, for anything you need."

She nodded her thanks, and Emily stood and said they should take the wine to the dining room while she brought in the food. At the table, Miriam sat rigid, the odd number, staring into a bouquet of pansies in the center of the table. She smelled chicken and gravy as Emily clattered in the kitchen and Herb stopped to put on the ethereal piano music of George Winston's *Autumn*. Emily brought in bowls of chicken and dumplings, crispy salad tossed with vinaigrette dressing, and country green beans with bacon bits that they passed around. Miriam spooned chicken and dumplings on her plate, wondering whether Emily had purposely chosen this Southern comfort food. She thought she could eat, but it was too hard to swallow around the lump in her throat, and she stared at her plate, wishing she'd taken less. Emily caught her eye, softly said, "It's okay," and patted her hand. Herb told a story about one of the journal authors who was resisting his editing changes, and Emily talked about the diligence of her English-as-a-second-language students. Miriam kept losing the thread of the conversation and sat mute but took comfort in their familiar voices and the undemanding exchange. She slipped back to thoughts of past dinners. She felt Tom's empty place beside her, though Emily had removed all of the chairs except their three. She heard the echo of Tom's chuckle at Herb's wry comments about the department, remembered the press of his thigh against hers under the table, how she'd enjoyed his quips on the drive home about Herb's outrageous political views. And saw the empty place again.

She left soon after dinner, and they knew not to urge her to stay longer. Emily gave her a container of leftovers, the universal salve for grief—Miriam wondered whether it was more comforting to the giver than the recipient. As she drove home alone, the finality of Tom's death rolled over her again.

The grief was ever-present, dulling her vision like a translucent gray linen curtain that didn't block the view, but blurred its brightness and faded the edges. If she slept more deeply than dozing, she would reach for Tom as she woke, a sleepy smile on her face—until she opened her eyes to empty sheets. Always, she missed him.

Several weeks after Tom's death, she woke, put on her robe, padded down to the kitchen, fixed coffee and toast, and sat at the table. She was sipping the coffee when she felt a quiver in her chest, as if she might sneeze. Her face grew hot and clammy with sweat, and a sour taste rose in her throat. She started to get up, thinking she might vomit, when she heard a loud bang from the porch. She fell back in her chair, mouth gaping, and heard the clatter of the revolver as it fell, then the thud of Tom's body. She slumped forward, head in her hands, squeezing her eyes shut. There'd been only one shot that morning, but now she heard the sound repeat, deafening, as if fired only inches away, her body jerking with each shot. She clapped her hands over her ears, shaking, panting, and drenched with sweat. When it finally stopped, she rose on trembling legs, lurched to the hall bathroom, and vomited. She sank to the floor, slumped over the toilet, still gagging, until it passed, then stood and washed her face. Pale and shaken, she went upstairs, determined to shower and dress for class. The trembling began again. She tried to calm herself. Whatever had overcome her was finished now. It wouldn't happen again. Maybe she'd heard a loud noise from the neighborhood, a transformer blowing, a car backfiring, and overreacted. Maybe reliving the horror of that morning had been a necessary part of healing. It wouldn't happen again.

A WEEK LATER, IT HAPPENED AGAIN. MIDWAY THROUGH HER afternoon class she felt the quiver in her chest and tried to stop it, closing her eyes and breathing deeply, steadying herself with her hands on the scarred wooden lectern, leaning over it as perspiration coated her body. She heard her students whispering and shifting in their seats; she opened her eyes and attempted a smile that became a grimace. One asked if she was alright, another left to get her a cup of water. She grabbed her things and bolted from the classroom, sat in her car, head down on the steering wheel until the gunshots ended, then drove home, barely making it inside before being sick. How could she teach, knowing she could be overcome, fall apart, at any moment?

She lay awake that night, alone in the wreckage of her life. At three a.m., she pushed back the damp, twisted sheets and sat up. She could go downstairs, make some tea, read over student papers. But exhaustion pinned her there; she flipped her pillow over and lay back down. Panic fluttered; she might never have more than tattered scraps of sleep again. She wouldn't be able to research or write. She couldn't teach. Terror and despair pressed into her; grief was devouring her. She needed real sleep, a few hours of oblivion.

Tom's doctor had prescribed barbiturates for insomnia. Tom said the sleep induced was more like a drugged unconsciousness that left him groggy and stupid the next day. Drugged unconsciousness would take her away. She thought of the line from Keats—*"To cease upon the midnight with no pain"*—and yearned for that. She went to the bathroom medicine cabinet and found the bottle—Seconal. She grabbed and opened it with an urgency blocking any consideration of consequences and gulped one down with a handful of water, then another. She took two more, returned to bed, and soon felt a warm blanket of darkness tuck itself around her.

CHAPTER 17

PITCHED PAST PITCH OF GRIEF

Three hours later, Miriam awoke to terrible cramps ripping through her belly. She held her arms around herself and struggled to the bathroom, whimpering. When the bleeding was over, she lay down again, empty and exhausted.

Pregnant. She'd been pregnant. And she'd taken Seconal. In the last couple of weeks, the possibility had skittered across the back of her mind, quickly suppressed. She'd ignored the nausea and fatigue as possible symptoms. Even the missed period; her cycles had always been irregular. Because a baby was what she'd wanted when Tom had been with her, not now that he was gone.

She lay still and numb in the gray light until eight, when she rose, shaking and frail, and called her doctor's office. The nurse said to come in right away when Miriam said she thought she'd had a miscarriage. Nearly overwhelmed by the effort of dressing, she wondered whether she'd be able to drive. Her mother would come in minutes if called, but Miriam couldn't face telling her she'd lost her only grandchild.

The doorbell rang. She looked down from the window of the front bedroom. Mac. Probably wanted to show her a new rose. If she didn't come to the door, he'd call. If she didn't answer the phone, he'd come over again. He'd probably already looked in the garage window and seen her car there. Ever since Tom's death, he'd been not very subtly checking on her.

She went slowly downstairs, clinging to the banister and opened the door. The shocked concern on his face told her how she looked.

"Honey," he said, taking her arm and steering her toward the couch, "Sit down. What's wrong? Should we go to the doctor or maybe the hospital?"

"I lost the baby, Mac," she said, tremulous, almost whispering, looking down at her hands.

"What?" he said first, confusion clouding his features. Then she saw him comprehend. He put his arm around her, and she let herself cry.

"Have you called your mother? I'll do it."

"No!" she nearly shouted.

Mac said, "It's okay," stroking her arm, trying to comfort her. "But don't you think she should be with you?"

"Don't you see—it would break her heart to know there was a baby and I lost it. It was my fault. I took some of Tom's sleeping pills last night. I was just so tired. I should have thought before I took them, but I didn't."

"Don't say it was your fault. It probably would've happened anyway with everything you've been through."

She would never know, would she? Miriam said she was going to the doctor, and Mac offered to take her before she asked. On the way there, she made him promise not to tell Rosemary, not ever.

Mac's brows lowered, jaw clenched, hands gripping the steering wheel hard. "Honey, I wish you wouldn't bear this by yourself. I know your mother. She won't blame you, and she could help."

"No, Mac. I couldn't stand to see her sadness."

He nodded, keeping his eyes on the road. She knew he wouldn't tell her secret and regretted the pain that would cause him. Add that to her tally.

. . .

DR. GREMILLION LEFT THE ROOM AFTER THE EXAMINATION, promising to return shortly. Miriam dressed and sat in the patient chair, staring dully at the framed diplomas and certificates on the wall. Dr. Gremillion knocked, then opened the door, closed it behind her, and sat down. "I can't be certain," she said, "but I'm afraid you're correct that you've suffered a miscarriage."

Miriam nodded, mute.

"Did you know you were pregnant?" Compassionate, taking it slow with her.

"I, I guess I should have. I had some nausea and fatigue, but . . . ." She let the sentence trail off. Baton Rouge was a big small town; Dr. Gremillion and her husband were family friends, attended the same church, and had come to Tom's funeral, so she knew.

"That's completely understandable with everything you've been through. Miscarriages are much more common than most people realize. This could have happened under the best of circumstances."

Miriam nodded, grateful for her kindness, however undeserved.

"This miscarriage shouldn't affect any future pregnancy—I mean, if, well, if you were to remarry," Dr. Gremillion stumbled, and Miriam saw her embarrassed realization that her usual comforting spiel didn't fit Miriam's facts. "You shouldn't worry that the same thing would happen again. There are things we can do for a high-risk pregnancy to protect the baby."

"So, you mean if I had come to you sooner, this could have been prevented? The baby could have lived?" The last words faded to a whisper.

"No, I didn't mean that. Miriam, you mustn't blame yourself for this. Sometimes there's a problem with the fetus and nothing can be done. It just happens."

Same thing people said after Tom's death. Don't blame yourself. Not your fault. And, as with Tom, she wasn't blameless.

Dr. Gremillion offered another kind, encouraging smile, and asked if she had any questions.

Miriam had to know. "I was having trouble sleeping, and I took a pill—Seconal—last night. I mean, I wasn't thinking about being pregnant. I was just so tired. Could that've caused the miscarriage?"

Miriam waited, fearful, expecting the disappointed frown or lowered eyebrows, maybe a lecture on necessary precautions when a pregnancy was possible. But, no, the doctor was kind.

"Well," Dr. Gremillion said, "Seconal is a powerful barbiturate, and of course I wouldn't advise taking it during pregnancy"—she saw Miriam flinch, and hurried on—"but I really don't think a single pill would be likely to trigger a miscarriage."

But she wasn't ruling it out. What about four pills taken together? Miriam desperately wanted to ask and be comforted by this compassionate woman, given the same answer, and told again not to blame herself. But Dr. Gremillion stood and opened the door, stopping to put a hand on Miriam's shoulder and assure her again that she didn't see any permanent damage done. No permanent damage. Only a dead baby. Only the last of Tom lost. The knowledge threatened to paralyze Miriam, so she got up stiffly, needing to be home now, back in her dim bedroom, to grieve this small victim of her absorption in her own misery. She walked down the hall to the lobby desk, urgently wanting to ask the doctor more, but saw her turn into the next examining room. Should she wait, tell the nurse she had another question? But what then? Dr. Gremillion couldn't give Miriam the absolution she craved. No one could. Mac rose from his seat in the lobby when he saw Miriam and helped her to the car. They were quiet on the drive, but she saw him stealing glances at her, loaded with troubled sympathy. He helped her inside and up the stairs to her bedroom. She thanked him, expecting him to retreat, but he lingered in the hall outside the bedroom and said he'd stay until she was safely tucked in. She took a gown into the bathroom to change, glancing with embarrassment at the stained and rumpled bedsheets. She was so weak she could barely stand; she'd never be able to change them. She undressed, then had to sit down on the bathroom stool and rest, listening to soft rustlings from the bedroom. She put on her gown, rested again, then pulled her hair back and washed her face. She sat again, marshaling the strength to walk out.

When she opened the bathroom door, she saw Mac had turned on the bedside lamp and closed the curtains, leaving the room in comforting dimness, though it was still morning. The bed was neatly made with fresh sheets turned down. She climbed in, gratitude outweighing embarrassment. In a few minutes, she heard him returning. He came in with a glass of orange juice and buttered toast on a plate.

"You should eat something, honey. If this doesn't look good to you, I can bring something else or get you anything you want from the store."

Her eyes welled; she blinked hard. "Thank you, Mac. I'll just rest awhile first." Her eyes were closing as she spoke, and she felt herself fading away.

"I'll come back later with some soup," she heard him say as he backed out of the room. "I can let myself in with the spare key you gave me, so you needn't come downstairs. I can stay in your guestroom tonight in case you need anything."

She managed a faint smile, eyes still closed. She fell asleep to the sound of him downstairs in the laundry room, starting the load of sheets.

Her first thought upon waking was the doctor's question: *Did you know you were pregnant?* She should have. She knew she wasn't taking the pills. But Tom had so seldom wanted to make love in these last months, being either mired in deep depression or caught up in a near frenzy of work on the journal or desperate efforts to publish, barely stopping to eat and skipping sleep entirely. Her thoughts of a baby had receded from conscious hope to the vaguest shadow of a possibility even before his death.

After his death, every feeling, mental or physical, had settled into the detritus of the murky depths she'd inhabited since then. Still, she'd thoughtlessly taken the Seconal and would have to live with that lapse, that failure. Seal the secret shame inside her, let it rot and spread like gangrene through what was left of her soul.

SHE CANCELED THE REST OF HER CLASSES THAT WEEK. THE following Monday morning, she struggled through her lecture, possibly the worst one she'd ever given, left the classroom immediately, passing students waiting to talk to her, retreated to her office, and closed the door. Agitated and unable to concentrate, she paced the small room, then left to check her department mailbox and found a note from the chair, Jim Wilson, asking her to come by his office.

He greeted her, closed his office door, and when they were seated, got right to the point, skipping more inquiries about how she'd been doing, sparing her the need to respond.

"With only a few weeks left in the semester," he said, "I know you don't want your students to lose credit for the course because of—well —lack of sufficient class time."

She hung her head. Failing her students, too.

He hurried on, voice sympathetic, not scolding. He said the new assistant professor, whom Miriam knew only slightly, had agreed to take over the survey course and would use her own notes for the fairly standard curriculum. A professor, Sid Clark, had agreed to complete the semester for Miriam's upper-level course. He'd asked for Miriam's lecture notes, correctly assuming that they would be detailed and prepared in advance. Jim would inform the students of the changes and handle the transition. She need not do anything more.

"Then you'll have the summer break, to, uh, continue to recuperate and heal," Jim said, "or if you prefer to take a longer leave of absence, of course, we can arrange that."

She assured him that she did not.

Stripped of her classes, she returned home and spent the rest of the week alternately crying and staring at whatever was in front of her—a book, television, notes for research—without comprehension, her brain incapable of absorbing any external information. The following Monday, she forced herself back to campus, determined to keep her remaining office hours. She would be there for students who wanted to discuss research, papers, courses for next semester. She could at least do that.

She walked quickly to her office with her head down, avoiding greetings, conversation, or condolences from colleagues. She entered her office and left the door open a slim crack so her students would know she was there. She'd barely sat down when a jittery restlessness drove her back to her feet. She stood and paced, sat and shuffled papers, stood again. She'd have to leave soon. What good could she be to anyone, wreck that she was?

She was gathering her things when she heard a timid knock and looked up to see Marcie Bienvenu, who'd changed her major to art history. Mentoring Marcie had confirmed Miriam's confidence in her diligence, scholarship, and prospective admission to a good graduate program. She'd met Marcie's family when they came from their tiny town in the heart of sugarcane country to visit Marcie, the first in her family to attend college. Like Marcie, all seven younger siblings had the glossy black hair and dark eyes of their Cajun heritage. They'd been mad with excitement about attending a football game in the famous LSU Death Valley stadium and seeing Mike the Tiger in his habitat. Their interest in the details of Marcie's research was limited, but their pride in her accomplishments, boundless.

"Dr. Johnson, do you have a few minutes to talk with us?" Marcie asked.

Us? Yes, of course. To Miriam's surprise, Justin Breaux entered with Marcie. Justin had been the starting quarterback that year, and his ability to lead the team through a winning season made him a demigod in a town obsessed with LSU football. His classic all-American good looks didn't hurt either. Miriam had been less than thrilled to see his name on her class roster, having learned from experience that football players expected, and often got, special treatment and a blind eye to frequent absences, along with a lack of consequences. But Justin's attendance and preparation for class and exams had been impeccable, and his intelligence and sensitivity had challenged her prejudices. Still, it was surprising to see him with the studious Marcie, who was attractive, not beautiful, certainly not in the way of the LSU Cheerleaders and Golden Girls Dance Team, who would have jumped at the chance to spend time with Justin. Miriam invited them to sit down, wondering what was coming.

Marcie began. "Dr. Wilson told us in class last Tuesday that, um, Dr. Clark would be finishing the semester with us." Miriam nodded tersely. She knew Sid Clark was unpopular with the students, for good reason, she thought, which was probably why he had been given the class. His own courses consistently drew only the bare minimum number of students required, leaving his workload relatively light. Even with the protection of tenure, Sid was likely insecure enough not to protest about the additional work.

Justin spoke up then. "Marcie and I thought that maybe there could be an alternative—if you're willing, of course."

He looked at Marcie, who said, "We considered that this is an upper-level course, with a good percentage of art history majors." Marcie gave Justin a quick smile, and Miriam sensed a private teasing between them—Justin was an engineering major.

Marcie proceeded to outline a plan for the students to research and prepare class presentations on their topics, along with a paper due on the day of the final exam. She explained that it would be good preparation for giving papers at professional conferences, and Justin commented that learning to give a good presentation was an asset in any career. Marcie pulled from her backpack a neatly typed list of topics with students' names handwritten beside them and an accompanying schedule for the presentations, filling the remaining classes. Miriam was stunned.

"Do you mean that the other students have already agreed to this?" she asked, taking the list.

Justin explained that the class had stayed behind to discuss the change among themselves after Dr. Wilson's visit the previous Tuesday announcing that Dr. Clark would take over beginning the next Tuesday. Marcie had suggested the presentations, and she and Justin had volunteered to prepare a list of topics for the class to consider at their usual class time on Thursday, which Dr. Wilson had designated an "independent study session."

"We voted, and every single student is in favor of this plan," Justin said, and Miriam had no doubt of his ability to marshal that unanimous approval. "Of course, if you could see your way clear to substituting the research papers for the final exam, that might be even more incentive for everyone to put a good effort into the presentations and papers," he added.

Fair enough, Miriam thought. But she wasn't sure whether Jim would approve of the plan. She was less worried about Sid, who would doubtless be glad to be relieved of the additional duties.

"Justin and I went to see Dr. Wilson on Thursday after the other students approved the plan," Marcie said, looking a little anxious, as if Miriam might be offended that they'd talked to her department chair before her. She wasn't. Miriam smiled and nodded.

"Dr. Wilson said that if you approved the plan, then he would too," Marcie said. "But he emphasized that it was entirely at your discretion. I think he said he'd talk with you about it this afternoon. We wanted to talk to you first."

"We know it's short notice with class tomorrow, and we wanted to be sure you knew we'd put in the preparation to make this doable," Justin said. Miriam looked again at the list of topics—they were excellent, just the right level of sophistication and difficulty. They'd spent a good bit of time on this.

Marcie said, "I'm down for Thursday, but I could try to have mine ready for tomorrow—it's a topic I've already started researching." Miriam looked up to find both pairs of eyes watching her, and she realized this was important to them.

"We don't want to pressure you into doing this if you need time off, Dr. Johnson," Marcie said, and Miriam had to look away from the deep sympathy in her dark eyes. Justin again stepped in with the instincts of one gifted in managing people, maybe like a quarterback, Miriam thought, a little grudgingly.

"We would certainly understand, after all you've been through, if you prefer not to finish the semester," he said. "But, honestly, Dr. Johnson, we want you to know how much all of us in the class value your teaching and would so much rather complete the course with you. We thought the presentations might be a way to minimize your lecturing for these last few weeks and at the same time give us the benefit of your knowledge and expertise as a scholar and a speaker at the big conferences."

Yes, Justin was smooth indeed, but it was the hope in Marcie's eyes that made it impossible for Miriam to say no. For the first time in many weeks, she felt something like hope, even a spark of anticipation.

And they were right—she routinely worked with her graduate students on their talks but hadn't yet worked with an undergraduate class. Her mental gears, rusted by tears, began to turn again, thinking of the things she could teach them through this new format.

"All right, let's do it," Miriam said, deeply touched by the joy on Marcie's face. "But tomorrow is too soon, even for you, Marcie, to have a presentation ready. Thursday isn't far off either, but if you think you could be ready by then, we could spend Tuesday going over some points on how to give a presentation. Would that work?"

Both agreed happily. Just after they left, she realized she hadn't thanked them and rushed out of her office. They were halfway down the hall, walking close together, oblivious to anything else, Marcie looking up at Justin with a shy smile, but it was the smitten expression on Justin's face that caught Miriam by surprise. He reached for Marcie's hand and held it as they walked. So, not only study companions. There was definitely more to Justin Breaux than she'd thought.

Seeing them reminded Miriam of the early days with Tom, when they'd walked the halls together, tantalized by their closeness, shoulders brushing, anticipating the evening, his eyes wandering down her new sweater and tight slacks. Laughing at Tom's waggish descriptions of blunders and infighting at the English Department faculty meeting. Stepping out into the sunlight together, quick kiss before separating for their office hours. Her yearning to see Tom approaching her office now was so strong she almost believed she could conjure him, but of course, he was gone. She would pour herself into what remained—her work, her students, and her art. She went directly to Jim's office to tell him she'd accept the students' proposal. He seemed relieved, possibly having weathered protests from some of the students about the substitution.

As the weeks passed, Miriam found herself looking forward to the classes, impressed by the quality of the presentations and the students' diligence. She wrote detailed evaluations of each presentation, commenting on points that should be further developed in the written paper. Maybe because she was focused on the presentations instead of attempting to lecture, the gunshots didn't recur in class. Her fear of them remained, but their debilitating power faded. The students were gratifyingly involved, as evidenced by an upsurge in office visits to discuss their papers. They'd asked for something she could give, allowing her a measure of atonement, at least for her failures in the classroom. They'd loosened the suffocating grip of despair. She could breathe again; not freely, not without pain, but she could fill her lungs now instead of each breath drawing shallow, as if blocked by an internal barrier.

CHAPTER 18

SORROW TOO DEEP FOR TEARS

Miriam slept through much of the summer after Tom's death, leaving her house for little more than necessary trips. Mac urged her with gentle persistence to come out and see the roses in his garden, and sometimes she managed to paint in that tranquility. She joined her parents for dinner often enough to barely satisfy them that she was coping. At these dinners, her father would ask her about her research or whether she had plans to attend the annual conference of the Art History Association. She knew he was trying to lead her back to the work that had been her passion, but she couldn't yet muster the concentration and will to immerse herself as she'd once done.

Her mother gently probed about friends and acquaintances, seeking signs of relationships, a renewed social life. Miriam consistently changed the subject. She wouldn't love or marry again. That part of her life was over. Miriam occupied herself with mindless tasks—cleaning out closets, waxing floors, polishing furniture, wiping baseboards, planting and weeding around the impatiens and caladiums, or watching television.

When the 1982 fall semester began, Miriam channeled all her will and strength into preparing her lectures, presenting them, and counseling her students. Each morning, she listed the tasks she had to complete that day and focused only on those. She went to bed each night by nine, exhausted, and slept until six the next morning. As if she were recovering from a devastating illness, even this limited existence required all her energy. The wounds weren't truly healing, but she was learning to live with them, each day bracketed by pain on waking and on retiring. Her grief burrowed deeply into her soul, but she didn't cry as often. As in Wordsworth's poem, her sorrow now lay too deep for tears—not lessened, but so engrafted as to be part of her.

She began to find her way back into her research. She eased herself into it like a hot bath, the warmth permeating the aches and weariness, gradually learning again to lose herself in the work, thankful for the refuge. Because Impressionism had originated in France, much of the relevant scholarship and original source material was in French. Although she'd become fluent in the language, she wasn't satisfied that she was deriving every nuance from her sources, so she attended an advanced French seminar.

As the semester progressed, Miriam drove herself deeper into erudite papers and texts examining esoteric points, followed complicated trails of references through treatises and obscure journal articles, assembled critical insights and forgotten facts into new interpretations illuminating the genius of Berthe Morisot and other original Impressionists. She saw more clearly in Morisot's work a yearning, a wistful consciousness of the irrevocable passing of the days. Miriam began a paper titled "Transience, Ennui, and Melancholy in the Paintings of Berthe Morisot," and planned to submit it to the Art History Association's prestigious *Art History Journal*. Her work was beginning to give her back herself, but the flush of excitement over a discovery or inspiration was still paired with the immediate desire to share it with Tom, followed by renewed anguish.

Thoughts of what might have been obsessed her. She constantly replayed and reimagined the last night and morning with Tom, substituting different words she could have said. If she'd confessed that last morning about not taking the pills, or even lied and said she'd forgotten to take one, and could be pregnant, he wouldn't have abandoned her, she was sure of that. She and Tom might be together now, eagerly anticipating the birth of their child. That thought was almost unbearable.

She finished the paper and submitted it to the *Art History Journal.*

ON A GRAY, RAINY SATURDAY MORNING IN DECEMBER, MIRIAM SAT at her kitchen table with a calendar and notebook. She counted the months and days, as she'd found herself doing repeatedly, calculating a likely due date, then checking it again and again. She wrote the date in her notebook: December 5, 1982—tomorrow. She traced her finger lightly over the day on the calendar and whispered, "Rosie." She always thought of the baby as a girl, named "Rosemary" after her mother, but called Rosie.

She put the calendar away and drove to the large Godchaux's department store on the edge of downtown. It was just opening, the clerks at the cosmetic counter straightening the displays, others walking to their departments, some carrying lunch bags. Miriam looked around furtively as she walked back to the infants' department. An idle saleslady leaned against the counter. She was middle-aged, overweight, and unattractive, despite heroic efforts with makeup (perhaps she got a discount) and liberal application of hair-styling products. She perked up when she saw Miriam and asked if she needed help.

"I'm looking for a dress for my newborn niece," Miriam said, eyeing the racks of tiny clothes.

"Oh, a baby girl—how fun!" the saleslady gushed and led her to a rack of the smallest clothes. "These are the little dresses—unless you wanted something more practical, maybe a romper?"

"No, I want a special dress. I'll look through these, thank you." Miriam turned her back dismissively, and the woman, miffed, returned to the counter. Miriam went through the dresses carefully until she found it, a long white christening dress, lace edging the collar and skirt, tiny pink rosebuds embroidered on the smocked bodice. On impulse, she added little pale pink satin slippers and approached the register.

The saleslady said, "A lovely choice. Is this your first niece?"

"Yes, and the first grandbaby on both sides," Miriam said. She didn't know why.

"Oh, well, that's a very special time then. Would you like these gift-wrapped?"

"No, I have paper at home. Thank you."

She drove home, pulled into the garage, and hurried into the house. She closed the curtains in the dining room that looked out on Mac's side yard. Then she turned on the bright chandelier and both lamps, went upstairs to fetch her sketchpad and pencils and returned to the dining room. She took the little dress from the bag, carefully cut off the tags, and laid it out on the table with the slippers. She gazed at them a moment, went back upstairs to her bedroom, and retrieved the photo album her mother had given her for her eighteenth birthday. The earliest photos were black-and-white with scalloped edges, mostly of a young Rosemary and baby Miriam. Some photos included her father, then a somber young man with closely trimmed dark hair and glasses with heavy black frames. Miriam paged through, pausing at the hand-colored studio portrait of her five-year-old self, posing proudly in her Easter finery—a starched pale pink voile dress with a petticoat underneath, white patent leather shoes, lace-edged socks, and a bonnet trimmed with silk roses and pink ribbon. She still remembered that outfit. How her mother would have loved having a granddaughter to dress up and spoil.

Miriam turned to the last pages, where she'd added pictures of herself and Tom, planning to one day give the album to their own child. She took the album with her downstairs, placed it on the table beside her sketchpad, and turned to her earliest baby pictures. Then she sat down and began working.

When she looked up from her sketchpad, two hours had passed. She stood on stiff legs, got a glass of water from the kitchen, and sat back down. When she paused again to refill her glass, it was midafternoon. She'd forgotten lunch, but she wasn't hungry. She continued working as the light faded outside. When she finally leaned back in her chair, finished, it was after six. She held the pad in front of her and whispered, "Rosie." The detailed drawing depicted a sleeping child, dressed in the christening gown and laid in her bassinet, perhaps while her parents dressed for church. A soft down of hair, delicately shadowed closed lids over round eyes like Tom's, plump cheeks, lips like Miriam's, pudgy little arms and tiny hands, one closed, the other open, as if in a dream—a baby sleeping securely, surrounded by love. Miriam stood, exhausted, carefully folded the little dress, and carried it with the slippers and the drawing upstairs to her bedroom. She opened the bottom dresser drawer she'd emptied of Tom's sweaters, put the clothes in with the drawing on top, covered them with a layer of white tissue paper, and closed the drawer.

WHEN SHE WENT TO CAMPUS IN JANUARY FOR THE WINTER semester's first faculty meeting, Miriam checked her campus mailbox and found a letter from the *Art History Journal*. She sighed, expecting it to be a brief rejection. She went to her office, closed the door, and tore it open before she even sat down. She stared at it, reading it again to be sure she'd understood correctly. The journal had accepted the paper with only minor revisions. She thought of past acceptances and how her first act would have been to rush over to Tom's office, letter in hand. How he would have insisted that they leave campus and celebrate, that minute if possible. How once, on a Friday with no classes remaining, he'd appeared at her office three minutes after she'd called with the news, taken her hand, led her to his car, and driven to Vinny's. They'd ordered charbroiled oysters with garlic bread and wine, then gone home and to bed, though it was only four in the afternoon.

IN APRIL, MIRIAM RECEIVED THE 1983 LSU STEPHEN J. GASTINEL

Award for Excellence in Teaching. She especially prized it because the award was made on the basis of student nominations.

In December, Miriam bought the pink ruffled dress, drew the one-year-old baby, brought the drawing and dress upstairs, placed them in the drawer on top of the prior year's, and covered them with tissue.

The following March, her article in the *Art History Journal* was chosen for the coveted AHA Prize for Emerging Scholars, given annually for a distinguished article published the prior year by a scholar younger than thirty-five. *You'll fly, Miriam. Nothing will hold you back.*

THE NEXT DECEMBER, FOR ROSIE'S SECOND BIRTHDAY, MIRIAM selected a toddler's dress in red-and-white gingham with strawberries embroidered on the pockets, white tights, and little red shoes. A Raggedy Ann doll wearing a matching gingham dress caught her eye, and she took that to the register too.

The same saleslady, whom Miriam now knew as "Ann," had moved from the infants' to the children's department (a change of venue Ann described as a "promotion," though her duties appeared identical). Without the slightest encouragement, Ann greeted Miriam like an old friend, undeterred by Miriam's monosyllabic responses. She asked Miriam far too many questions about the toys Rosie liked, what kind of cake she would have for her birthday, and other specifics that Miriam was forced to fabricate, each response piercing her heart.

Miriam softened a bit when she noticed Ann didn't wear a wedding ring and never spoke of a child herself. Ann's delighted cooing over the purchases as she rang them up pleased Miriam, irrational as that was.

"She's so lucky to have you for an aunt!" Ann declared as she handed Miriam the shopping bag.

At home, Miriam cut off the tags and carefully ironed the dress, then laid it with the shoes on the dining room table next to the doll. She sat a moment staring at the items, her eyes filling, then blinked back the tears and went upstairs for her sketchpad and pencils. She sat down again, thought about the composition, then began. Her hand gripping the pencil felt stiff and awkward; after a few tentative lines, she tore out the page, crumpled it into a ball and went to the kitchen for a glass of ice water. She resumed drawing, slowly at first, but with increased fervor as the drawing took shape and Rosie emerged on the page. Miriam continued working while the shadows lengthened, shading, sharpening her pencil to add the fine details, pausing to evaluate, then switching pencils for a softer or harder lead as she made the final adjustments.

When she finished, she looked at the drawing for a long time. Rosie was holding the Raggedy Ann doll tightly with both hands, and looking up, perhaps at the one who'd given her this new treasure, and laughing, thrilled with her birthday gift. Miriam's shoulders ached when she finally stood, slow and weary, gathered the gingham dress, shoes, and doll, tore the page from the sketchpad, carried it all upstairs, and added another layer to the drawer, covering it with tissue.

The next night, Miriam had the usual Sunday dinner with her parents. She was dismayed when her mother said that her friend Aimee's son was coming home for the holidays, and maybe Miriam would like to have dinner with him? Miriam again tried to explain that she wasn't interested in dating. Her father had been unexpectedly supportive, pointing to Miriam's dedication to her career and her accomplishments. When Rosemary protested that she just wanted Miriam to be happy, Miriam knew she meant that she wanted Miriam to have a family. Rosemary wanted grandchildren. And there was nothing Miriam could do about that.

CHAPTER 19

In December 1986, Miriam chose the yellow polka-dotted cotton dress with the wide sash and an appliqué of a white cat sewn on the bodice. Back at home, she drew Rosie in the dress, pigtails tied with bows, standing outside the front door. Rosie was looking up and reaching out a hand, as if for a walk, perhaps down the street to visit her grandparents. Miriam was sipping a glass of wine and studying the finished drawing when her mother called.

"Miriam, could you go with me to see a dress they're holding for me at Sussman's? I need something for the New Year's Eve party at the Country Club. I thought maybe we could go in the morning, then have lunch afterward?"

Miriam reluctantly agreed. She'd planned to use tomorrow to make up for the time she'd spent drawing today, but her mother didn't know that—she'd know only that it would be Saturday and Miriam had no . classes.

. . .

At Sussman's the next morning, Miriam quickly agreed that the dress was perfect. When they returned to the car, Rosemary said Godchaux's was starting their annual white sale early and asked if they could go by to look at sheets. Miriam tried to divert her mother, first by suggesting an early lunch at a nearby restaurant she knew her mother liked, then by saying she really needed to get to her office. Rosemary said that they could be quick by having lunch at the Godchaux's coffee shop and drove straight to the store. Miriam made sure they went directly to the linen department on the second floor, rushing her mother past the clothing departments on the first floor, relieved not to see Ann.

Miriam was beginning to relax as she and her mother walked through the aisles, her mother stopping to show her several sets of sheets, when Miriam saw Ann rounding the corner of the aisle. "Mom, come see this set over here," Miriam said, walking rapidly toward the next aisle. But Ann had seen her.

"Miriam!" Ann called, "Did you come for the white sale? Look at this set—I'm so glad they're still here. I was sure they'd be gone by the time I could get up here on my lunch break!" Ann winked and added, "Today is payday."

Miriam tried offering a few complimentary words on the sheets and said she had to run, but Ann, excited about her acquisition, kept talking. "I've loved this set since it first came out and never dreamed it would go on such a good sale. I might paint my bedroom a shade that would match. I wonder if they still have the comforter," she said, digging through the pile.

Miriam was edging away while Ann was preoccupied, but bumped into Rosemary, who had come up behind her. Rosemary politely introduced herself to Ann.

"Oh, I'm so glad to meet you," Ann gushed, "I'm Miriam's sales consultant when she comes in to select the birthday dress for her niece every year."

Miriam felt sick. Rosemary raised an eyebrow and said, "Oh?"

Ann was momentarily distracted by her joyful discovery of the comforter matching the sheets. Miriam tried nudging her mother toward the next aisle, but she remained solidly in place. Ann, snatching the comforter, picked up where she'd left off.

"I always tell Miriam how lucky her niece is to have her for an aunt. She chooses the most beautiful little outfits every year." Ann said she'd better go pay because she had to be back on the floor in ten minutes. She left them, tossing Miriam a cheery, "See you next year!"

Rosemary put down the sheets she'd been considering and took Miriam's arm, steering her toward the coffee shop. After they'd perused the menu in silence and ordered, Rosemary asked what on earth Ann was talking about.

"You don't have any nieces," Rosemary said. "Is there something you haven't told me?"

Miriam didn't see a way around it. "I didn't want to tell you because I knew how sad it would make you. After Tom died, I had a miscarriage." There, she'd said it. She watched her mother's face and saw the spasm of sadness that shifted to compassion.

"I'm so sorry, Miriam. I'd noticed that every year around this time, you seem sad. But why would you buy clothes?"

"I know it seems crazy. I guess for one day a year—the day that would've been her birthday—I like to think about what might have been." That wasn't quite it, but Miriam didn't know how to articulate what she felt.

"Oh, Miriam, I wish you'd shared this with me sooner. Maybe I could have helped."

"I didn't want you to be hurt too." She wasn't going to tell her mother that the miscarriage was her fault, that she'd triggered it. Not now, not ever. She rushed on with the explanation that occurred to her as she spoke.

"Anyway, I buy one dress a year and then I donate the dress to the Goodwill Store so that a little girl somewhere can have it. Maybe her mother can't afford nice things for her daughter and would enjoy dressing her up." Neither her mother nor anyone else would ever know about the drawings.

"Well, that's a sweet way to honor the occasion," her mother said, looking like she might cry. "But maybe it's time for you to move on, find happiness again. You're beautiful, intelligent, and have so many qualities that would make you a wonderful mother. I'm sure there's someone out there who could be right for you."

"No, Mom. Like I've told you before, I don't have the slightest interest in remarrying." They paused a moment as the waitress put down their chicken salad sandwiches and bustled off.

"Are you sure you're not just afraid, Miriam? No one would blame you for that, but please don't rule out being happy again. Tom wouldn't want that."

"Tom was the only one for me, Mom. Please let's not talk about this again." Miriam picked up her chicken salad sandwich and took a large bite.

Her mother watched her a moment longer, then picked up her sandwich, offered a shaky smile and said, "Maybe after lunch we could go back to linens so I could show you that set of sheets I liked and you could show me the ones you liked. Would you have time?"

"Sure, Mom, we could do that."

They each bought a set of sheets, Miriam more out of solidarity than for actual need or desire and started home. Rosemary was uncharacteristically silent on the drive, and Miriam knew she was searching for a way to reopen the discussion. When they arrived at her house, Miriam grabbed her shopping bag, thanked her mother for lunch, and opened the car door.

"Miriam, I know you're in a hurry, but could we maybe have a cup of coffee together before I go?"

Her mother's hopeful smile (and turning off the engine) made it too hard to say no.

They made coffee and put the mugs and shortbread cookies Rosemary had bought at the coffee shop on a tray and brought it to the sitting room. When they were settled on the couch sipping coffee, Rosemary said, "Something's been bothering me, and what you told me today, well, makes me feel even worse."

"What, Mom?"

"I just want to say that I'm sorry I didn't stand up to William about how he treated Tom. I should have. It was wrong for me to stay quiet."

Miriam stared. Tom had been dead for over four years. Why say this now?

"And with what you told me today," Rosemary said, staring into her coffee mug, "I wonder even more how different things might have been for you and Tom if you'd lived somewhere else, away from us."

Miriam, shocked, set her mug down hard enough that coffee sloshed over the top. "What? Why would that have mattered? I thought you'd be devastated if we moved."

"Yes, I would have been devastated, but William and I were wrong to be so set on keeping you close to us. I know you had your position at the university, and William insisted on giving you the house. Maybe we made it too hard for you and Tom to really consider living anywhere else."

How could her mother say this now? Miriam felt betrayed by this belated regret, with its implied criticism of their staying.

"I'm just saying," Rosemary continued, "that Tom was a gentle, unselfish man, and maybe our family didn't think enough about what he needed. Maybe we tried too hard to force him into our plans."

Miriam's shock flared into anger, and she shot back, "I didn't think enough about what Tom needed? I was forcing him into my plans?"

"No, Miriam, you were a good wife, I meant--"

"Yes, that's exactly what you're saying. That I might have a happy family now if only we'd moved to New York. Away from here." Miriam was nearly shouting now.

"No, Miriam, I'm not saying that at all!"

"Thank you, Mother, for laying Tom's death at my door. And Ro— the baby's, too!"

"Miriam, please, let me explain," Rosemary pleaded, tears welling.

"Please leave!" Miriam stood, grabbed the tray from the coffee table, and fled into the kitchen, mugs and plates clattering. "Leave!" she shouted. She heard her mother walk quickly from the room and out the front door. When she heard the car pull out of the driveway, she ran upstairs to her bedroom and lay down, furious and sobbing.

Gradually, her anger receded. Her mother would be home by now, probably still crying. Miriam got up wearily, washed her face, and walked the two blocks to her parents' house, trying to clear her head. Although it was Saturday, her father would be at his university office for at least another two hours. When she knocked, her mother answered, pale and fragile, eyes red-rimmed, but smiling to see Miriam.

"Mom, I'm so sorry, I shouldn't have said those things."

"No, Miriam, I'm the one who's sorry." Rosemary opened the door wide and waved Miriam inside. They sat on the couch together.

Rosemary said, "I know I pressured you to stay in every way I could. I was trying to excuse what I did at your expense. I guess I want forgiveness for my mistakes without admitting that I made them."

"No, Mom, it wasn't you. I wanted to stay here, near you and Dad, with a job I loved, in a house and town I loved. I always thought Tom might love it here, too, if he gave it more of a chance. But you're right that I didn't truly give his wishes a chance."

"No, Miriam, that wasn't what I meant. You couldn't have changed what happened. That came from within Tom. Sacrificing what you loved wouldn't have saved him."

That wasn't what her mother had said earlier. She'd said things might have been different if Miriam and Tom had left. Exactly what Tom thought. What Miriam had always denied. Now she'd have to live with knowing that her mother believed that too. And that was hard.

"I always thought we had more time."

"So did I, Miriam."

They sat together in silence, and Rosemary put her arm around Miriam and pulled her close. Miriam felt the loss of the baby settling into her mother, cutting a jagged wound. She felt her prayer that Miriam would love again, have a family they could both cherish. Miriam couldn't give her that. After a few moments, Miriam hugged her mother, then said she needed to get back. Rosemary nodded, stood, walked her to the door, and kissed her goodbye.

"We'll see you for Sunday dinner?" Rosemary asked.

"Sure," Miriam said, waved, and walked home. Back inside, she cried again. Knowing her mother would be crying too didn't help.

Now that her mother knew about the dresses, maybe it was time to end the ritual. As the months of 1987 passed, though, the compulsion grew stronger. The night before Rosie's fifth birthday, Miriam found herself sitting in front of the fire, planning the composition. She closed her eyes and let the images of Rosie come, seeing Mac's garden on a sunny December morning, the fountain sparkling in the sun, Rosie playing amid the azaleas, camellias, and bridal wreath bushes as Mac tended his roses and Miriam painted. Rosie hiding behind a red rosebush, then giggling and peeking out from behind it when Miriam pretended to search for her, blond hair shining, blue eyes bright, rejoicing in the game.

When Miriam went upstairs to bed, sleep didn't come. She rose in the gray dawn, dressed, and went down to the kitchen for coffee and toast. After the sunrise, she gathered her brushes, palette, easel, and a painting of a red rose bush she'd begun and put aside over a year ago. She set up in Mac's garden and began painting. Mac was delighted to find her there when he came out at eight, and she stayed until ten. Then she took down her easel and told Mac she had to run errands and grade papers the rest of the day.

She drove to Godchaux's and selected a bright red wool dress with brass buttons down the front, red tights, and black patent leather shoes. She was initially relieved that Ann was absent, but as the unfamiliar saleslady rang up her purchases, she missed Ann's silly chatter about the outfit and Rosie's birthday party. Missed how Ann unknowingly played along with the fiction that a living child would wear the dress, delight in the stuffed tabby cat with the red bow Miriam bought. Back at home, after preparing the dress, Miriam set up her easel in the dining room, then ate a ham-and-cheese sandwich to stop the faint trembling in her hands. She studied the painting, the dress, pictures of herself at age five, and pictures of Tom.

It was the only time she painted Rosie instead of drawing her. Rosie's face emerged from behind the rose bush, eager and excited, watching her mother, the stuffed cat lying forgotten in the grass.

When exhaustion released the tears, Miriam angrily jabbed her brush on the palette, sat still for a moment to compose herself, then continued, like a fighter returning to the ring in spite of being too damaged to triumph. She painted until weariness began to blur her vision and make her too clumsy for the fine brushwork. After a fitful night, she rose before dawn to finish the painting, then hid it in the pantry to dry before it could be varnished and put away on top of the red dress.

THROUGH THE YEARS, MIRIAM OFTEN DREAMED OF ROSIE, especially on the nights after drawing her. A series replayed, like a collection of home movies a parent might watch repeatedly to relive memories. Sometimes Rosie was the same age in the dream as in that year's drawing, sometimes not. Sometimes the dreams were a collage of scenes from different stages of her ghost child's life. Sometimes Tom was in the dreams, sometimes her parents joined them, sometimes Mac.

Miriam's national standing as a scholar continued to grow. She achieved her goal of writing a comprehensive book on Berthe Morisot, and in 1998, the LSU Press accepted the manuscript for publication. Miriam applied for and received a grant from the AHA Publication Fund to subsidize high-quality printing and color plates of Morisot's paintings for the book. When *Berthe Morisot: Revolutionary Artist and Woman* was published in 1999, it was awarded the Outstanding Book Award of the Association of American University Presses and the AHA Book Award, honoring an especially distinguished book making a substantial contribution to the study of art history.

How proud Tom would have been. He would have second-guessed the Press's editor, argued for changes he considered indispensable improvements, and fiercely overseen every detail of publication. She pictured Rosie, rolling her eyes at Tom's obsessiveness, sharing a laugh with Miriam in the kitchen when they overheard him on the phone with the editor, proud of her mother's accomplishment and of her father's indefatigable insistence on perfection in the execution.

When Miriam received the first copy of the book, she sat down with it at home, took it out of the padded envelope, and stared at the beautifully rendered cover, illustrated with a copy of her favorite Morisot painting, *Young Woman on a Divan*. The reclining woman in the painting, gazing into the distance, lost in thought, faint smile, as if daydreaming of the night before or to come, a mixture of innocence and speculation. Miriam traced her fingers over her name on the cover, then opened the book, enjoying the feel of the heavy, slick paper, the beautiful colors of the paintings, taking time to sink into this culmination of years of striving. A deep peace suffused her; she hadn't expected that.

She gave copies to her parents and Mac, and sent one to Marcie, now a tenured professor at Columbia University, who emailed enthusiastic praise and congratulations. When Miriam delivered her parents' copy to them, her father took it with obvious pleasure and sat on the couch with Rosemary beside him. They paged through it reverently, Rosemary commenting with delight on the beauty of the volume.

"This is a great and significant accomplishment," her father pronounced. "Scholars will be turning to it for many years. Your book will be the standard for research on Morisot—hell, on any of the Impressionists!"

Rosemary beamed. Her father stood and shook Miriam's hand, smiling broadly, and said, "Congratulations, Professor!"

Her mother still held the book, and Miriam noticed she faltered at the dedication page, then turned it quickly.

The book was dedicated to Miriam's beloved husband, Thomas S. Johnson.

MIRIAM CREATED THE LAST DRAWING IN 2000, FOR ROSIE'S eighteenth birthday. She selected the blue silk dress carefully, a coming-of-age dress for a young woman on the cusp of independence. After she'd completed the drawing of Rosie posing on the front porch, she'd settled with a glass of wine to gaze at the drawing, knowing it was the last one. She closed her eyes and saw a tall, beautiful Rosie in the auditorium at University High School as the graduation ceremony ended and the graduates dispersed to find their families. Rosie, leaving the graduates' section, rushing to Miriam, Tom, her grandparents, and Mac, all smiling and congratulating her. The celebratory lunch, talking about Rosie's plans for college in the fall, Tom choking up, Rosemary, William, and Mac glowing with pride and love.

PART V
NOW

CHAPTER 20

SECRET PLANNING

As January began, Miriam felt herself deteriorating and knew she had at most only a few months left. She knew too that Camille remained unconvinced that medical school was an attainable goal, though Miriam thought she'd seen a cautious hope growing. Miriam hadn't been prepared to care as much as she now did about Camille's future, though she should have known that every promising student she'd worked with during her long career had become important to her. But she'd never had one with the obstacles that Camille had to overcome to complete a long and arduous, not to mention expensive, curriculum like medical school.

Miriam had no more time to waste. Duncan had brought another draft of her will he'd fine-tuned after their last discussion. She read it over again and was satisfied. She'd sign it and have that done. She called and made the appointment. Then she called Mrs. Doucet—Ruby, as she'd told Miriam to call her—who said she could come by that afternoon. They'd met before to talk about Camille and possible curriculums, but now it was time to tell Ruby more specifically what she planned to give Camille. Miriam needed to know Ruby would support the plan and encourage

Camille, especially when she no longer could. She'd ask Camille to do the grocery shopping after class today to get her out of the house.

Miriam sat for a moment after calling Ruby, organizing her thoughts. Hanks looked at her through the French door, tail wagging and grinning as if he knew what she was planning. She let him in and said, "Yes, boy, you'll still have a fireplace and a good backyard too." That is, he would if she could ensure that Camille would accept what she wanted to give her.

That afternoon, Ruby arrived, laden with bags in both arms and a ready smile. "I got to cooking last night and thought I'd bring you some more of my chicken noodle soup. Adelaide said she thought you liked it."

Miriam assured her that she did, and they unloaded the meal-sized containers of soup. Then they sat at the kitchen table, and Miriam asked if she'd talked with Camille more about her education.

"We have talked several times since you and I last spoke, and I can see Camille's thoughts changing," Ruby said. "She's beginning to see the LSU Bachelor of Science as a real possibility, and even tentatively thinking about medical school. But she's worried about the expense and how she can support herself and put in the study hours at the same time." Ruby paused, with an expression Miriam couldn't interpret.

"I sense a 'but,'" Miriam prompted.

"Only a selfish reservation. Adelaide has done so much better with Camille as her friend and study companion—and with your help. I honestly just hate for her to be left in the two-year curriculum while Camille moves on. But I agree that Camille must do what's best for her."

"Well, what do you think about Adelaide switching to LSU's nursing program?"

Ruby pondered this. "Six months ago, I would have said no way. Before she and Camille became friends, Adelaide hung around with a group of girls who were much more interested in clothes and boys than in their classes. But I've seen a real change in her over the last several months, partly because of the extra studying but, more importantly, because she's become committed to nursing. It's not just a good job to her anymore, it's something she feels in her bones that she wants to do."

Miriam said she'd sensed the same and that she thought Adelaide would make a wonderful nurse. Then she went further. "I haven't spoken of this with Camille, but I'm going to leave her the resources to pursue her education. She'd have the funds for school and living expenses, so she wouldn't have to worry about supporting herself. My only concern is that she may not accept the help."

Ruby considered this. "I understand your concern. Camille is very independent. She was raised to make her own way. Which reminds me —." Ruby paused, thinking.

"What is it?"

"I knew Camille's grandparents, especially her grandmother. She was bound and determined that Camille would have what she needed to get a good education, especially after Camille decided she wanted to be a nurse. Her grandmother saved every penny she could for years to build up a college fund."

"But I had the impression that Camille didn't have anything."

"Me too, Miriam. Both her grandparents were sick for months before they died. Maybe that's what happened to their savings?"

"Could be," Miriam said, thinking of her own medical expenses. Even with insurance, the costs mounted quickly.

Ruby seemed lost in thought. She said, "Let me think on this some more, Miriam. Are you going to talk with Camille about your help before, uh—"

"I was hoping to leave that to my attorney to do after I'm gone, but do you think it would be better for me to do that?" Miriam hated to ask because she didn't want to hear Ruby say yes, but she trusted Ruby's opinion.

"I know that's hard," Ruby said, putting a comforting hand on Miriam's shoulder, "but I think you have to. You're the one she's most likely to listen to."

Miriam nodded and said, "She values your opinion highly too, Ruby. Could you help?"

Ruby said, "If you'll let me know when you've talked to Camille, I'll see what I can do to encourage her to accept your help. I'll pray and think on it until then."

Miriam thanked her, and Ruby gave her a hug and left, promising to stay in touch. Miriam was grateful to have such an ally, but the talk had left her exhausted. Her strength was indeed waning faster these days.

She was tired of the business of dying and wished she could just quietly fade away, like the view of her backyard at twilight. But not before she finished with her last student. That she would not give up.

Camille drove Miriam to Duncan's office the next morning to sign her will. Miriam met with Duncan in his conference room while Camille read her chemistry textbook in the lobby. Miriam congratulated Duncan on his creativity and practicality and thanked him for agreeing to serve as trustee of Camille's trust. When she confided that she was afraid Camille wouldn't accept the gifts, Duncan echoed Ruby's advice that Miriam should talk with Camille.

"I can be a backstop and will urge her all I can to accept the bequests when I go over the will with her. But it won't be the same as her hearing it from you."

Miriam left his office relieved to have the will completed and another ally but knowing that he was right. His talking to Camille after Miriam's death wouldn't be the same as Miriam talking to her now.

Miriam spent the afternoon while Camille was in class thinking about how to approach her. She was tempted to return to her original plan to let Duncan tell Camille about the will. But she found she couldn't leave it there. She knew she was avoiding the discussion because she was afraid of Camille rejecting the gifts and how hard that would be for her to bear. It was so much easier to envision a happy revelation after her death than to deal with the possible refusal now.

Well, taking the easier way out had never been her style, nor was shrinking from a difficult conversation. When Camille returned, Miriam asked if they could talk. Camille looked apprehensive, perhaps worried that Miriam was going to reveal further deterioration in her health—which she could, but wouldn't. Unfortunately, she knew that was already evident to Camille.

"Camille, have you thought further about your education?"

"Actually, I have. I've talked with Mrs. Doucet about it, and she said she was sure I could handle the premed curriculum and that I have, uh, a natural ability for that field."

Very good, Miriam thought, encouraged. "Excellent, and I hope you believed her. I know you've been concerned, as anyone would be, about the financial burden of putting yourself through medical school. I want to offer you a solution to that."

Camille looked up, surprised.

Miriam decided to just say it. "I've created a trust in my will that will pay your education and living expenses until you graduate from whatever level you choose—nursing school or medical school—and have begun your practice."

"No, Miriam, I couldn't accept that," Camille said immediately.

"Camille, I know you've taken care of yourself and earned your own way. That's admirable, but I want you to be able to focus solely on your studies without the distraction of providing for yourself."

"Thank you, Miriam, and it means the world to me that you believe in me. But it would be wrong for me to accept that."

"Whyever do you think that?"

"My grandparents raised me not to take or expect anything I hadn't earned myself. And I don't want anyone to think that I took advantage of you."

Miriam was mildly insulted that Camille seemed to be thinking along the same lines as her cousins. "Duncan will tell you that I acted with full capacity in making my will," she said stiffly.

"Oh, Miriam, I didn't mean that! I know that you wouldn't let me influence you to do anything you didn't want to do. But—"

"You've worked hard and excelled in your coursework, including before we met. Of course, if you don't truly want to go further than the two-year degree, that's nothing to be ashamed of, and we can certainly leave it at that." Miriam was lying through her teeth. She wasn't going to let Camille deny herself her dream.

"No, I did think that before. But now I want to do more. It might take me longer, or I might have to stay out of school to work and save money for a couple of years."

Miriam noticed that Camille looked unhappy with that alternative. "Camille, how do you feel about being a doctor? I don't want to push you in a direction that you're not passionate about pursuing. Of your intelligence and ability, I have no doubt. But that underlying passion is something only you can judge."

"Miriam, I think about being a doctor every day now. I want it more than anything. I thought if I could make it through the LSU nursing program and become a registered nurse, then I could earn more to save for medical school or maybe have enough from working part-time while I was in school."

Miriam could see that Camille had given this a good bit of thought and was struggling to find a way to make medical school possible. Good, that should make her job easier.

"Mrs. Doucet told me that your grandparents saved for years for your education, that they were determined that you would be able to accomplish whatever you desired."

"Yes, they did. And they always told me not to stop until I reached my goals."

Miriam softened, seeing Camille's grief in her shiny eyes. "They wanted you to be able to reach those goals even more than I do," Miriam said. Possibly true, but not necessarily. "What happened to the savings they had for your education?"

"They didn't have much insurance to help when they got sick, and the drugs and treatments were very expensive. My grandmother used up their own savings on my grandfather's care."

"And when your grandmother got sick? You took care of her, didn't you? And you took the money out of your college fund."

Camille nodded, mute, looking down at her hands, twisting them in her lap, wrongly ashamed of this unselfish deception.

Miriam said, "She didn't know, did she?"

"No," Camille said, almost in a whisper. "She wouldn't have let me. I told her the doctor gave us discounts or that they had a special fund for poor patients. She was so sick she didn't have the strength to question it."

"So what do you think your grandparents would say if they knew I want to help you, to give you what they tried so hard to give you?"

Camille was quiet. She looked out the window at Hanks, lounging under the oak tree.

"I know they were so proud of you," Miriam said. "It would break their hearts if they knew you were too overburdened supporting yourself to follow your true vocation. Please let me do what they would have wanted."

Miriam could tell this argument was reaching Camille. But she wasn't saying yes. Miriam had one more card to play.

"Camille, the trust for you in my will says that anything left in it when your education is completed goes to a fund I've created to help homeless animals—The Hanks and Petey Companion Animal Fund." Camille looked up and smiled at that. "If you accept the trust's help while you're in school, you could always consider giving something back to the fund once you're earning a good living."

Miriam could tell that Camille was thinking about that. Hanks, always helpful, chose that moment to come to the French door and look in at Camille, grinning, tail wagging.

"All right, Miriam, I'll think about it. Thank you for caring about me so much. Even if I never take anything from the trust, that will always mean so much to me."

Miriam didn't care for that last "assurance," but she didn't think she could push farther today. The house would have to be another conversation. Still, they'd moved away from Camille's initial refusal to a maybe. That was progress.

Miriam napped in her chair before dinner and woke to find the room growing dark and Camille nowhere to be found. Petey and Hanks were missing, too. Camille should be rustling around in the kitchen by now, getting their dinner ready. She got up and saw the kitchen and the rest of downstairs was dark, but saw a light on upstairs and heard footsteps. She went up to investigate. The light was coming from her office, where Camille had no business being. Miriam stood in the doorway and coughed. Camille turned from where she stood in front of several of Miriam's paintings she'd placed on the display shelf, phone in hand.

"What are you doing?"

"Oh, uh, I was going to talk with you about this, but you were resting, so I thought I'd do it at dinner."

Miriam raised an eyebrow, waiting.

Camille picked up a sheet she'd printed that said, "LSU Faculty Art Exhibit" at the top. "I heard about this exhibit of work by LSU faculty and thought you should consider it for your beautiful paintings. I was going to fill out the application for you."

"You were what?" Miriam could barely believe Camille could be so presumptuous.

"Miriam, they're so lovely. Please let them be shown. They shouldn't be kept hidden away in a closet."

The words were so much like what Mac and Tom had told her that she was silenced, but only momentarily. "Camille, I distinctly remember telling you that the painting is my private hobby and that I don't show the work."

"So you wouldn't even consider—"

"Absolutely not! Now let's go downstairs, and please also recall that I told you this room is off limits."

Camille went meekly downstairs with her, but Miriam had the unsettling feeling that the subject would arise again. Well, let it. She'd just refuse again. Frankly, she was shocked that Camille would pull something like this.

The next morning, Miriam sat at Tom's desk after Camille had left, holding an unopened envelope she'd found in a drawer. The return address was the publishing house in New York where Tom had interviewed, and the postmark showed that it had arrived only a day or two before his death. She put the letter down on the desk without opening it. She'd assigned herself the much-delayed and dreaded task of cleaning out Tom's desk. She couldn't put it off any longer because she didn't want anyone else doing it. At least she could skip the top drawer, now empty, that she'd cleaned out those months ago for

Camille's use. She picked up the envelope again, confirming that it hadn't been opened. She put it back down. She'd finish cleaning out the desk before she opened it.

She moved quickly through the drawers, tossing dried-up pens and yellowed typing paper in a trash bag. When she found the last manuscript Tom had been working on, a low whine escaped her. She ran her fingers over his penciled markup and his notes in the margin. She sniffed the pages as if Tom's scent might still be on them. She sighed and consigned the manuscript to the trash bag too. Next went a pile of partially graded student papers—she should have checked for things that needed to be returned. Worse, there was a folder of papers for the journal that Tom had been editing. She wished Herb had, for once, ignored his empathetic kindness and asked her to look for them. They couldn't have any value all these years later, so she tossed them too, along with the last set of student evaluations.

She returned to the drawer where she'd found the sealed envelope. Other old envelopes were jammed together there. Most held rejection letters, either from journals where he'd submitted papers or from positions he'd applied for, many of which she hadn't known about. She threw them all into the trash bag. Apparently, he'd told her about only a small part of what had been an extensive job search. All of the positions would have necessitated moving. None was likely to offer an opportunity for her comparable to what she had at LSU. Had Tom been considering leaving her? Even now, the thought hurt.

She carried the trash bag out, then returned for the envelope from the publisher. She opened it and read, "We are pleased to tell you that a position as copyeditor has become available and we invite you to apply for it." Not an offer, but the tone was warm, and Tom was obviously favored for the position. Why hadn't he opened the envelope? Had he intended to open it later, with her, and then forgotten about it? That seemed unlikely, but he'd been so lost in his misery then.

What if he'd opened it? She was beyond hiding from herself now that she might have refused to leave Baton Rouge.

She put the letter in her pocket and retreated to her chair in the sitting room. She was crying and Petey came rushing in, meowing. She scooped him up and sat with him in her lap, stroking him and gazing out the windows, remembering Tom's haunted eyes.

CHAPTER 21

Miriam found herself leaning on Camille now for even simple things, like getting dressed in the morning. Dr. Viator had said it was time for additional sitters (sitters!), which had eased the burden on Camille. Irene, the night sitter, was kind, competent, and dumb as a bag of rocks—basically the most Miriam had hoped for in a caregiver before she'd met Camille. Elaine, who came when Irene or Camille was off, was much like Irene. Kind and capable of anything except an engaging conversation.

Unfortunately, though, it was now undeniable that Miriam needed a whole team to take care of her. And despite her inner crabbiness about Irene's and Elaine's limitations, Miriam was grateful for their professionalism, tact, and skill. She instructed Duncan to provide them each with a generous gift after her death to compensate for any lack of grace on her part.

What bothered her most now was her continuing failure to persuade Camille to agree to accept help with her education. Miriam hadn't mentioned the house to her yet. The brevity of her remaining time weighed on her heavily. She'd always been able to push her graduate students to heights beyond what they'd thought they could achieve, and she'd never given up on a promising student. Six months ago, Miriam had accepted that the disease was devouring her existence. Now she fought it because she wasn't finished. But she'd lose the fight, and soon. She'd talk with Camille again tonight.

Camille arrived home that afternoon looking distracted, even anxious. Miriam wondered whether she'd been considering the approaching end of her position here and what she'd do next. Maybe worrying about how she'd manage the rigors of a curriculum far more challenging than her current one. Camille had cut back on her classes this semester, without consulting Miriam, and she knew Camille had done it to spend more time here. Miriam regretted that sacrifice but admitted that she might not have argued if given the opportunity. Not only did she depend increasingly on Camille's physical help, but she looked forward to the pleasure of their time together, the distraction from her thoughts of past failures or fears of her steady and accelerating debilitation.

Before Miriam could approach Camille, she came to her, looking nervous.

"Miriam, I have a letter that came for you today."

Miriam noticed the letter had been opened.

"Um, it's about that LSU faculty art exhibit."

"The one I told you I wasn't interested in, you mean?"

"Well, yes. Your work was accepted."

"So now you'll have to notify them that I won't be participating."

"Please don't make me do that, Miriam. Please, I'm begging you. The work is too beautiful to go unseen."

After her initial surprise at the intense longing on Camille's face, Miriam had an idea. "Camille, you know I've kept my paintings to myself all these years because they're private. The last thing I want to do at this late juncture is publicly display them. You were wrong to submit them to the show behind my back."

Camille looked contrite, but she wasn't conceding. "I know, Miriam, and I'm sorry. But I don't want you to pass without seeing others enjoy what you've created. Please, is there anything I can do to change your mind?"

Ah, there it was. Miriam pounced. "Hhhmm, well, there might be."

Camille waited, twisting a strand of hair in her fingers like she did when she was nervous.

"If you apply to LSU for premed, I'll consider the show."

Camille pulled some papers out from under the envelope and held up the completed application. "Done," she said.

Miriam realized Camille had anticipated the bargain, clever girl. "I said I'd consider it, not that I'd do it," Miriam tried in a last grasp at control.

"Sorry, Miriam," Camille said, her grin reflecting a distinct lack of sincerity. "The deadline to withdraw was yesterday. Thank you so much for accepting! And, yes, I already mailed in my LSU application but made this copy for you."

"Well played, Camille." She'd let it go. She could always say she was too sick to attend. She should ask to see which paintings Camille had submitted, but she was tired now and didn't want to think about the show further.

THE MORNING OF THE SHOW, CAMILLE SAID THE FEBRUARY weather was still cold and insisted on helping Miriam select a warm outfit to wear, choosing a thick wool sweater and slacks that somewhat obscured her weight loss. Now dressed and settled in her recliner with the paper, Miriam waited for Camille, who had rushed back upstairs to get ready herself. Miriam wondered in passing about the rush—they had plenty of time before the show opened. Camille murmured something about having a new dress, and Miriam nodded absently.

After taking longer than usual to get ready, Camille entered the sitting room shyly, wearing a beautiful pale blue silk dress unlike anything she'd worn before. Camille's jet-black hair fell loose and shiny on her shoulders instead of in her usual practical ponytail, and she wore pearl earrings and a new shade of lipstick.

Miriam's mouth dropped open in shock and, enraged, she bolted upright in her chair, dropping the newspaper, and nearly shouted, "Where did you get that dress?"

Camille's expression changed from proud to shocked dismay, face flushing, eyes wide, shrinking from the silk dress withering around her.

"I—I found it at the Goodwill Store. It didn't cost nearly what it would at a regular store."

Miriam took a deep breath, mortified. Yes, the Goodwill Store— where she'd taken it with the other dresses when she'd emptied those drawers months ago. Damn, how could she be such an idiot?

"Camille, I'm so sorry. I don't know what came over me."

Camille frowned. "I hope you don't think I'm wasting money on fancy clothes. I mean, this dress cost more than anything I've bought before, but it was so beautiful, I—"

"No, Camille, I would never think that. I just—"

"I've saved a good bit of my salary, especially since you won't let me chip in for food. I buy all my clothes at the Goodwill Store, just like when me and my grandmother shopped together."

"Camille, no, I've never thought you wasted a dollar of your pay, and—"

"Or maybe you think I have no business buying a dress this nice. That I should stick to school or work clothes." Camille's face was reddening again.

"No, you deserve to have nice clothes—of course you do. I can't explain what I was thinking."

Camille looked unconvinced and in a barely audible voice mumbled, "Can't or won't?"

Miriam quickly said, "The dress is perfect for you. I'm so sorry if I made you think I thought otherwise." She hoped she hadn't ruined Camille's joy in having the dress and was mortified to feel tears rising. When she dabbed at her eyes with a tissue, the anger left Camille's face and she patted Miriam's shoulder and assured her that everything was fine. Camille's shift to compassion made Miriam uncomfortable but not above playing to the sympathy. "The illness must be confusing my mind. I don't know what I was thinking." Camille looked skeptical but said nothing.

On the drive to LSU, Miriam said, "You look beautiful," her voice small and shaky, sad apology in watery eyes. "The dress is gorgeous on you, I'm so glad--" she tried, but faltered and had to stop. When had she become so pathetically weepy? Camille glanced at her, concerned.

Camille had insisted that Miriam bring the blasted cane she'd begun using on the now rare trips outside her home. The weakness had made her less steady, and Camille had pointed out that using a cane was less embarrassing than falling (thanks, Camille). Even with the cane, Miriam linked her other arm in Camille's, and they walked slowly into the large exhibition room. Professors Miriam recognized, along with others she didn't, stood by exhibits of their work, talking to viewers. The largest group was clustered around one exhibit, some even jostling others to get a better view of the paintings. An empty chair was placed beside that display.

"I asked them to have a chair for you, Miriam," Camille said, guiding her to it. At first, Miriam wondered why the chair wasn't by her own exhibit instead of this popular one, but as they came closer, she saw the paintings were hers. They'd been artfully arranged, though she felt uncomfortably exposed when she saw the most personal one—Rosie behind the rose bush—at the center. She knew she should have asked Camille which paintings she'd sent. She could have had this one removed.

As they moved closer, she heard viewers' comments, spoken in hushed, respectful tones—"never seen anything like it"; "look at how she uses the light"; "why haven't I heard of this artist before?" When she sat in the chair, people immediately began approaching her to praise the work. Their expressions of awe and wonder overwhelmed her, especially those of the professors she knew. After years of teaching students to appreciate the genius of other artists, she could barely comprehend that these people, art lovers all, were finding such beauty in her work. When Tom and Mac had pleaded with her to show the paintings, she'd wanted only to hold them close, not to expose her amateur creations to critical evaluation. She hadn't painted to display her work; she'd painted because she had to. She was incomplete without her art, though she'd called it a hobby, an indulgence she made subservient to her professional work and domestic chores.

Then Miriam heard a familiar voice and was astonished to see

Camille leading Marcie and Justin through the crowd. Their broad smiles faltered a bit when they got a good look at her. Marcie leaned over to hug Miriam and said, "We were in New Orleans for the AHA conference and couldn't fly home without seeing your exhibit. I can't believe you never told me you painted! The work is unlike any I've seen —moving and extraordinarily beautiful." Marcie paused, looking at the paintings, eyes round, mouth slightly open, as if entranced. People coughed and shuffled behind her, and Marcie glanced back, said she and Justin would see Miriam at lunch, and they yielded to the line. Miriam saw that they lingered for long looks at each painting, then left after a brief conversation with Camille.

Miriam sat through another hour of being barraged by admirers, gratified but embarrassed by the attention. She was glad when the ever-vigilant Camille told the undiminished crowd around the work that Dr. Johnson was sorry to leave, but that her health didn't allow her to stay longer. An old friend and fellow professor from the Art History Department helped Camille walk her out and sat on a bench with her while Camille got the car, all the while praising her work, even asking if she'd mind if he included photographs of the paintings in his course. On the way home, Camille said Miriam had time for an hour's nap before meeting Marcie and Justin for a late lunch. Miriam still felt dazed from the show, but also exhausted, and gratefully napped in her chair with Petey on her lap.

Marcie and Justin were waiting at Vinny's when Miriam and Camille arrived. After effusive compliments on the exhibit (even from Justin), Marcie handed Miriam a box that she opened to reveal an engraved brass plaque surrounded by a pretty crystal frame. "Did you know you received the AHA Distinguished Lifetime Achievement Award for Writing on Art?" Marcie asked. Miriam was startled and vaguely remembered a letter from Alice, her department chair, in the pile of unopened mail. Marcie said, "When I saw Alice at the conference, she said she'd sent you AHA's letter but hadn't heard from you. I volunteered to bring you the award."

The server came to take their orders. After they toasted Miriam with their water glasses, Marcie said, "For a long time, I've wanted to tell you something I've often thought." Marcie paused, eyes shiny, took a breath, and said, "You changed my life. Without your support and encouragement, I would have never even tried to go to graduate school, to envision the career I have. I'll never forget that."

Miriam demurred. "Marcie, with your talent and intelligence, you would have found your way."

"No, because I wouldn't have even seen the path without you, Miriam, let alone think I could follow it. My greatest wish has been to be the kind of teacher that you were." Marcie turned to Camille and said, "You told me Miriam has been tutoring you and talking with you about your education. Listen to her, Camille. Miriam knows her students, and you won't regret following her advice. Trust me on that."

Miriam was grateful, especially to have this unexpected ally, but the praise was almost too much. She should say something more, but she had no words. Justin saw it and knew what to do.

"Now, if I can interrupt a moment to brag, we thought you might like to see some pictures of our son graduating from MIT." Justin showed her a picture on his phone of a handsome young man with Marcie's dark hair and Justin's broad smile, and Miriam expressed appropriate admiration. They ate and talked about Miriam's painting, Marcie's research, and colleagues seen and talks given at the conference. Saying goodbye was hard since it was clearly the last time.

Back at home, Camille beamed, proud of her surprise. "I first talked to Marcie when she called on the landline one day while you were napping. She said she hadn't been able to reach you on your cell, and the emails didn't tell her much about how you were doing. So I started texting her updates, and sometimes we'd talk. I hope you don't mind."

Miriam assured Camille that she didn't. The visit had lightened her; she wasn't forgotten and, maybe, she'd made a difference. Camille put the plaque on the mantle in the sitting room, admiring how the light sparkled on the crystal frame.

A FEW DAYS LATER, MIRIAM NOTICED THAT PETEY WASN'T EATING his breakfast but was drinking heavily from his water bowl. She picked him up and felt how thin he'd gotten beneath his plush fur. Camille made a vet appointment for him for the next day and admitted that when she'd taken him for his annual exam, the vet had said his kidneys were beginning to fail, not unusual for a cat his age. He would be fine, Miriam told herself, stroking his soft head. Petey nuzzled her arm as if to reassure her.

But the next morning Miriam woke to find that Petey had slipped away in the night beside her without a sound. Miriam's wail brought Camille running to her room. They sobbed together as Camille gently wrapped Petey's body in a towel and showed him to Hanks so he wouldn't look for his friend. Hanks sniffed Petey, whimpered, then lay down on the rug, head on his paws. Camille took Petey's body to the vet clinic, and after she left, Miriam let the tears fall. Even though she'd felt the daily drags of age and disease pulling at Petey these last weeks, it had never occurred to her that he would die first.

Camille returned and sat on the bed beside Miriam, who rolled on her side, facing away. Camille rubbed her back, murmuring, "There, there," those meaningless words eloquently expressing the lack of any real comfort, but infinitely better than what Camille said next.

"Maybe God wanted a cat, Miriam. I've never seen one as loving as Petey."

Miriam was glad she was facing away so Camille couldn't see her rolling her eyes. If indeed cats were permitted inside the pearly gates, heaven would be overrun with them by now. God hardly needed her Petey. Maybe he'd taken him as a cruel foretaste of the desolation awaiting her. With Camille's help, she finally got up and dressed. Downstairs in her recliner, she stared out the windows, unable to shake the heavy sadness. Camille came and sat beside her, chemistry book in hand.

"Miriam, I just can't figure out this problem," she said, frowning and wrinkling her brow. "Can you help me?"

Miriam appreciated the rather transparent effort, but she couldn't focus on the page. She said she couldn't get it either and apologized.

Nonplussed, Camille went to the kitchen to make tea, her fallback when all else failed.

Adelaide came by after lunch to bring banana pudding from Ruby. "I called Momma at work and told her the cat had died, and she felt bad. She came home at lunch and made the pudding," Adelaide said. "Momma cried for three days after that dumb little furball dog of hers died last year, so she knows what it's like."

After Adelaide rushed off for class, Camille and Miriam had the pudding, still warm and soothing, like one of Ruby's big hugs. Miriam thought about how Ruby folded kindness into everything she made.

THE NEXT NIGHT, AS SHE WAITED IN BED FOR CAMILLE TO RETURN to read, Miriam resolved to shake off the paralysis of sorrow. She still had things to finish. Petey was only a cat; she was well aware of that. No one was overwhelmed by grief for a cat, for God's sake. But she was. It hurt to breathe. Only a cat. Only a cat. No. He was Petey, her friend and family.

Camille came in with her Bible and *Bleak House*. As had become their habit, she opened the Bible first. At least Camille had kept her promise to keep the Bible readings brief.

"This verse is one of my favorites," Camille said.

Miriam wondered how many "favorite" verses Camille had—she'd heard this same introduction repeatedly. But she had no quarrel with the selections chosen.

"'As the branch can't bear fruit by itself, unless it remains in the vine, so neither can you, unless you remain in me.'" Camille read, then looked at Miriam and said, "You know this part about how the branch can't bear fruit by itself, how it has to be part of the vine? I was wondering, would you feel up to going to church on Sunday? I could drive us. We could go to your church."

Miriam hadn't been to church in many years, but she realized that she'd again been oblivious. Of course, Camille attended church, or had until Miriam had begun monopolizing her weekends. She attempted to dodge the proposal by offering Camille time off on Sunday to attend her own church and saying Camille needn't bring her along.

"No, I'd like to take you. And I'd be glad to go to your church."

Miriam didn't really feel like going there or anywhere else. But Camille wasn't asking much, especially if they went to Miriam's church. Miriam really didn't care to attend a new one, where she'd have to face Camille's friends, who would doubtless guess that she was the reason Camille had been absent.

Miriam knew Camille thought church would give her comfort after Petey's death. It wouldn't, but she'd go.

CHAPTER 22

Miriam said she wasn't feeling well enough to attend church the following Sunday, so she and Camille watched the sermon online in the comfort of the sitting room. Miriam felt guilty afterward and resolved to go the next Sunday. Now that Sunday had rolled around, she regretted her decision, hoping no one she knew would remain at her old church. She didn't want to be seen, shrunken and debilitated as she was. The mirror told her that she was still recognizable, but clearly in poor health. But she had promised, and they were going. She wasn't going to disappoint Camille again.

They went to the "contemporary service," something new since Miriam had last attended the large downtown Presbyterian church many years ago. Apparently, "contemporary" meant that the dress was casual, quite casual for some. Observing the guitars and drums in the choir area, she realized that it also meant the music was contemporary —like what played on Camille's favorite radio station. Miriam liked it well enough, though a traditional hymn or two would have been nice. She was just settling in after the opening songs and prayer when the assistant minister, a rather large man with an even larger smile, said, "Let's greet each other—get out of your pews, and hug ten people!"

Goodness. What were they now, Baptists? She stood next to Camille, who, of course, was smiling and hugging or pumping the outstretched hands around them. A woman with short gray hair and a pleasant, vaguely familiar face enveloped Miriam in the big Louisiana hug that commonly accompanied arrivals, departures, celebrations, consolations, and even chance meetings in the grocery store.

"Is it really you, Miriam?" the woman asked. "I remember your parents. They were such fine people." The woman introduced herself as a retired LSU professor who'd served on the faculty senate with Miriam's father. She beckoned to others to come and greet Miriam. A few looked curiously at Camille, and Miriam wasn't sure how to introduce her, not wishing to refer to her as a caregiver. A young man reached across Miriam to shake Camille's hand, asking, "Are you Ms. Miriam's daughter? Or, uh, granddaughter?"

Miriam was about to respond, though she still hadn't decided what to say, when Camille answered smoothly, "No, I'm a student of Dr. Johnson's," flashing her lovely smile.

Miriam was relieved when the assistant minister finally called everyone back to their seats, though it hadn't been wholly unpleasant to be back in the warm embrace of people who, at least for this hour, were determined to offer only loving acceptance to others here. As the choir sang the bright new songs in voices ringing with honest worship, Miriam remembered the old feeling of well-being she'd once had in this sanctuary.

The bulletin said a guest minister was speaking this week, Dr. Jackson, a noted theologian and professor at the Princeton University Seminary. Miriam had heard religious speakers who were smooth and shiny, as articulate and skilled as any good politician and almost indistinguishable from one. Then there were others, rare and memorable, who spoke simply, humbly, and cogently of great truths, whose faces seemed to glow with an inner goodness tinged with earthly holiness. Dr. Jackson was one of the latter. He looked about seventy, and his kind, well-weathered face and attentive manner probably led his students to seek him out when they needed a sympathetic ear and good advice.

"Well, you already know I've promised more than I can deliver this morning," he began. "The title of the sermon, 'Understanding God's Love and Forgiveness,' makes no sense. We can never understand the magnitude of that love and the comprehensiveness of that forgiveness—we're just not made that way." He paused, inclined his head as if considering this, then continued, "As Paul says in Ephesians 2, without God, we are all dead in our transgressions, where we're led by our desires, walking in the course of this world—following the prince of the power of the air." His eyes roamed the room, as if seeking connection with each of them, then, raising his voice a notch, he said, "*But God* has saved us by grace, making us alive together with Christ. Why? Because of his great love for us."

Dr. Jackson seemed to look directly at her. She looked down.

"In spite of all our flaws, we're God's workmanship, created in Christ Jesus to walk in good works that God prepared for us beforehand. God knew it would be difficult for us to comprehend his love for us, the 'children of wrath,' fixed on our own desires. So what did he do?" Dr. Jackson waited a beat, then said, "He sent his beloved son, Jesus, to redeem us, yes, but also to show us his love in a tangible form—to bring it even dimly into focus for us."

Unexpected tears rose and Miriam blinked them back. Sentimental idiot—the illness making her maudlin.

"We forget that we can ask forgiveness for anything and it will be granted. It's an open-ended offer. What stands between us and God's love is our own turning away. The corrosive sin that we refuse to forgive in ourselves and don't trust him to forgive—we forget about his immeasurable grace. We don't really believe his love extends that far."

Dr. Jackson looked down for a moment, then up at them, blue eyes shining. "And yet, there is *nothing* you can do that God cannot use to bring you closer to him."

The sermon continued, but that simple sentence snagged Miriam like barbed wire. *Nothing*? Really? She'd once tentatively, fearfully asked for forgiveness for failing Tom, failing Rosie. Then, instead of listening, she'd turned away, slammed and bolted the door against any hope of an answer. She couldn't ask for what she didn't deserve. And it was too late now.

Or was Grace still there, waiting quietly outside the door? Waiting, like Petey had when he curled up outside the closed door of her office, not budging until she opened it. Did Grace, like a big white cat, stretch up and press paws against the door, push to see if it might open? Finding the door latched, did Grace stay on the other side, never tiring, never deserting, waiting always for the door to open just a crack, enough to push through, and flood the heart with light?

The congregation stood for another hymn, and when the offering plate was passed afterward, Miriam put a generous check into it (hoping it wouldn't trigger a call from some well-meaning membership committee person—she should have brought anonymous cash). As they were leaving the sanctuary, she gazed at the light filtering through the stained-glass windows and felt again that brief, blessed breath of peace. Camille had been right to bring her.

Back in the car, Camille tentatively observed that once a month, she and her grandparents had gone to the Piccadilly Cafeteria on Government Street after church. Miriam had been thinking more of taking out the rest of Mrs. Doucet's chicken noodle soup at home, but it was early enough that the restaurant wouldn't be crowded, so she said it was a fine idea. As they left the parking lot, Camille suggested that they go to Capitol Park before leaving downtown.

"Look, Miriam, the roses are blooming—would you like to get out and see them?"

The bright March sun was warm enough, and how long had it been since someone had asked her to look at a rose? Yes, she would. They walked on the path by the well-tended bushes, and Camille paused to smell the blossoms, exclaiming on the unique scents of the different varieties, as delighted as a child. Miriam smiled and obligingly sniffed the roses too, leaning on her cane and closing her eyes, seeing Mac's garden. And remembering an afternoon in this same park with Tom, when he'd pulled her from her office to escape to this beauty. The way they'd frisked about among the rosebushes, exploring the varying scents and colors just as Camille was doing now. How the sun had shone on his dark hair, the way he'd reached for her hand, then pulled her into a long kiss. She blinked and realized Camille was standing in front of her now, eyes searching her face, anxious.

"Miriam, are you alright?"

"Yes, of course. Just enjoying the roses."

Camille looked doubtful.

At the Piccadilly Cafeteria, they pushed their trays through the line of smiling servers who called them "honey" and "sweetheart" as they made their selections—roast beef Dilly Dishes for each of them. Miriam insisted that Camille take the slice of chocolate meringue pie she was covertly eyeing. They sat in a booth with padded red vinyl benches, and Camille attacked her dinner for a few minutes (amazing how the girl could eat), then looked at Miriam and said, "It was a good sermon, wasn't it?"

Miriam agreed and pushed some food around on her plate. Her own appetite was dwindling daily.

"I used to think how strange it was that a great God would love tiny, sinful us so much," Camille mused. "When the minister would say that God wants a personal relationship with us, I'd think, why? And why would he want praise or love from us?"

Miriam nodded, feigning interest to distract Camille from noticing how little she'd eaten—she didn't feel like being fussed over.

"You know what helped me understand? Hanks. He's just a dog, and I never expected to love him so much. And not only that, but I really care that he loves me too, even though he's just this big dumb animal—I mean, he's smart for a dog," Camille amended, as if Hanks could hear and understand her. "It makes me happy that he's so excited when I come home, and the one time I had to board him, it made me sad when I picked him up and he was mad—he didn't even wag his tail, and he turned his head away from me. I felt really bad."

Miriam got the gist, but Camille wasn't finished.

"And once I stupidly left out the new shoes I was so excited to find at the Goodwill Store, and Hanks chewed them up. When I scolded him, he hung his head and looked so sorry that I forgave him instantly —in fact, I started patting him and telling him it was okay because I hated to see him so sad." She laughed at the memory, then turned serious again. "I mean, the gap between me and God is a lot bigger than the gap between me and Hanks, but it helps me understand how God could really love such inferior, limited beings as us and forgive us no matter how many times we commit the same sins."

Miriam nodded without comment. A simple comparison, hardly a theological gem, but she too had struggled with the concept that a perfect and omnipotent God would find anything in puny humans to love or care about. Yet Petey—a mere cat—for years had been the most beloved being in her world, regardless of his lack of conversational skills or analytical thinking.

Later that afternoon, Miriam sat in her recliner finishing the Sunday paper, the scratchy old wool Hudson Bay blanket on her lap. She'd dragged it out of the back of the closet because she was always cold now. She was considering whether she had something else as warm but more comfortable when Camille came bounding down the stairs, eyes bright, holding a bag.

"I got you something when I was at the Goodwill Store yesterday." Seeing Miriam frown, Camille added, "It's still in its original packaging, Miriam—not everything there is used. And it's something you really need." She thrust the bag into Miriam's lap.

Miriam picked it up. Should she explain that she wasn't bothered by the store, but by Camille's spending money on her? She took out a clear plastic storage bag that held a lovely thick, rose-pink fleece throw, as soft as anything she'd ever felt.

"Camille, this is lovely, and so kind of you." She didn't have to pretend delight in the gift. She threw off the old blanket, shook out the throw, and laid it on her lap. So light and soft, so warm and lovely. She stopped herself from offering reimbursement, knowing it would spoil the moment.

Camille smiled, radiant, then picked up the old blanket and said, "I could take this to Goodwill next time I go—if they want it." Miriam laughed.

THAT NIGHT, MIRIAM SLEPT POORLY, WAKING OFTEN AND WISHING she could have Petey beside her again for just a few minutes, feel his soft fur, his warmth as he lay still sleeping, then woke to nuzzle her hand, demanding his first attention of the day. She thought of what Camille had told her one morning when Miriam had arrived in the kitchen, her face haggard from a long night of wakefulness. She'd told Camille that every time she'd drifted off, she'd woken up again, as if some malevolent force kept deliberately yanking her back.

Camille had said, "That happens to me sometimes too. It can be a good time to pray. Sometimes I think God is tugging at my sleeve, maybe wanting to talk, calling me to him. It's quiet, no distractions. So I just put whatever I'm worrying about aside, clear my mind, and pray."

Maybe she should try to pray, maybe for Petey's sweet soul. The Bible was uninformative on animals in the afterlife, but she yearned to believe that she would see Petey again. Except that she wasn't likely to be going to any afterlife for the pure of soul like Petey. Miriam closed her eyes and saw again that door within, sealed by the guilty memories —how she'd turned away from Tom's desperation, ignored the warning in his words that last night, swallowed the pills without considering Rosie's life.

She dozed and woke again when the night was slowly ebbing, replaced by the thick gray light of dawn. It was still too early to get up, certainly too early to wake Camille. Morning was so different without Petey. If she were lying on her back, like now, he'd flip over on his side and hug all four legs around her arm, nuzzling his face against it. She'd never had a cat as actively loving as Petey. Well, enough. She closed her eyes, thinking again about that big white cat of grace—was he waiting still, watching with divine patience for the smallest crack in the door? She remembered her second-grade Sunday school class, how she'd fervently sung "Jesus Loves Me," led by old Mrs. Boudreaux's off-key, high-pitched warble, joined by the boys in the front row singing in mocking falsetto, snickering, jabbing and jostling each other. She remembered how she'd gazed at the picture of Jesus dressed in a shining white robe, arms outstretched, benevolent smile and kind eyes. How she'd been so secure in her belief, a child's unquestioning faith.

Dr. Jackson said there was nothing you could do that God could not use to bring you closer to him. Sometimes she wanted to be closer, to regain that old child-like belief that those arms were open to her. Sometimes she felt a breath of it. She and Tom had attended church together all those years ago. When Tom died, she'd stopped going. She'd turned away from any comfort faith might offer, turning instead for salvation to what she could control—her work, her students, maybe her painting too. She'd tried to fill her soul with only what the world could offer. Now she realized that had never been enough.

She yearned for sleep; she was so tired. She closed her eyes, slowed her breathing, and lay still, inviting it to come, take her away.

She saw Petey entering a lush garden with tall, leafy trees surrounding a sunlit clearing filled with bright red, white, and blush-pink roses. Petey trotted forward with purpose, like when he used to run to the door to greet her. His green eyes were restored and intent, gray tabby tail brandished high. A man in a shining white robe strode toward Petey, and when they met, bent to reach out a hand to him. Petey rose on hind legs to nuzzle the hand, then dropped down to be stroked and scratched under his chin. The man smiled indulgently at Petey, then paused, as if listening, straightened, and turned to look toward the surrounding trees. The foliage rustled and a little girl emerged. She had bright blond hair and blue eyes and wore a red wool dress with brass buttons, just as Miriam had painted her. The little girl ran to the outstretched arms and He embraced her, then stood with his arm around her, keeping her close, his face shining with present and powerful love.

Shaken by mingled joy and awe, Miriam opened her eyes and blinked in the early morning light, dazed. As she lay pondering what she'd seen (dreamed?), she felt that big white cat of grace push through a crack she must have opened in that long-closed door. A pure, radiant joy slammed through her like floodwaters, undiluted by guilt, untainted by grief, and she heard herself whispering, *thank you, thank you, thank you*, during the few seconds it lasted. The receding flood left a changed landscape; the poisonous undergrowth of isolation, grief, and remorse all washed away, leaving a certain knowledge. Me, she marveled, all undeserving, yet beloved. For the first time in many years, Miriam prayed and felt heard. Forgiven. She lay still, drifting in and out of sleep, and another image came to her. She'd paint it before she died. She slept again until Camille came in to help her dress for the day.

After breakfast, Miriam asked Camille to help her set up her easel to paint in the office. Camille was understandably surprised—Miriam was very weak now and hadn't been painting.

"Are you sure, Miriam? I thought maybe we could watch a movie today, and I could read to you later."

"I know I can't start a new painting, Camille, but there's something I need to get on canvas. I'm going to work with one of the paintings I have."

Camille searched her face, anxiety evident—was she worried that Miriam might spoil the painting? Well, nice that she cared, but Miriam wasn't going to explain. Camille could see it after she was dead, which wouldn't be long.

So Camille helped her, following Miriam's instructions to pull out the night scene of the white rose painting. It would work well. Miriam dismissed Camille, who left the room reluctantly. She painted, moving slowly and deliberately, stopping to nap before lunch. She painted after lunch, stopping again to nap for a couple of hours, then painted until evening. She left one of the cloths she kept in her office closet for cleaning brushes draped lightly over the canvas when she finally stopped, exhausted.

"Really, you won't let me see it?" Camille wheedled as she cleaned the brushes and put away the paints while Miriam watched from the comfortable office chair, feet up on the ottoman.

"No, and I want you to promise me that you won't sneak a look at it. You'll see it after I'm gone," Miriam added, realizing from Camille's expression that she didn't find this comforting. But Camille promised.

Miriam worked on the painting steadily through the week. It was hard—she didn't usually paint people. Yes, she'd drawn the annual pictures of Rosie, but that was different. Miriam's weakness slowed the painting, but it wasn't impossible. It helped that the figures, though more than shadows, weren't in sharp focus like the rose bush.

The second week, she was glad to be nearly finished; her diminishing strength and the pain radiating from her lower back made it difficult to sit even an hour at the easel. She shortened the painting time, resting or napping in her bed or the office chair between sessions of thirty or forty minutes. Camille graciously kept the brushes and paints always ready, recognizing Miriam's urgent desire to complete this last work.

Finally, the painting was finished. Miriam gazed at it for a long moment before replacing the cloth, feeling a deep peace suffuse her. The white rosebush still shone in the foreground, its beauty undiminished. Deeper in the garden, a small lantern sat on a checked cloth on the ground, lightening the surrounding darkness to a silvery twilight. There, among the rosebushes, sat three people having a night picnic. The figures were insubstantial and muted, as if formed from the mist—a young Miriam, Tom, and Rosie. They sat close, attuned to each other, bound by love and a quiet happiness. Rosie looked up at Tom, lips parted in a smile, eyes bright, as if listening to a story, and he looked down at her, one arm around her shoulders, the other extended, as if in the telling. Miriam watched them both, smiling too, one hand resting on the picnic basket, as if savoring this moment before pulling out sandwiches. A cloud illuminated by the moon behind it, when studied carefully, took the softly glowing shape of a large white cat, benevolently watching the group sitting among the roses, and it seemed to smile. Camille mightn't understand that part of it, but Miriam thought she'd like the painting anyway.

She replaced the cloth over the painting and settled herself in the chair. Camille appeared with a tray bearing Miriam's afternoon medications, ice water, a cup of herbal tea, and a few of the thin ginger cookies Ruby had brought them. Miriam noticed that Camille looked worried and remained standing.

"Miriam, would you be all right if I took a couple of hours off this afternoon? If you'd feel better, I could see if Elaine could come."

"You needn't do that."

"It's just that my grandparents' friends who own the house I rent told me they're ready to sell it, so I'll have to find another place. I didn't realize what a good deal they were giving me until I started looking around."

"Camille, remember what I told you about the trust for you? That it would pay all your living expenses while you're in school?"

"Yes, but I still need to find somewhere with reasonable rent even if the trust, um, helps me with it." Miriam could tell Camille was still reluctant to accept help from the trust.

"Actually, you won't need rent. I'm also leaving you this house."

Camille's mouth fell open. She closed it, took a deep breath, and said, "But I could never afford to live in a house like this."

"Like I said, you won't have to. The trust will pay for all its costs and maintenance. And it will pay for rent on an apartment when you go to New Orleans or elsewhere for medical school. The house will be waiting for you if you come back to Baton Rouge to live after you've finished."

Camille was silent as if trying to grasp what Miriam was saying. Then she said, "Miriam, this is a beautiful home and anyone would love it. But I'm not sure I should accept such an extravagant gift."

"Well, I suppose my estate can sell it and all the contents. The money would go to the trust, of course."

Camille pondered that.

"You could have a roommate if you liked. Adelaide might enjoy living with you here, especially since you wouldn't have to charge her rent." Camille stayed quiet, but Miriam could tell she was tempted. "Obviously, Hanks likes it here."

Camille looked at her and nodded, still unsure.

"You'd be under no obligation to keep the house. It would be yours free and clear—not part of the trust. You could sell it whenever you chose."

"Are you sure about this?" Camille asked almost in a whisper. "I do love the house—and being here would always remind me of our time together."

So that was the key. For these months, maybe she'd replaced Camille's family, however poor a substitute she'd been. Hoping for a further enticement, Miriam said, "And I'm leaving you all of my paintings, too. You'd have room for them here."

Camille's eyes filled with tears, and she went to Miriam and hugged her. When they separated, Miriam said, "Camille, I truly don't want you to feel that you have to keep the house forever. You might decide to move somewhere else to establish your practice. But it would make me so happy to think of you here, even temporarily."

Camille wiped her eyes, nodded, and said, "Thank you, Miriam. But what if I don't get into medical school or even finish the LSU nursing program? Would you still want me to have the house?"

"Yes, of course. I'm giving it to you, whatever you do with your life. It's not contingent on your success, Camille. I want you to have it because I—" Miriam stopped short of saying, "love you," though that was true. "Because I care for you and am deeply grateful for all you've done for me."

"Thank you, Miriam." Camille pulled out another tissue, blew her nose, then sat in the desk chair. "You're sure I can't see the painting?"

"Of course you can, after I'm gone." Camille frowned but brightened again when they began talking about her studies. She'd ordered textbooks for the next level of classes and was studying them this semester while her course load was lighter. Miriam loved the way Camille lit up like the sunrise when she talked about what she was learning and what the next semesters would bring. Miriam wasn't sure whether Camille was referring to her nursing curriculum or LSU's premed courses, and she didn't want to ask, hoping Camille would tell her. Miriam was giddy with relief and happiness that Camille would accept the house. But it hadn't escaped her that Camille still hadn't said definitively that she would accept the support from the trust, and Miriam desperately wanted that assurance.

AFTER DINNER THE NEXT NIGHT, WHEN MIRIAM WAS SETTLED IN her chair, waiting for Camille to come in and watch a movie with her, she heard Camille on the phone in the kitchen.

"Yes, Elaine comes tomorrow, so I can be there. Thank you, Mrs. Doucet!"

Camille hung up and came in, her face bright with excitement and a letter in her hand. "I have something to show you, Miriam," she said, handing her the letter. Miriam saw the LSU insignia on the return address. She opened it, noticing Camille was practically vibrating with excitement. It was Camille's acceptance letter to LSU for the fall.

Camille sat on the couch beside Miriam's chair. "I'm going to start this fall, but I spoke with admissions, and I can go part-time the first semester. Or longer if need be. So I'll still be here for you."

Miriam didn't think that would be necessary. She'd be gone by then. She said, "Does this mean you'll--?"

Camille broke in, grinning. "Yes, Miriam, I'm going to accept your help. I talked to Mrs. Doucet about it. She was friends with my grandmother, and she said it would have broken her heart to know I didn't have what they'd planned for my education. She said you are God's way of fulfilling my grandparents' dreams for me."

Camille paused, then said, "And Marcie called to tell me I could always talk to her about my education. She knows about colleges and studying for advanced degrees. So I told her about what you were offering to give me."

Miriam hadn't expected that. But she couldn't ask for a better advisor than Marcie. Or a better ally and friend.

"Marcie said I should accept your support. She didn't even think about it. She said school is the one chance to focus full-time on learning and gaining the knowledge that will help for the rest of my career." Camille, clearly rapturous at the thought of uninterrupted studying for medical school, continued. "Marcie said, if you don't have to be distracted by a job that takes time from your studies, then don't be. Accept the help and use all your time to learn."

Relief washed over Miriam along with a joy almost reaching the level of what she'd experienced that dawn two weeks ago. She held out her arms, and Camille leaned over and hugged her. Miriam babbled something about how happy she was.

Camille laughed and said, "I just hope I can handle the coursework when, I mean if, you aren't tutoring me. She sat back down and took Miriam's hand. "Thank you," Camille said, and the gratitude shining in her eyes brought light to Miriam's soul. "Like Marcie said, you've changed my life, Miriam. You always saw a doctor in the cleaning lady. I only hope I can do what you believe I can."

"You can and you will."

Camille said, "Mrs. Doucet is going to help me and Adelaide figure out which classes will transfer and what to schedule for the fall. Will you be okay with Elaine tomorrow?"

"Of course. Is Adelaide going to transfer too?"

"Yes, she just got her acceptance. She's really excited about it. She says there are a lot more cute guys at LSU." Camille giggled. "Seriously, though, she's very excited about studying to be a registered nurse."

Miriam was satisfied with how she was leaving things. Good job, teacher, she told herself. She wished she'd be there to watch Camille continue her studies, to witness her success, but was thankful she'd been permitted to see Camille on the cusp of this next phase and her excitement about entering it.

MIRIAM HAD SPENT SEVERAL DAYS—OR HAD IT BEEN A WEEK?—IN bed, rising with assistance only as necessary, floating in and out of consciousness, mercifully cushioned by the morphine hospice adminis-tered. She knew the end was very near now and knew Camille felt it too as she helped her get settled that night. Irene was on duty, bless-edly unobtrusive, and it hadn't been as difficult as Miriam had feared to have her in the room at night. Irene would sit quietly in the chair after Camille retired, keeping the room dark except for the soft glow of her phone or Kindle, the nightlight, and the hall light. Every hour or so, Irene would walk quietly to Miriam's bedside and check on her; sometimes Miriam woke for a moment and sometimes not. If Miriam needed medication, Irene gave it to her. It wasn't so bad.

Miriam was waiting for Irene to replace Camille in their nightly changing of the guard when Camille came back into the room wearing her robe and slippers and told Miriam she was staying with her that night. Irene would be in Camille's room across the hall if they needed her, and would still check in every hour, but Camille told Miriam—rather than asked—that she was going to stay in the reading chair that night.

"All right," Miriam murmured, with a faint smile. The old Miriam would have resisted further, but now she felt a peace she hadn't had in many years, maybe ever. It still hurt when she reached out for Petey and found only emptiness, but remembering how she'd seen him in that clearing was balm enough. Tonight, she felt death looking over her shoulder, as if waiting for her to turn out the lamp. Camille came to her bedside and smoothed the covers, tucking them around her to ward off the ever-present cold. Hanks followed Camille and lay down on the rug by the bed like he did when Camille read to her. Funny how he'd insinuated himself into every ritual. Tonight, even Hanks seemed subdued and somber, lying quietly with his head on his paws instead of his usual tail-wagging alertness.

"Sleep now, Miriam," Camille said gently, stroking her hair with light fingers trailing love. "Do you need anything?"

"No, dear," Miriam assured her as she closed her eyes. Then she opened them again to find Camille still standing there, watching her, the tears allowed to spill once she thought Miriam had fallen asleep. When Miriam reached out to take her hand, Camille sobbed and held it fast, bending to kiss it, murmuring, "I love you, Miriam."

"I love you too, Camille," Miriam whispered, the last thing she needed to say. She closed her eyes again and let the darkness take her. As she slipped away, she heard Hanks get up to pace anxiously in and out of the room, then to patrol the hallway as if he could protect her from what was coming.

She awoke in the darkest hour. She felt a disturbance in the air as someone approached her bedside. Opening her eyes and seeing nothing, she glanced at Camille's chair, expecting it to be empty. But it wasn't. Camille was still, her breathing deep, exhaling in the gentle snore that she denied. Miriam turned when she felt the coolness brush her forehead, expecting Irene's capable hands.

Tom stood by her bed, looking down at her. The old love was in his eyes, undiminished by her failings. She wanted to stand beside him, take his hand. Although she hadn't been able to get up unaided for days, she found herself moving easily, lightly, rising in one swift motion like when she was a bride on their Florida honeymoon, delighting in another day. She took Tom's outstretched hand and walked with him toward the light.

ACKNOWLEDGMENTS

In the years I've worked on this novel, many people have offered encouragement and generously read, discussed, and advised, too many to name, but I'd like to specifically thank a few.

I'm grateful to John W. Jarrett, Publisher of Silent Clamor Press, for his unhesitating enthusiasm and belief in the novel, so generously expressed, his responsiveness to every question or idea, and his reassuring kindness through the publication process. I'm thankful for Silent Clamor Press Editor Fatima Hussan, whose meticulous and insightful work included ferreting out sentences that needed smoothing, suggesting formatting improvements, and pointing out places that needed a few more lines for better transitions or development. I'm gratified and deeply thankful to be a Silent Clamor Press author.

I thank John Matthew Fox for his developmental editing that better shaped and sharpened the novel, and for his encouragement and confidence in its worth.

My Zoom-enabled, four-state writing group, CINCO, generously read, reviewed, and critiqued the novel, providing valuable insights and suggestions. I deeply appreciate the friendships and all I've learned from the talented long-time members of the group--Mike Saeugling, Jasper Rine, Jim Roberts, and Cynthia Nooney.

Warmest thanks to Gail Tsukiyama for being a mentor and friend, reading prior and recent drafts of my manuscript, offering encouragement and astute comments, always inspiring and kind.

Other treasured readers include my sister, Carol Cole Czeczot, and friends Jane Kester, Judy Thompson, and Ed and Virginia Caress. All of them have buoyed me up when I've felt weighted down by rejections and doubts, and given me hope that an audience existed for this novel.

I thank Michelle Latiolais for thoughtful and insightful advice, support, and encouragement.

Many thanks to the dedicated staffs and faculties of the Community of Writers Summer Writers Workshops, the Bread Loaf Writers Conference, and the Iowa Summer Writing Festival. I learned so much every time I attended each of them, found community, and made good friends.

My husband, Mark, always believed and never stopped telling me that the novel would be published. He listened to innumerable versions through twelve years of writing and revising, and offered advice, feedback, and faithful support. Mark, I wouldn't have made it through the long evolution of the novel without you and will be forever grateful. I love you, and dedicate this book to you.

ABOUT THE AUTHOR

Mary Hester holds a Master's degree in English from Louisiana State University, where she taught English and technical writing. She practiced law for many years and was listed in *Best Lawyers in America*. After living in Baton Rouge and New Orleans for over forty years, she now resides in North Carolina with her husband Mark and their rescue dog Blue. *Painting Grace* is her debut novel, written over twelve years with guidance from her writing group and mentors.

At Silent Clamor Press, we seek to illuminate the human experience with excitement, elegance, and unflinching honesty. If this work has resonated with you—offering a profound journey or a new way of seeing the world—consider sharing your reflections with others. Your voice enriches the ongoing conversation that keeps literature vital and transformative.